STILL BURIED

The Still County Thrillers
Book 2

LAUREN STREET

STERLING & STONE

STILL BURIED

Chapter One

WELCOME BACK TO HELL.

That was Rita's first thought as she stepped out the doors of Casper/Natrona County International Airport and into the sweltering July heat. She didn't remember it being this hot when she was a kid. Or maybe that was because she'd hide out in the basement of her father Otto's house, where it was always cool. Or head to the local swimming hole when she was a teenager. Why did it have to be so hot and sticky? Wasn't it enough that Wyoming had some of the harshest winters in the U.S.?

Rita rolled her suitcase along the sidewalk, searching for Jason's Kia. He was supposed to be here to pick her up at two. But there was no Kia. And certainly no Jason.

She checked her phone. No new text since last night's confirmation: *See you at 2.*

"Well, it's two," she said. "So where the hell are you?"

She pulled up his name in contacts and was about to hit the call button when she paused. A black pickup pulled up to the curb, *Quick Cash Auto Repair* written on the side. Cash himself was in the driver's seat.

She glanced around. He wasn't there for her, was he?

He lowered the passenger side window and raised a hand.

Shit, he was.

He parked, then hopped out and walked around to her.

"You're not Jason," she said.

"I see that being in the Big Apple for three weeks didn't dull your keen powers of observation, Sheriff."

She glared at him. "Shut up. Where's my deputy?"

"Held up at work."

She stiffened.

"Not literally. He asked me to come get you."

She scowled. "He couldn't have asked someone else? Like Mary Lou?"

"Mary Lou wasn't about to leave an air-conditioned office for no reason."

"No reason?" Rita asked. "What am I? Chopped liver?"

"Her words, not mine. Now, are you getting in? Or am I leaving you here to fry on the sidewalk?"

"I'm getting in."

He grabbed her suitcase, walking back around to the driver's side and storing it in the cabin behind the front seats.

Rita opened the passenger door and climbed in. His air conditioning was cranked high enough to raise penguins. And it felt goddamn amazing. Jason's Kia did not have the same refrigeration powers. She would forgive him for making her ride with Cash.

Cash got into the driver's seat. "So, how was New York? I hear that the stench of urine in Times Square is particularly wonderful this time of year."

"Have you even been to New York?"

"I've watched the Mets' approximation of what they think baseball should be. Does that qualify?"

Rita snorted. "You really should travel. There is a world outside of Still County, Wyoming, you know."

He grunted. "I got all I need here."

Rita wondered if that included her. But she wasn't about to ask. "Besides, the only sights I saw were the inside of a courtroom for three weeks."

"So, no comment on the urine?"

She didn't answer. An awkward silence filled the truck. He broke it first. "How was the trial?"

"Over." That's all she wanted to say about it. It was her last pending case, and she didn't want to rehash the circumstances. Kid, dead of neglect. Father now behind bars where he belonged.

"You see Dale?"

She glanced over at him. Three months ago, Dale had shown up when she first arrived in Still. He'd only stayed the weekend, but somehow, he'd managed to befriend everyone she knew, including Otto and Cash.

"You have a lot of questions."

"Haven't had anyone to talk to for three weeks."

Yeah, right. She didn't believe that.

"No, I didn't see him." Dale had a weird ability to make friends wherever he went. Rita was the opposite. She tended to piss people off.

"At all?" He sounded surprised.

"Did you forget I was working?"

"You stayed an extra week."

Was he keeping track? She hid her smile by looking out the window at the countryside, mountains in the distance. "Yeah, the trial ran long."

"I'm kind of surprised you came back."

Her smiled fell, and she glanced over at him. "Why?"

He shrugged, gesturing. "Thought you might want to leave all this behind."

Was he referring to himself? "And by *this*, you mean—"

"The mountains."

Uh huh.

"No, I'd miss it too much."

"You talking about the mountains?"

She grinned. "Of course."

Although she would miss him too. She just wasn't about to say so.

He grunted, then they lapsed into silence. Rita focused on the landscape. Her eyes grew heavy. Her flight from LaGuardia had been at 7:20 a.m. So she'd been up early. But she hadn't slept well either. Cash wasn't wrong. She had debated whether to return to Still. After all, what was here for her?

Her relationship with Otto was strained. She had no idea what was going on with Cash. She was still bitter over Apex Global, the clandestine multinational who handled murder cases their own way, such as breaking into her sheriff's office—not that she had proof.

When she'd gone for drinks with her former colleagues in New York, her sergeant had invited her back. But Rita didn't think he meant it; it was the kind of thing you said to former friends. They'd all moved on, talking about cases that had occurred after she left. She'd felt isolated and alone. And no one wanted to hear about the elk that had wandered into downtown and refused to let anyone into Elk Mountain Equity for a day and a half.

Not that that was all that happened. But she wasn't ready to share that Otto had hidden a half-sister from her. One who was murdered before Rita could even meet her.

She closed her eyes and yawned.

A second later, Cash nudged her. She blinked at him,

surprised to see that they were back in Still. She'd slept most of the way back.

"Almost home," he said.

He hit the main drive, pulling up to the stop sign outside the Bighorn Mining building.

"Stop," she said.

He braked.

A new sign stood in front of the location.

It was an artist's rendering of the Bighorn Mining building looking revitalized. And the words, *Lisa's Place — Supportive Housing for Still — Sponsored by Apex.*

She stared at it. "What the fuck?"

"Showed up while you were out of town."

Rita got out of the truck. Heat hit her like a furnace blast. She walked over to the sign. It was about ten feet wide, supported by two metal rods embedded in the dirt.

Lisa's Place — Sponsored by Apex.

How fucking dare they?

They killed her sister, and now they were exploiting her for good PR?

She grabbed a rod, pulling at it. It refused to budge. She tried the other one. Managed to loosen it. Then she pushed the goddamn thing over. When it was lying on the ground, she walked across it, cracking the plywood.

Then she returned to the truck and climbed back in.

She was sweating now.

Cash had an amused twinkle in his eyes. She'd forgotten how sexy the crow's feet of his tanned skin looked when he smiled or laughed. "Feel better?"

"No."

He pulled back onto the street and for a bit before turning left down the alley and pulling into the parking lot behind Bighorn Bean.

She opened the door and got out again. This time she

was prepared for the heat. Not that it was more manageable.

He got out behind her and pulled her suitcase out, setting it on the ground. "You need a hand getting that up the stairs?"

"That your way of inviting yourself up?"

"Well, no. But after watching you struggle with that sign, I'm concerned all that easy East Coast living made you soft."

She glared at him. "No thanks. All I want is a shower and to cozy up in my own bed."

He grinned. "I can give you a hand with those, too."

"I bet." She stepped over to him, then gave him a quick hug. He leaned in for a kiss, but she backed away. "Thanks for the ride, Cash. I appreciate it."

"Yeah."

She grabbed her suitcase and made her way to the door of the apartment, unlocking it. Then she climbed the stairs to the door at the top. She was finally home.

Chapter Two

ONCE INSIDE HER APARTMENT, RITA CLOSED THE DOOR AND dropped her suitcase. It was stifling inside. Sun poured in through the front window. She should have drawn the blinds before she left.

It was probably warmer inside than outside. She walked over to the window, unlatched it, and slid it open. She didn't have air conditioning, but she did have a fan. She clicked it on, trying to push the warm air out.

The apartment, which she rented from Abigail, owner of Bighorn Bean, wasn't much larger than the camper she'd lived in at Otto's, but it was clean, had everything she needed, and was literally across the street from her job. Plus she woke each morning to the smell of fresh coffee and baked goods from the coffee and baked goods place on the first floor.

The two biggest selling features of the place were that it had actual running hot water, and it lacked an Otto.

While she'd come back to Still to care for her father, it didn't mean she had to live under his literal shadow. She walked to the kitchen sink, surprised to see that the fiddle-leaf fig she'd placed in a couple inches of water was still alive. And not only that, it had new growth.

She'd found it on the side of the road shortly after visiting Lisa's grave. It had been housed in its planter, either having fallen off a truck or been discarded.

She'd never cared for plants — her mother, Carol, had been the one with the green thumb. Rita had just planned to keep driving, but something about the plant had pulled at her heart strings.

Perhaps it was just the melancholy of the moment, but she felt like she'd been meant to find the plant. So she'd stopped the Honda, walked back down the road, and picked it up.

She'd thought about taking it into the office before she left for New York. But ultimately, she figured if it was meant to be hers, it would survive.

"Miss me, Figgy Stardust?"

She felt the soil. It was still damp. She picked the plant up and took it over to the window, placing it on the sill in full sunlight.

"Yeah, I know. I need a social life."

Rita went to the bathroom and turned on the shower. She wasn't just sweaty from her bout with the Apex sign. No matter how fresh she felt at the start of the day, she always felt grimy and sticky after air travel.

She stared at herself in the mirror. Her face and body had healed fine after her pummeling at the hands of Apex security. Boyd had said they acted on their own. But knowing what she knew now, she didn't believe him.

She leaned closer to the mirror, spotting the scar on her nose. Faint as it was, it was still visible. At least to her.

She wondered how Jason was doing. A gunshot wound had made her deputy a shadow of his usual buoyant self. At least for a while there. He had returned to work after less than a month, and Rita had worried that it was too soon.

Maybe he just wanted Walter, Still's other police officer, to feel guilty for betraying her and Jason to Apex. Before Rita left for New York, he had been buying Jason breakfast every morning.

Or maybe Mary Lou was right. Jason just needed to get back to routine. God knows, Rita took a beating and went straight back to the desk.

Rita peeled off her clothes, reached into the shower, and flinched. The water was ice cold.

Usually it heated up quickly. She turned the knob. Waited. Nothing. She turned off the water, grabbed her robe from the hook on the back of the door, and pulled it on. Then she got her phone from the back pocket of her discarded jeans.

She called Abigail. "My water's cold."

Abigail laughed. "Welcome back, Sheriff."

God, did she have no manners? "Sorry. Hey, Abigail."

"You sure you want it hot? Have you seen the temperature?"

Rita grimaced. She had a point. "I just got off a plane."

"The heater went out. Henry is supposed to be stopping by to take a look at it sometime today."

"Thanks."

"10-4."

"Ha ha," Rita said.

Abigail laughed again and hung up. Rita set her phone on the counter next to the sink and stared at the shower. If she really wanted a hot one, she could go to Otto's. Or Cash's. Either would oblige. But she didn't want their company.

She was tired. And needed to get acclimatized to Still

again. She wanted to do that on her own. She turned the tap on again, discarded her robe, and stepped in. The water was still shockingly cold. She made quick work of it, scrubbing away the sweat and invisible airline grit.

She shampooed her hair, rinsed off, then got out. She toweled off, then pulled on her robe, walked over to her bed, and collapsed. A cold shower hadn't been a bad idea. She felt cool enough that she needed a blanket. She rolled over, taking the quilt with her.

Closed her eyes, still feeling like she was on an airplane. She tried to relax. But fifteen minutes later, she was still awake.

Shit.

She shouldn't have napped in Cash's truck. That and the time change were playing havoc with her circadian rhythm.

She glanced over at the clock on her nightstand. It was almost 6 p.m. Or 8 p.m. in New York. She was surprised how easy it had been to adapt to Eastern Standard Time. Like putting on an old boot.

Rita rolled over again, trying to will herself to sleep and lean into the sensation of flight that still lingered in her body. But she was wide awake. Maybe it was better to stay awake? She was going to have enough trouble adjusting as it was.

Maybe some food would help her settle. After all, it was technically supper time. She got up and walked to the refrigerator.

Inside was a jar of jam, some olives she didn't even remember buying, a couple bottles of beer, and a questionable-looking apple. That's right. She had been planning to take the apple with her to the airport but forgot.

She opened the cupboard. It wasn't much better. Ramen. No thanks. Bread that was growing colonies of mold. One single sleeve of opened crackers. She grabbed those, not caring how stale they were, then poured herself a glass of water, taking both back to bed with her.

She was starting to feel sweaty again. Maybe she should take the fan with her into the bedroom. But she decided against it. Mainly because it seemed like way too much work.

She set her glass and the crackers on the bedside table next to the clock. Then she got her phone from the bathroom, stopping at the closet on her way back. She slid her phone into her robe pocket and pushed aside her uniform to find the safe she'd installed.

She punched in the combination.

It contained two items. Her service weapon, and the box of letters Lisa had written to Rita when she discovered they were half-sisters.

Rita touched both as though to make sure they were really there.

She still hadn't opened a single letter from Lisa.

As long as the letters were left unread, it felt like a part of her sister was still alive. Like she had something to say in this world. Once she'd read them, that would be the last of her. And Rita wasn't ready for that yet.

She swung the safe closed and locked it.

Then she returned to her bed. She climbed under the covers, stuffed a couple of crackers into her mouth, and chewed. She plugged her phone into the charger and opened up her texts.

She didn't know why she lied to Cash about seeing Dale. They'd had dinner twice. But it hadn't gone well. He'd wanted her to come back to New York. Rekindle what they once had.

She'd always known their relationship had meant more to him than it had to her. As awful as that sounded.

She read over his last text. *Please reconsider.*

She leaned her head back against the pillow. How had she survived fifteen years in New York City? By lying to herself. Convincing herself that that was where she wanted to be, when she hadn't wanted to be there at all. She'd only gone there because she didn't know where else to go.

Because she hadn't wanted to be here either. At least not then. But ever since she'd moved back to Still, Rita had come to realize that no matter how much she hated it here, Still was home. And it always would be.

She closed her eyes, trying to picture Dale.

But all she saw was Cash.

Then she was asleep.

Chapter Three

RITA OPENED THE FRONT DOOR OF THE STILL COUNTY Sheriff's Office and stared. What the hell?

The entire office looked like it had been through one of those TV shows where a decorator comes in and changes the room. Gone were all the unused desks and broken chairs. The walls had a fresh coat of paint. A new whiteboard hung on the wall next to Jason and Walter's desks. Photos of recent vandalism and graffiti clung to it with brightly colored flower magnets.

A cat climbing tower was now located in front of one of the narrow windows. Ted the cat was curled up in a ball on the top platform, illuminated by a single shaft of sunlight. He opened a single eye and stared at her, then closed it again, not even bothering to yawn.

"Hello to you too," Rita said. So much for rescuing him. Apparently, she wasn't even worth acknowledging. "Asshole."

He rolled over so that his back was to her.

Mary Lou was on the phone at reception.

Rita gestured to it. "For me?"

Mary Lou shook her head and covered the receiver. "Not unless you want to assure Mr. Wilson that no one replaced his cows with communist spy robots."

Rita pursed her lips and shook her head. "No. Seems like you've got it handled."

Mary Lou pointed. "Coffee's in the pot."

Rita headed towards the kitchen. Then stopped. Jason's sister, Edith Mae, sat at one of the desks, staring at her laptop. Large headphones covered her ears. Some kind of music was blasting her drums.

She glanced up at Rita. "Hey." Then she turned her attention back to her screen. Rita blinked and continued on to the kitchen. She pulled a mug from the cupboard and poured a cup of hot coffee.

She glanced over at the dishwasher. The sign that said *broken* was still in place. At least some things hadn't changed.

Mary Lou walked in and joined her, holding out her empty mug. Rita filled it for her.

Mary Lou gestured to the dishwasher. "It's getting fixed tomorrow."

"Jesus," Rita said. "Hope *I'm* not getting replaced."

"I'm sure Hunter Green thinks about it on a daily basis."

Rita wrinkled her nose. Best thing about being in New York was not having to speak to the D.A. For a little while there after Lisa's case, he'd become a bit of a micromanager, checking in with her almost daily.

"What happened to this place? It's all tidy."

"Edith Mae needed something to do besides shoplifting and helping Arbuckle pick up bottles and cans from the side of the road."

"So you hired her as decorator?"

"It was a trade."

Rita put the coffee pot back. "I hate to ask. But what was the trade?"

Mary Lou ignored the question. "What are you doing here? Thought you weren't coming in until Monday."

"I couldn't sit cooped up at home. I'd just annoy myself."

"So, you thought you'd annoy us instead?"

"You didn't answer my question."

"Nor did you."

"You first. I'm the boss."

Mary Lou eyed her. "You sure about that?"

Rita growled.

Mary Lou grinned. "Edith Mae needed a workspace."

"For what?"

"She's advertising her services as an IT specialist. Whatever that is."

"And working out of our office? I don't think that's a good idea."

"You're the one that told her to get a hobby aside from shoplifting."

"Shoplifting isn't a hobby."

"It was to her." Mary Lou leaned forward and lowered her voice. "Besides, it's good for Jason to have her around."

"He regressing?"

"No. But Edith Mae being here might be helping."

Okay, Rita could understand that. "Were the bright flowery magnets her idea?"

Mary Lou grinned. "Of course."

"And the cat tower?"

Mary Lou took a drink of coffee.

"That was you?"

"Well, if the furry bastard is going to live here, he needed something to sleep on besides my lap."

"That thing must have cost a hundred bucks."

"Two."

"It better not have come out of our budget."

"He's a member of the team."

"Mary Lou."

But she had already walked out, stopping by Ted to give him a scratch on the head. Jesus, why couldn't Matt have had a dog? She had a feeling the cat was going to be here longer than she was.

Rita walked towards her office. A new chair sat behind her office. She made her way to it and sat. Not bad. A package sat on her desk. It was from Seattle. She knew what was in it without opening. She'd couriered it herself.

Rita picked up the package and walked to her door. She held it up. "Why is this back?"

Mary Lou's mouth turned down. "Flora passed away before it arrived."

"Jesus."

"I spoke with the facility. They figure the stress from Matt's murder did her heart in."

Rita clenched her teeth together. Flora's death was yet another casualty of Apex. Months later, and they were still catching innocents in their snare.

She thought back to that moment three months ago when she had talked to Flora. How frail her voice had been. Her only son dead. Not understanding why anyone would want to kill her son for doing the right thing.

"She left everything to Matt. So the state will take it all. The facility thought we might have a better use for that."

Rita ripped open the courier envelope. The five hundred dollars they'd taken from Matt's home for security. She stuffed it into another envelope, sealed it, and wrote her name across the flap. Then she walked over to Mary Lou's desk. "Sign it, would you?"

Mary Lou did. "I'll put it in evidence."

"Thank you."

The room had a new steel door as well. Much as the county didn't like spending money on the SCSO, Rita wasn't about to have Apex break in again. Not that there was any proof of that. Or so everyone kept telling her.

Mary Lou nodded her head towards the other item in the envelope. "What about Matt's wallet?"

Matt had been cremated, his ashes shipped to Flora. She wondered where those were now.

"I don't know yet. Evidence for now. As for the money, I was thinking we could donate it to Arbuckle. If I recall correctly, Matt used to give him a few bucks when he saw him in town. I don't think he'd object."

Mary Lou nodded.

Rita glanced around. "Walter and Jason coming in?"

"They've been. They're at the Still Haven Inn."

"More vandalism?" It had started right before she had left for New York. School had just gotten out, so they had all figured bored kids.

"Whoever it is, they're dedicated to the cause."

"Jesus, I'll say. I'll join them."

Mary Lou raised her brows. "Cooler in here than out there."

"Gotta acclimatize sooner or later."

"Well, before you go, a call came in yesterday afternoon. Thought you might want to take it."

"Me?"

"Uh huh. Psychotic woman on Main Street vandalizing a sign in front of the Bighorn Mining building."

"Oh."

"Apparently, she looked a lot like you. You wouldn't happen to know anything about it?"

Rita shrugged. "It took me by surprise."

Mary Lou narrowed her eyes. "Destroying the sign, or seeing it there?"

Rita shrugged. "Both."

Mary Lou snorted.

Rita grabbed the keys to the patrol truck and went out to the parking lot. Her Honda was parked back there in the only sliver of shade. She left it at work now. Much easier to simply walk over from her apartment.

She got into the SCSO vehicle, flicked on the air conditioning, and headed towards Miner's Way.

Chapter Four

RITA PULLED UP TO THE STOP SIGN IN FRONT OF THE Bighorn Mining building. Two construction workers were attending to the sign that she had kicked over.

She pursed her lips, then flipped the indicator, turning left. She pulled up at the side of the road and got out. And immediately regretted it.

Before she even crossed the road, she was sweaty.

So she might as well commit.

She approached the men. One was tall, slump-shouldered with jug ears and sad, droopy eyes. The other was a short redhead.

"You come to take prints?" the redhead asked.

Rita snorted. "Hell, no. I want to know about Lisa's Place."

The tall one shrugged. "Apex hired us to remodel, bring the plumbing and electricity up to code."

"When's it supposed to open?"

He wiped the sweat from his brow. "Dunno. We just got started."

"Either of you know who Lisa is?"

Ginger chuckled. "Probably the one banging the boss."

Rita tightened her lips, refraining from kicking over the sign yet again. "Thank you for your time, gentlemen."

She walked back to the truck. When she got in, she sat for a moment watching the two men walk to the building. Seconds later, they disappeared inside. She drummed her fingers against the steering wheel, wondering if Lisa's place was Helen's idea.

Or Otto's.

Not that she wanted to ask either of them. And she couldn't really see them agreeing to help Apex with such a project.

Maybe Jason would know.

She started the car up again, this time not allowing anything to distract her from the drive to Still Haven Inn. She turned onto Miner's Way, then took an immediate left, pulling onto the well-tended drive.

She spotted the graffiti immediately.

FUCK THE RICH was spray-painted in bright yellow neon across the inn's large slate and glass sign. Rita thought it was an improvement. It brought the pretentious level down a smidge.

Walter was taking photos. Jason was off to the side, engaged in conversation with the owner, Milly Toole.

Rita parked in the front lot and got out.

Milly glanced over at her, mouth tight. "Can you please park around back in the staff area?"

"No. I'm not staff."

Milly glowered at her.

A wide smile crossed Jason's mouth. "Sheriff. I thought you were off until Monday."

She shrugged. "Changed my mind."

Milly folded her arms across her chest. "Good thing. Because those hooligans are at it again."

Rita glanced at the sign. "Can't say I disagree with the sentiment. Color could be more subtle, though."

Milly seemed unamused. "It's the third time this month. What are you all going to do about it?"

"I told you what to do about it before I left for New York."

"And I told you," Milly said, "I'm not installing security cameras. My clientele prefers privacy."

"Which clients are those? The Apex bigwigs, or the cheating spouses?"

Milly's nostrils flared. "Is it too much to ask for some police surveillance?"

"For vandalism?"

"Yes!"

"Not sure how the rest of Still would react if they found out that's where their tax dollars were going."

"Well, I don't agree with my tax dollars going to people who won't help themselves. Whatever happened to personal responsibility?"

"You talking about Lisa's Place?"

"I sure am."

"Isn't Apex behind Lisa's Place? You know, the company that keeps you in business? Take it up with them if you're unhappy with their community service."

Milly looked like she'd eaten something sour.

"Mrs. Toole has hired an extra security guard," Jason said.

"Well, there you go," Rita said. "A step in the right direction."

"Yes, but they can't be everywhere at once."

"Neither can we," Rita said. "If you won't install security cameras, I don't know what to say. Whatever happened to personal responsibility?"

Milly froze, then muttered something under her breath and walked away.

Jason sighed.

"Sorry," Rita said. "Didn't mean to hijack your investigation."

"You didn't. I told her the same thing you did. Security cameras."

"So, no luck finding the mystery taggers?"

Jason shook his head. Together, they walked over to Walter.

"Sheriff," he said, nodding. His face was already shiny with sweat, and it hadn't even begun to get sweltering. He gestured to the two of them. "We've been documenting everything for you, haven't we, Jason?"

Walter was obviously still trying to earn back Jason's goodwill.

"We have," Jason said.

Rita's radio crackled. She pulled it from her belt.

It was Mary Lou. "Got another report of vandalism. Out near Apex."

"Swell."

"Does that mean you're on it?"

"10-4."

"Glad you remembered the call sign."

"I wasn't gone that long."

Mary Lou didn't respond.

Rita restored her radio to her belt. Then she glanced at Jason and Walter. "What do you say we take this party on the road?"

Jason nodded. "I'll grab the cruiser. Meet you here, Walter."

Rita raised her brows. "You park in the staff lot?"

Jason nodded. "She thought it might draw too much attention."

Rita looked up at the sign with its giant neon FUCK THE RICH message. "Yeah, it's the SCSO vehicle that's going to get attention."

Chapter Five

Rita pulled up in front of Apex Global, parking on the shoulder of the road. Jason pulled in behind her.

The vandalism was obvious.

Painted across the road in the near identical spot to where Matt Kirkland's body had been found months earlier was the phrase SMASH THE CAPITALIST PIGS. It was in the same neon yellow as the Still Haven tag.

Beside it were three other similar messages that had recently been tarred over. But instead of covering the last message in broad sweeps, only the letters had been covered. DIE APEX PIGS was still easy to read.

Rita got out of the cruiser and walked over.

Walter followed her, snapping photos. "You disagree with this one?"

"Nope."

"Me neither."

Jason looked at her. "Maybe we should check your place for paint."

"Maybe you should."

He instantly looked worried.

"Just kidding," she said, squeezing his shoulder.

He nodded, then his face tightened. "There's something you should know."

Something other than the Lisa's Place sign? The remodel of the SCSO? Edith Mae as a temporary fixture? She couldn't imagine what.

He hesitated, then nodded towards the gate. Rita spotted him right away. Ken. Only he wasn't dressed in uniform. But a suit. Not an expensive one like Boyd's. But it was obviously the look he was going for. Still had the requisite asshole-mirrored shades on though.

Her heart thudded into her throat. "What the fuck is he doing here?"

"Out on bail," Jason said. "Conditions not to contact you except in the course of employment."

Rita touched the scar on her nose. Jason spotted the motion, and she dropped her hand. She turned her back to the Apex gate, taking a breath. She would not let Ken see that he had rattled her.

"I meant to tell you earlier," Jason said.

"Not your job," Rita said. "Hunter could have given me a goddamn head's up."

Behind them, the gates opened, and three Apex workers emerged with traffic cones, tools, and buckets of tar. They walked towards the graffiti.

Rita straightened her shoulders and met them. "Not until we get photos."

The workers nodded.

"Want me to talk to him?" Jason asked.

Rita shook her head. "Nope."

She wasn't going to let him know that his presence rattled her. She wasn't going to let him see her sweat ever again. Regardless of the temperature.

She strode over to him, pleased to see he hesitated

when he saw her as well. She smiled. Good. He was nervous. Let him be.

"Where's your partner, Clyde? Still in jail?" She spoke first, wasn't about to let him take lead of anything. Even a conversation.

Ken cleared his throat. "No. Bailed out. But he was recalled."

"Recalled?" It made him sound like a defective product. But, then again, that was about right. "To where?"

"New York."

She almost flinched. They had both been in the city at the same time. How odd. Of course, it wasn't surprising they didn't run into each other. New York was no Still, Wyoming. There was anonymity when one was surrounded by millions. It was harder to hide in places like this.

And really, she shouldn't be surprised he was gone. Apex always protected their own. He'd never be back now. What was more surprising was that Ken had stayed. "So why are you here?"

"A condition of my release."

"Clyde not have that condition?"

"He did."

"So?"

He shrugged.

Something else was going on here. He hadn't stayed because he suddenly got a conscience. And then she got it. The suit explained it all. "You got a promotion."

Ken said nothing.

"You got Boyd's job?"

"Not yet."

Not yet. So he'd applied. "Temporary?"

He nodded. "Acting chief."

So that's why he stayed. He was hoping to make it permanent. "You know they killed the last one, right?"

"Suicide."

"Uh huh." Rita knew Ken would never get the job. He didn't have the bandwidth. He was nothing more than a bully with fists. Apex needed someone with the cunning of a shark.

She gestured to the cameras. "They catch anything?"

Ken folded his arms across his chest.

"Ah, jurisdiction."

He nodded.

Jason stepped forward. "No. Someone shot their cameras out."

Ken glared at him.

Rita glanced up at where the security cameras used to sit. Jason was right. They were in pieces. She laughed. Good on the vandals.

"It's not funny," Ken said.

"It is a little," Rita said. "Apex going to replace them?"

Ken clenched his jaw. "They already have. Twice. And this kind of bullshit isn't good for morale."

"*That's* bad for morale? What about murder?" She'd be surprised if Apex employees had any morale left. Three workers dead within a year. One murdered by another employee. And not just any employee. The big boss. She knew a bunch of Still residents had quit after Boyd was officially named as Lisa's killer. But that still left plenty of others that had come from outside to work at the company.

He ignored her question. "Are you finished with the photos?"

Rita glanced over at Walter. "You good?"

He grunted, nodding. Then he went back to the cruiser without a word.

Ever since Apex shot Jason, Walter wanted nothing to do with them. She wasn't sure if that was for her benefit. Or because he thought they'd come after him next.

"You got any leads?" Ken asked.

Rita glanced over at the graffiti. The Apex workers had begun the process of tarring the road. "Where's that graffiti located, Jason?"

"Two hundred and one feet from Apex's front gate."

"Yeah, so that would make this a SCSO case."

"I believe so, Sheriff," Jason said.

"Which means, Ken, I don't got to tell you a goddamn thing." She had no interest in helping Apex out with their vandal problem. Or any problem. She'd been down that road before, and it got her beaten and her deputy shot.

If this was costing Apex money, she didn't give a shit.

"Listen," Ken said. "I know we got off on the wrong foot."

"Which foot is that?" Rita asked. "The one where your Apex pals shot my deputy? Or the one where you tried to frame a homeless man for the murder your boss committed?"

Ken flushed. "I knew nothing about those."

"Or maybe it was the one where you lured me to the reservoir with my dad's phone and tried to kill me."

He sealed his mouth shut.

"I thought so. Come on, Jason."

She turned and walked back to the truck. God, it was hot already. By afternoon, it was going to be stifling. She stopped outside the vehicle.

"Breathe," Jason said.

She glowered at him. "When did you become my caretaker?"

"Sorry, sheriff."

She saw hurt in his eyes.

"Fuck. I'm sorry, Jason. I'm pissed at Ken, not you. I tried to get Apex investigated for your shooting."

"I know. Hunter Green told me. But he wasn't about to stir up a hornets' nest."

"No." Hunter's message had been clear. Apex would be staying, and there was nothing she could do. She'd find a way to take them down, but she'd have to play it smart and patient. The latter wasn't her strongest suit.

She wiped her brow. "Let's get back to the SCSO. It's too damn hot to stand around talking outside."

Jason patted her back. "See you at the office."

She grunted and got into the truck, then turned on the ignition and blasted the air conditioning. She turned the vehicle around, then glanced back at Ken. He was gesturing to one of the workers where to apply the tar. The man looked like he wanted to take his brush to Ken's face.

Rita understood the impulse.

Ken looked up and met her gaze. Her stomach soured, and she hit the gas. Maybe she should've stayed in New York after all.

Chapter Six

RITA GLANCED OVER AT EDITH MAE'S DESK. IT WAS EMPTY. "Where did our resident thief go?"

"Merritt's drugs," Mary Lou said.

Rita blinked. "I thought the point was to keep her away from that place."

"She's installing a security system for them."

"Bullshit."

"Seems she knows all the blind spots."

Rita couldn't argue with that. Edith Mae had been keeping Merritt's on its toes, ever since she had returned from New York the first time.

She walked over to Jason and Walter's desks. Walter had printed out the latest photos from Apex and Still Haven and was adding them to the whiteboard with flower magnets.

Rita studied the photos. Apex, Elk Mountain Equity, Chester's Gas and Go, and the Still Haven Inn had all been hit by graffiti. At first, she thought only Apex was being targeted, but the inclusion of the others had widened the playing field.

"Let's review," she said, claiming Walter's chair before he could sit. "What do we know about our favorite local artist?"

Walter stood, tapping the whiteboard. "We've got nothing on the paint. Checked the local stores and even a couple hardware stores up Casper, but no match yet."

"Maybe they ordered online?" Rita said.

"Manufacturer says this particular paint color has been discontinued for three years," Jason said. "He's trying to track down some old bulk orders. See if anyone in the area ordered them."

"Good. What about witnesses?"

Jason shook his head. "Arbuckle spotted someone suspicious dumping some bags in the woods near the inn, but it turned out to be garbage."

"What else do we know?"

"They have access to a vehicle," Walter said. "Given the timing and distances of the targets, it can't be someone on foot."

Rita stared at him a moment.

He shuffled from one foot to the other. "What?"

"Excellent observation," she said.

He flushed.

"I think it's obvious it's the same artist," Rita said. "Anything distinctive about the handwriting?" They all leaned close, examining the photos. Large block letters. Nothing distinctive about them, aside from the color and the location.

Walter shrugged. "Hell if I know. We could request a handwriting analyst from Casper, but they'd probably tell us to fuck off. Honestly, this is probably worth about 20 hours less than we've already invested."

"You're not wrong. We got anything else on the books at the moment?"

Mary Lou opened her mouth.

Rita jumped in before she could speak. "Besides Wilson's communist cows? Or the vandalism of the Lisa's Place sign?"

Mary Lou shook her head. "Nothing."

Ted meowed.

Rita glanced over at the cat tower. "You don't get a say. You haven't even welcomed me back."

Ted lifted a leg and began licking his asshole.

"You getting your manners from Ken?" she asked the cat.

She turned back to the others. They were all staring at her. "What?"

"Should we give you two a moment alone?" Mary Lou asked.

Rita gave her the finger. Mary Lou laughed.

"You think the two are related?" Jason asked. "The Lisa's Place sign and the graffiti?"

"No," Rita said. "They aren't."

Walter eyed his chair, so she got up and rolled it back to him. Soon as he caught it, he sat. "Sooner or later these kids are gonna get caught red-handed."

"Yeah, but let's hope it's us and not Apex that does the catching," Rita said, heading to her office.

She had one voicemail. She dialed in and listened. Hunter Green. He'd heard she was back in town and thought he'd touch base.

Rita considered calling him back. But she'd probably just growl at him. So she deleted the message and spent the remainder of the day catching up on paperwork. Towards the afternoon, Jason tried to convince her to work a speed trap with him. But no way in hell was she going outside if it wasn't urgent.

Walter had volunteered. Apparently, he'd rather melt in a hot car than risk her asking him for help with the files.

She finished up just before five and waved to Mary Lou. She was in the kitchen, feeding Ted. Rita didn't bother to wait. What had started as a five-minute "feed the cat" moment had turned into a half-hour ritual. Feed the cat, change his water, check the litter box, floof his bed (whatever Mary Lou meant by that), give him some pats so that he knew he was a good boy.

Rita had no doubt that Ted knew.

The more mice he caught, the more praise Mary Lou lavished on him. She half suspected Ted was angling for a new home. And he'd chosen Mary Lou as his mark.

"Rita!" Mary Lou caught her at the back door.

"Yeah?"

"Did you RSVP for Saturday night?"

Rita hesitated. "I'm not going."

"Of course you are."

Rita glared at her. "I'm not."

"I told Otto I'd bring you myself."

"You shouldn't have done that."

"I'll pick you up at six."

Rita refrained from stamping her foot. "I might have come to Still for Otto. But as far as I'm concerned, the cancer can have him."

"You don't mean that."

"I sure do." Okay, maybe not really. But that still didn't mean she was going. She walked out the front door.

Her phone blipped.

She pulled it out and looked at it.

Mary Lou: *You're coming. No arguments.*

Rita turned back to the office. Mary Lou was watching her from one of the windows. She refrained from making a face. She was trying to be more mature. It was one of the agreements she had made with herself when returning from New York.

Time to start acting like an adult.

Rita walked across the street and was coated in sweat by the time she arrived at the back of Bighorn Bean. She unlocked the door and went straight to the shower. The water was still cold.

This time she didn't care.

When she finished, she toweled off and got dressed. Jean shorts and a well-loved Dolly Parton tee.

Then she surveyed the sad state of her fridge. It hadn't magically improved since the day before. Her stomach rumbled, but she didn't have the energy to go to the store.

Mainly because she didn't want to deal with anyone else who was surprised she came back. She knew a good portion of Still didn't believe she had gone to New York for a trial. They figured she was running away. Again. And not that she had needed to know this. But part way through her trip, Otto had texted her to let her know folks were making bets as to whether she would return or not. She wondered if Walter was one of them.

She walked over to her tiny couch and sat. She'd stayed with her friend Lara in New York. Not that she'd seen her a lot. But when she wasn't on night shift, she'd gotten used to having someone to talk to. She glanced over at the fig.

Bad enough that she was talking to a cat. She wasn't about to start talking to the plant.

She pulled out her phone. Scrolled to Cash. *Wanna get supper?*

He responded almost immediately. *Busy. Another time?*

She frowned, wondered what he was doing. Was he on a date? A twinge of unwarranted jealousy burned in her gut. That surprised her.

He was probably just working late.

She messaged back: *Sure.*

She stared up at the ceiling, then called The Shaft.

One of the servers answered. Rita couldn't remember her name. Deborah, maybe? She ordered a burger and fries to go.

Deborah told her ten minutes.

Ugh, that meant going out in the heat again.

Maybe she should call and cancel.

But she was starving. Nothing she had eaten in New York held a candle to the food from The Shaft. Rita rolled off the couch and made her way downstairs. She crossed the street and walked down the alley to the parking lot behind the office. Victor and Stu were in the empty lot across from the office, chucking rocks at the sign announcing a new grocery store would be arriving in 2018. But the only thing that had arrived was the sign.

Rita walked over to them.

Victor, long hair as greasy as ever, his soul patch still spotty and looking more like pubic hair than facial hair, smiled smugly. "Hey, Sheriff Jone-Ass. Planning to seize our rocks?"

He cupped his genitals.

She ignored the gesture. "Jone-Ass. Funny. Haven't heard that one before. Wanted to ask you about the graffiti around town."

"We didn't do it," Stu said.

"Didn't think you had. Not sure you could handle the spelling of 'capitalist.'"

"Then what do you want?" Victor asked.

Rita turned her attention to Stu. "Don't supposed you've heard any rumors about who the artist, or artists, might be?"

Victor raised his chin. "Even if we did, we wouldn't tell you, pig."

Stu reached into his pocket and pulled out his phone. "They hit Dad's shop."

"What?" She hadn't heard that.

He nodded. Thumbing through photos but shielding the screen so that she couldn't see what he was scrolling past. Finally, he found what he was looking for. He turned the screen so she could see it.

"Dad had me clean it up."

The photo was of a broken window in the front of the store. He flicked to the next photo. Same yellow neon paint sprayed on the wall.

PEOPLE BEFORE PROFITS.

Funny, considering everybody knew that the Rancher's Pantry was barely surviving. They were the very mom and pop-type shop that giant corporate stores were gobbling out of existence.

"Can I get a copy of that?"

Stu hesitated.

"Don't help her, asshole," Victor said. Rita wondered if he was going to grow up to head a company that oppressed others. He was well on his way with his attitude.

"I'm not, asshole. I'm helping my dad." He looked at Rita. "What's your number?"

Rita told him. He texted the photos over.

"Thanks, Stu. Anything else you can tell me?"

"No, ma'am."

Victor muttered something under his breath.

"Thank you, gentlemen. Be safe out there."

She walked back to the parking lot, unlocked the Honda, and got in. She paused to let the two of them cross in front of her, heading back to Main Street. Apparently, the allure of chucking rocks had grown stale after their interaction with Rita.

Victor flipped her off. Stu glared at him and pulled his hand down. She laughed. At least one of them might turn out not to be a piece of shit.

She turned right, waved at them, and then drove out to The Shaft.

Chapter Seven

She spotted Cash's truck in the parking lot.

So much for being busy.

Maybe he just didn't want to have supper with her. She tried not to feel hurt. He could have told her that.

Except, they weren't dating. They'd only hooked up once since that time at his house, and they'd both been pretty drunk. They hadn't talked much about it, if at all. Besides, it was her that was keeping him at a distance.

Although at least this time, she had told him that she was going to New York. That had to be an improvement, right?

She thought about turning around and going back home. She could stop by tomorrow and pay for the discarded meal. But she was hungry. And the Rancher's Pantry would be closed by now. And she wasn't going to drive into Casper. So it wasn't like she had a whole lot of food options.

Unless she wanted to go to the drugstore and pick up a chocolate bar. Or join Otto.

Nope.

She turned off the Honda and got out.

Thankfully, it was both cool and dark inside the restaurant.

She walked over to the bar and waved to Ruby Joe.

"Welcome back, Sheriff. You cost me twenty bucks."

Rita stared at her. "You bet against me?"

Ruby Joe shrugged. "It had all the hallmarks of an earlier flight to New York."

"It did not. This one was planned."

"Uh huh."

"I had a trial."

"If you say so."

"Besides, what would I be running from?" Rita asked. "Apex doesn't scare me." Okay, it might a little. But she wasn't about to tell Ruby Joe that.

Ruby Joe pointed across the room.

Cash was seated at a table. Alone.

But then a beautiful, dark-haired woman in expensive looking jeans and a plaid shirt exited from the hallway that led to the bathrooms. She walked over to Cash and sat across from him.

Oh.

He did have a date.

Rita wasn't sure how long she stood there staring, but it was long enough for the woman to notice, then say something to Cash.

Oh shit.

Cash turned, caught Rita's eye.

Shit, shit, shit.

Rita turned back to Ruby Joe. But she was gone. Fuck, where did she go? She emerged from the kitchen with a paper bag. It seemed to take her forever to arrive at Rita.

Rita slapped a twenty on the bar and grabbed the bag. "Thanks, Ruby Joe."

"Anytime."

She hustled out, not turning around. She didn't want to know if Cash was following her. She also didn't want to know if he wasn't.

She unlocked the Honda and climbed in. The moment her ass hit the seat, she flinched. Damn it. The material had already gotten hot against her bare legs. She winced and started up the SUV. Then her phone pinged.

She didn't want to look.

But she had no willpower.

It was Cash. *Not what you think.*

She texted back: *How do you know what I'm thinking?*

Because I know you.

Dammit. He did too. She chucked the phone onto the passenger seat and drove, ignoring the other pings that followed.

By the time she got back to the SCSO and parked, her phone was quiet. She picked it up, gathered the paper bag, and walked home. When she entered her apartment, she was both sweaty and had lost her appetite. Not even the fries smelled tempting. What had she been thinking, buying a hot meal?

She chucked the paper bag into the fridge and went to her bedroom, tossing her phone on the bedside table. It was still early, but whatever. She was still on New York time. She stripped off her clothes and climbed into bed, pulling the comforter over her head.

She was asleep within seconds.

Chapter Eight

Rita woke early. Soft blue moonlight poured in through the bedroom window. She'd fallen asleep despite the blind being open.

It was too early for even the birds.

She dragged a pillow over her face, hoping to fall back asleep.

But she might as well have turned the lights back on and had a cold shower. She was wide awake.

She flung the pillow aside and glanced over at her phone. Then she plugged it into the charger and pulled up her messages. And saw the thread of texts she'd missed from Cash.

Call me.

Please.

Rita?

Alright, you're pissed.

I'm headed to bed. Call me tomorrow.

God, they were ridiculously similar to the ones Dale had sent her months earlier. Was she that predicable?

She set the phone down, not even sure what bothered her the most. Was she looking for a reason to be mad and to write him off, sabotaging the relationship before it could resume?

Or was she mad that she had obviously jumped to some kind of conclusion? *Not what you think.*

Couldn't she trust that he meant that? Give him the benefit of the doubt? She pulled a pillow back over her head. And eventually fell back asleep.

She woke to voices and the smell of coffee. That meant it was after 7 a.m. The apartment had fairly good insulation, but when the chatter got loud enough in the Bighorn Bean, it served as a fairly efficient alarm clock.

Rita got up and turned the shower on.

Still cold.

Alright, this was becoming tiresome. She made a mental note to call Abigail again. Then she braved her way through another icy shower, washing quickly, then hopping out and getting dressed in her uniform.

She still had nothing for breakfast. She wasn't about to dive into ramen or stale crackers. And even though coffee and fresh baked goods awaited below, she didn't feel up to seeing anybody just yet. So she opened the fridge and grabbed the paper bag.

She didn't even get a plate. Or bother to heat up the burger and fries. Just flattened the paper bag and used that instead. God, she was practically feral. So much for maturity.

Both the burger and the fries were cold, but delicious.

Or maybe it was just that she was starving.

She scarfed it down, watching the local morning news on her phone. Well, as close to local as could be. It was News 13 out of Casper. Apparently, her colleagues there were dealing with drug overdoses this morning. The graffiti in Still didn't even rate a mention.

Rita finished up her breakfast and brushed her teeth. Then she walked to work and got the Honda. Might as well kill two birds with one stone.

She drove to the Rancher's Pantry, air conditioning blowing. The grocery store was located near the Divine Horizon church. Across the street from the store was an empty lot with yet another sign. The one had been there before she left for New York.

It read, *STILL SHADOWS: COMING SOON — DESIGNER HOMES. FORGE YOUR OWN DESTINY.*

And unlike the land where Stu and Victor had been throwing rocks, this spot showed promise of development. A bulldozer sat silent on the dirt, and some of the trees and brush had already been cleared.

What Still needed with designer homes, Rita had no idea. Didn't Apex already have their own private little community? Maybe they really were having trouble attracting new employees from town. Was this them needing room for more flatlanders?

Or maybe it had nothing to do with Apex at all. After all, this wasn't their land. At least she hadn't heard any rumors that it had been sold. Maybe someone else was developing Still Shadows, hoping to attract the ultra-wealthy who wanted to get away from the hustle and bustle of the city. That's what was happening in Jackson Hole and other parts of Wyoming.

It was never a good thing for the locals.

Rita pulled into a parking space at the grocery store and got out of the Honda. The broken window hadn't been replaced. It was now covered with plywood. Flecks of neon paint could still be seen on the other window. But Stu had done a good job of getting rid of it.

Then Helen rolled out a cart of tomatoes, setting it in place on the sidewalk. Rita froze. Not moving.

But Helen hadn't spotted her and had returned to the store.

God, she had a whole list of people she didn't want to run into. Maybe she should have stayed in New York.

She hustled inside, grabbing a basket and taking refuge in the bakery aisle. She hadn't seen Helen since the night she had arrested George for Matt Kirkland's murder.

She should have asked Cash to stop at a grocery store in Casper before he brought her home.

She walked quickly down each aisle, finding the basics — toilet paper, bread, peanut butter, eggs, milk, butter, and a few cans of SpaghettiOs.

She was about to head to produce, but saw Helen hovering around the bananas. So she walked to the cashier, keeping an eye out for Stu's father. Usually he was either walking along the front end or holed away in his upstairs office, spying on his customers (or employees) in the checkout lanes through a little window.

Rita emptied her basket on the conveyer belt. A teenage girl rang her through while a pimply-faced teenage boy bagged the groceries. "Peter around?" Rita asked.

The girl immediately looked worried. "Is there a problem with the service?"

"Service is just fine."

The girl nodded, then grabbed the phone on the half-wall next to her register. She pressed a button and spoke, her voice echoing throughout the store's speakers.

"Mr. Walters, the sheriff would like to speak with you."

Rita winced. If Helen didn't know she was here before, she sure the hell did now.

The girl turned to her and smiled. "He'll be with you shortly."

"Thanks."

She nodded. "Twenty-nine sixty-three."

Jesus. No wonder Still residents had started shopping in Casper. Rita pulled out her card, tapped the point of sale.

From behind her came, "Rita."

Shit. She turned. "Helen."

"I'm glad to see you. I wanted to talk to you about something."

"Afraid I'm working."

Helen glanced down at the bags of groceries.

Rita shrugged. "Just got back from New York."

"Yes, Otto said you had gone. A case or something."

Trial. But Rita didn't bother to correct her.

Peter strode up, glancing at Helen. "Problem?"

Helen shook her head. "No."

"Then the produce needs attending."

God, wasn't he a fantastic boss. Rita hoped she didn't sound like that when talking to Jason or Walter. Well, Jason anyway.

Helen stepped away, disappointment dulling her eyes. When she was out of earshot, Peter turned to face her. "What do you want, Sheriff?"

He barely masked his annoyance at being interrupted with whatever he was doing up in his office. She wondered if Stu had told him he'd told her about the vandalism.

"Heard you had a bout of vandalism."

Peter folded his hands in front of his pot belly. "Yes, Stu told me he informed you."

That surprised Rita. But then again, maybe he was more fearful of his father than he was the police.

"When did it happen?"

He shrugged. "Couple weeks ago?"

"You can't be more specific?"

"No."

God, he was as verbose as Victor. Maybe he and Stu had been swapped at birth.

"You didn't report it."

"Insurance covered it. Probably just stupid kids being stupid kids. Not the first time we've been vandalized. Won't be the last."

"Have you had messages like that before? People before profits."

"Not like that."

"So, no suspects? Disgruntled employees?"

"Brats that never had to work a day in their pathetic entitled lives."

God, he was a charmer.

"Besides, I treat my employees well. I'd be surprised if any of them would do something like this."

If his treatment of Helen was anything to go by, Rita wasn't sure his employees would agree. "Don't suppose you do any business with Apex."

His brow furrowed. "Apex?"

She nodded.

He shrugged. "Some of their employees shop here, of course, but not the company proper. The suits tried to lowball me on bulk purchases. When I wouldn't budge, they chose to order anything they needed from Casper." He shifted impatiently. "So Apex can fuck themselves."

No lost love then. Maybe she should consider him a suspect.

"Is there anything else, Sheriff? I need to get ready for an audit."

"IRS?"

"No." He seemed genuinely offended by the assumption. "Store audit."

"No, that's it. Thank you, Peter."

He grunted and left without saying goodbye.

Helen was hovering. Rita picked up her groceries and walked out to the Honda. She got them stored in the trunk, then hopped in. She was driving out of the parking lot when she spotted Helen exiting the store, looking for her.

Rita drove past her, pretending not to see.

Chapter Nine

RITA PUT HER GROCERIES AWAY.

She'd parked behind the Bighorn Bean because she hadn't wanted to cart her groceries across the street from work. When she finished that, she dialed Cash's number. She felt strangely mature. He couldn't very well say she was running away from him if she called him back, could he?

There was no answer. Voicemail.

She wondered if he was still asleep.

And if the woman she'd spotted him with last night was with him. Tucked up in bed beside him. Or on top of him.

"Stop it," she said.

She got the beep, inviting her to leave a message. But she hung up instead. So maybe she wasn't that mature.

She stared at his texts.

Then typed out: *I called.*

And hit send.

She put her phone away, then headed to work, crossing the street and entering the office through the front doors.

Jason was already there, standing in front of the white-board, reviewing the photos.

"I've got another one for you," she said.

He turned. "Apex again?"

She shook her head. "The Rancher's Pantry. A couple of weeks ago."

She pulled out her phone and emailed the photos to him. He studied them, frowning, before sending them to print. "That doesn't really fit the profile."

"That's what I thought. Profits before people? The Rancher's Pantry is hanging onto existence by a thread."

Jason retrieved the photos she'd sent from the printer and added them to the whiteboard.

God, she wanted to laugh at the ridiculousness of this crime and how badly they all wanted to catch the culprit. She hadn't cared that much when they'd targeted Apex.

In fact, she had laughed when Ruby Joe told her that Apex sent a formal request to have the graffiti on the road repaved. She'd informed them it wasn't in the budget. And that eventually summer sun and winter snow would help it fade.

Apex obviously hadn't liked that answer, because the next morning the graffiti had been tarred. The next time, they never bothered to make the request. Just went out and covered it up. Let them spend their tainted money on cameras and road repairs.

But the Rancher's Pantry was Still property. Peter had inherited the store from his father. He had to have been pissed that he was targeted.

Jason glanced over at her. "What are you thinking?"

"Every business in town is probably connected to Apex in some way. Payroll runs through the bank. Apex folks refuel at the Gas and Go." Rita wiped the sweat from her forehead. "But until I found out about the Rancher's

Pantry, I would have thought someone had a vendetta against Apex."

"Yeah."

"Not even any rumors of who it might be?"

Jason shook his head.

Rita dropped into Walter's chair, spinning back and forth. "Okay, that's surprising."

Usually the town rumor-mill would have been in full-swing with theories. Or actual knowledge.

So if it was from someone from Still that was targeting Apex, the town was holding the secret tight to its collective chest.

And if it was a disgruntled Apex employee, then the town either didn't care or was on board with it. After all, the company killed Lisa.

They heard the back door open. Voices. Walter and Mary Lou.

Rita got up from Walter's chair.

Mary Lou stopped when she entered. "You're here early."

"Couldn't sleep," they both said at the same time.

Rita glanced at him. She knew why she wasn't sleeping. A combination of jet lag and emotional unintelligence. But Jason? "You having nightmares about the shooting again?" she asked him.

His cheeks deepened to a dark red. "Heat."

She knew he was lying. But she wasn't about to call him out about it in front of the other two.

Mary Lou walked over to the cat tower and petted Ted. Rita could hear him purring from where she stood.

"How come you get purrs and I get full view of his asshole?"

"I'm the one that feeds him," she said.

Rita couldn't argue with that.

Walter sat, gesturing to Mary Lou. "She's gone full cat lady."

Mary Lou glared at him. "You're just jealous."

"Of a cat?"

Mary Lou turned back to Ted. "Ignore him."

Walter held up a flash drive. "I stopped by the bank this morning and picked up CCTV footage from the incident the other night."

Rita blinked. "You policed outside of work hours?"

He flushed. "Didn't want to walk over later. Too hot."

Of course.

"Plug it in," Rita said.

Walter swiveled around and signed into his computer. Then he loaded the footage. On screen were two shadowy figures dressed in all black.

Rita peered closer, but the footage was grainy. Maybe they were wearing masks. Maybe not. "Well, we learned something new. There's two of them."

"Can't tell if they're female or male," Jason said.

"Could be Armenian dwarves," Walter said.

Rita glanced over at him. "That's oddly specific."

He grunted. "I've got court today in Casper, so I'll be out of pocket until this evening."

Rita nodded. "Have fun with that."

She went to her office and sat down, turning on the computer. Glancing at her phone. Still no response from Cash.

She set it aside, glancing out the window. Right when a black car pulled into the front lot. She got up and walked over to one of the narrow windows, looking out.

It was a black Audi.

And it had to belong to Apex.

A woman got out of the driver's seat. She looked anywhere in age from early twenties to late thirties. She wore the equivalent of a business suit. She walked around to the rear passenger seat and opened it up.

Another woman got out. If Rita had thought the first woman's suit was expensive, it probably cost mere pennies compared to the one worn by her passenger. She could have been anywhere from mid-twenties to mid-fifties.

Shades hid her eyes, and she walked with the air of a woman who rarely heard the word no. Definitely Apex.

The first woman retrieved an iPad from the car, clutching it to her chest. Then she hit the fob, locking the vehicle, and ran after her passenger.

The first woman stopped suddenly and glanced over at her.

Rita didn't care she was caught staring. This was her patch. She held the woman's eyes until the woman turned away.

Rita grinned. No way was she going to break contact first.

She walked back to her desk and sat. Whatever Apex wanted, Mary Lou could deal with.

She signed into her computer, pulled up her emails.

But before she knew it, Mary Lou was standing in her door. "You got company."

"I saw. Tell Apex to go away. I'm busy."

Mary Lou snorted. "I happen to know you have nothing going on."

"They don't need to know that."

"They'll just come back."

Rita sighed. That was true. "You're right, send them in."

Mary Lou nodded, then retreated back to her desk.

Rita pulled up the voice app on her phone, setting it to record and placing it on the desk.

By the time Mary Lou brought them both to her office, Rita was on her feet.

Glasses entered first. Stepping forward, hand outstretched. Rita caught a whiff of perfume. Damn, this woman even smelled expensive. "Angela Ruiz."

"Sheriff Jonas." Rita took her hand, shook. Firm, dry, confident. Rita hoped her own hand conveyed as much.

The other woman hovered behind her, eyes fixed on her boss.

"And you are?" Rita asked, releasing Ruiz's hand.

"My assistant, Peggy Saunders," Angela said. "She'll be taking notes."

Rita lifted her phone. "So will I."

"I presumed as much."

"Have a seat," Rita said, gesturing to the chair in front of her desk.

Angela Ruiz sat, removing her glasses and crossing her legs. She had large, expressive brown eyes.

Rita sat. "What brings Apex to our SCSO this morning? Hopefully not another dead employee." She tried to keep the venom out of her voice. She failed.

She thought she saw a flash of empathy in Angela's eyes as the woman said, "I heard about Lisa. My condolences."

Rita dropped her eyes. She'd rather Angela take the hard approach. She wasn't sure what to do with Apex employee's sympathy. "What can I do for you?" Rita asked. Sooner she got this over with, the better.

"I thought I should come by and introduce myself."

"Why? You replacing Farmer?"

Angela laughed. "Heavens no. I've replaced Philip."

"Philip?"

"Yes. I'm the new CEO of Apex Global."

That took Rita by surprise. She hadn't heard about a change in leadership.

"Philip was asked to step aside," Angela continued.

"Is that corporate speak for cleaning up after a scandal?"

She smiled. "The board wished to go in a different direction."

So Angela wasn't that different from Boyd at all. Or Price either, she imagined. Not that she had had much face-to-face experience with him. But Angela was still putting Apex first. Keeping its secrets.

"In other words, you want to reassure Still that Apex is a valued member of the community," Rita said.

"Exactly."

"And that nothing is wrong with the water."

Angela's smile faltered. "The EPA investigated. They found no contamination that originated at Apex. I cannot speak to the contaminants they found from decades of mine runoff."

That was true. Rita had seen the report herself. "Investors need to know there's nothing to worry about."

"Exactly."

"And that's the real reason you're here," Rita said. "Nothing to do with the community. Everything to do with reassuring the investors."

"There were many reasons Apex parted ways with Victor. The memo was only one reason."

Rita was quiet a moment. "I supposed you paid him out."

Angela nodded. "I believe he is sitting on a yacht in the Bahamas this very minute."

Unless that was code for dead, Apex had obviously made him a financial offer he couldn't refuse.

"What bothered Apex more?" Rita asked. "That he killed Farmer, or wrote the memo?"

Angela inclined her head. "I'm sure I don't know what you're talking about."

"Ah," Rita said. "It was neither, was it? It was that he got caught. And Apex business was spilled publicly."

There was a flash of something in Angela's eyes that belied the smile on her face. Rita had no doubt that despite her friendly appearance, she was ultimately cut out of the same shit that made Farmer and Price.

Rita sat back in her chair. "What is it that you want, Ms. Ruiz?"

"I'm here in a new spirit of collaboration and cooperation."

"Which means what?"

"I want a more mutually beneficial relationship with the SCSO."

"Why?"

"Community."

Bullshit.

Rita glanced over at Peggy. She averted her eyes. "Your assistant ever talk?"

"Only when necessary." Probably how she kept her job. Keeping her mouth shut.

"As much as I'd like to believe you, Angela," Rita said, turning back to the subject at hand. "I don't believe a goddamn thing coming out of your mouth."

"Then why do you think I'm here?"

"To mark your territory. Intimidate me into keeping out of Apex business."

"I'm sorry that you've interpreted my good faith attempt at bridge building as hostile."

"Well, be comforted. I have no interest in Apex's business. Stay out of my way, and I'll stay out of yours."

"I believe I can earn your trust. You'll see that I'm a very different beast to Mr. Price."

"But still a beast," Rita said.

Angela stood, slipping her shades on. "Give me time, Sheriff. I will prove you wrong."

"I've got all the time in the world," Rita said.

Angela smiled and held out her hand.

Rita stood, taking it. Angela's hand was just as confident as the first time Rita had taken it. Although, she may have shown a little more strength this time.

"Thank you for your time," Angela said.

Rita grunted.

Rita went to the window and watched them depart. They stood for a moment on the front steps, while Peggy picked Ted-hairs from Angela's skirt.

Angela glanced over at the window again. Caught Rita watching for a second time. This time it was Rita who turned away first.

Chapter Ten

RITA WALKED OUT OF THE OFFICE. MARY LOU AND JASON had stopped what they were doing to look at her.

"How'd it go?" Mary Lou asked.

"It's a new spirit of collaboration and cooperation with Apex."

"What does that mean?" Jason asked.

"Hell if I know," Rita said. "That was Angela Ruiz. She's taken over from the now deposed Victor Price."

"How nice of her to pay our little backwater a visit," Mary Lou said.

"Right?" Rita grabbed the keys to the truck. "I'll be back in an hour."

No one asked where she was going. Most likely because they knew. She'd done it a couple times a week before she'd left for New York. Go out and visit Lisa's grave. Today, she retrieved Matt's wallet and the envelope of money that Mary Lou had placed in evidence. Then she headed out to the truck.

Driving out past The Shaft.

Still Cemetery was another ten minutes along the road.

The lot was empty when she arrived. She walked the rows until she arrived. There was a bouquet of fresh roses in a mason jar. They had just started to wilt.

Helen, probably.

She read the card.

Nope.

Arnold. Lisa's brother.

Good kid.

Rita got out Matt's wallet and her pocketknife. She dug up the grass, peeling it back, making a hole. She stuffed Matt's wallet inside. Then she put the dirt back and lay the grass flat.

She hoped he didn't mind. He and Lisa being buried together. They had died for the same cause.

Maybe they could rest easy together.

Then she walked back to the truck. Got in and drove back into town, stopping at Elk Mountain Equity. She hadn't seen Arbuckle since returning to Still, but she didn't want to be hanging onto the cash if it could do him some good.

She hoped wherever he was, he was cool.

Inside, she approached the counter and spotted Margot. On the wall behind the front counter was a plaque with Margot's photo on it. Beneath it were the words, "Margot Hawley, Branch Manager."

Rita glanced back at Margot. Gone was the timid young woman with caked-on makeup she'd first met a few months ago. In her place stood a radiant, confident young woman.

"Sheriff," Margot greeted her.

"Rita," Rita said.

Margot nodded her head in acknowledgement.

Rita gestured to the photo. "Congratulations on the promotion."

"Well, thank you for the recommendation letter."

"My pleasure. Where did Donald wind up?" Rita knew that Donald's wife had left him. Lisa hadn't been the only underage girl he'd harassed. More had come forward in the month after Lisa's death. No one wanted to press charges.

But word had gotten out.

"The bank shipped him to Cheyenne."

Rita snorted. "Promotion?"

Margot shook her head. "Teller."

At least one company around did things that made sense. "What are you doing working the counter?"

"We're short-handed today. And I really don't mind. I always enjoyed dealing with our customers."

"And that," Rita said, "is why you got the job as manager."

Margot laughed.

"Arbuckle Kinder have an account?" Rita pulled the envelope out of her shirt pocket. "I have a deposit for him."

"Let me check." Margot scrolled through some menus on her computer and then frowned. "He has one, but it's inactive."

"Can you reactivate it?"

Margot nodded. "He'd need to come in and sign some paperwork."

"I'll let him know." Rita tore open the envelope and extracted the five hundred dollars. "Can I get a receipt for that?"

Margot took the money, typed some more, then printed out a deposit receipt, handing it to Rita. "Just tell him to swing by, and we can get him set up with a new card."

"Will do," Rita said, pocking the receipt. "Thanks again, Margot."

Her phone rang when she hit the bank's vestibule. She hesitated, wanting to take the call inside where it was cool.

Mary Lou.

"Hey."

"Moses called."

Rita blinked. "Biblical Moses?"

Mary Lou sighed. "Moses Grant. He owns the land where the Still Shadows custom homes are being built."

"Okay."

"He wants to meet with you at the site. Says he has something to show you."

"He say what?"

"Nope. My guess is vandalism."

"Okay. I'm at the bank. Tell Jason to meet me here."

"Will do."

"Also, who names a place Still Shadows? Sounds like a graveyard or the title of a vampire TV show coming soon to the CW."

"If you're about to make fun of *Supernatural*, you and me are going to have a problem, boss."

"Never saw it," Rita said, disconnecting. She waited inside until she saw Jason. They met at the truck. She tossed him the keys, then climbed into the passenger seat.

Soon as he had the vehicle started, Jason yawned. Dark circles ringed his eyes.

"Jesus," she said. He looked over at her. "You look like shit. You still going to therapy?"

He nodded, pulling into the road, making his way along Main. "Yeah."

"Is it working?"

"I think so. There's just a lot to sort through." He smiled. But it looked forced. Something was definitely going on with Jason. She made a note to chat with him off-hours. Maybe even take him for a drink.

Jason turned left, then turned right and parked in the Rancher's Pantry lot. They both sat for a moment. Not that the silence was awkward. Neither of them wanted to get out of the air conditioning.

Finally, Jason shut off the ignition, and they got out. Rita spotted a heavyset man in his sixties, leaning against the bulldozer. He had weathered skin and broad shoulders. His plaid shirt was tucked into his jeans. He had a surprisingly relaxed air about him, like he had all the time in the world.

"That Moses?" she asked.

"Yeah."

Rita walked across the road, hand out. "Morning. Mr. Grant."

He shook her hand, his fingers strong and callused. "Sheriff."

Rita glanced around for the graffiti but saw none. Then she eyed the bulldozer. "They vandalize your machine?"

"Pardon?"

"Figured you got hit my mischief-makers."

He shook his head. "Nah. Found this this morning."

He gestured for them to follow, then led them to a pit. Next to it lay a skull, speckled with dirt.

Rita crouched next to it.

"Thought at first it was fake," he said. "You know, kids joking around."

Rita nodded. Studying the skull. It probably would have been her first thought as well. Only this skull didn't look fake. At all. The bone was cream colored. A tooth was missing. The nose had what looked like bits of cartilage adhering to it.

There was a hole in the occipital bone. If this was real, whoever it was had been shot in the back of the head.

Moses pointed at the bottom of the pit. "I took his head clean off with the digger. Or hers."

The rest of the skeleton lay partially exposed.

Rita turned to Jason. "Call Casper. Tell 'em we got a body."

"More than one," Moses said.

"What?" Rita and Jason said in unison.

Moses walked over to a mini mountain of dirt and vegetation. Three skeletal hands stuck out of the pile.

Rita looked back in the pit. That skeleton had both hands.

They were looking at a minimum of three bodies.

Chapter Eleven

RITA STUNK.

She was soaked through with sweat. Dirt clung to both her uniform and skin. Even her throat felt raw. She'd kill for a drink of water.

The sun was starting to set on Moses' property. Although now it looked more like an archaeological dig than a crime scene, despite the yellow tape. Rita walked the perimeter, watching over the scene as Casper's forensics crew crawled like ants over the piles of dirt.

Moses was long gone.

He'd stuck around for a while, but as soon as the afternoon sun began to bake the ground, he headed home for "a cold one." After all, they'd taken his statement and knew where to find him.

Across the street, the Rancher's Pantry parking lot was packed. Several pickups were parked so that their truck beds faced the property. A few had lawn chairs set up and sun umbrellas. Kyle Jenkins even had a cooler full of beer.

Peter was doing a humdinger of a business day. Some Still residents at least tried to pretend they had forgotten the milk or the bread, and that's why they'd wound up at the Rancher's Pantry. They ended up in the parking lot, gawking alongside everyone else.

Rita wondered if the killer was in the parking lot, watching. Although that greatly depended on how long those bodies had been in the ground. She'd been assured they were recent, as in not a historical gravesite, but anything further would have to wait until the bodies were examined in the lab.

But she had an inkling she might know the identities.

There was a missing poster hanging on a bulletin board at the SCSO from Otto's time. Three missing Apex employees. If this wasn't them, Still had more problems that she ever thought possible.

A car screeched to a halt on the road, not even bothering to park. A woman jumped out of the car. Gray-haired, puffy faced.

Rita walked towards her. The woman held a photo that looked like one of those school studio shots.

Like the one Mary Lou had used for Lisa's missing poster.

And, judging from the hairstyle of the girl in the photo, it was at least twenty years old.

The woman met her eyes. "Did you find my girl?"

Rita had seen the same haunted expression as in this woman's eyes too many times to count. The only thing worse than burying your child was not knowing if they were dead or alive. In a way, you buried them a little each day, all the while battling the hope they might walk through the door again.

It wasn't the grief that killed the parent of a missing child. It was the hope.

Rita held out her hand. "May I see?"

The woman handed her the photo.

"What's her name?"

"Tammie Mitchell."

"She's beautiful."

"Thank you."

Rita looked the woman in the eye. "I don't have any information myself at the moment."

The woman opened her mouth, then stopped.

Rita gestured to Jason. He walked over, wiping sweat from his brow.

"Jason here is going to take all your information down. And as soon as I know anything, I'll have someone from the SCSO give you a call."

The woman's shoulders fell. No doubt she'd been fobbed off by more than one police officer over the years.

"I don't even know if the bodies are male or female yet," Rita said.

The woman sniffed.

"Would you like me to keep Tammie's photo, or would you like to take it with you?"

The woman hesitated, then said, "Keep it."

Rita nodded, handing it to Jason. Then she gestured to the cruiser. "Take Mrs. Mitchell's details for me?"

He nodded.

Rita touched Tammie's mother's arm, then Jason led her away.

"Sheriff Jonas," a woman's voice said from behind her. Rita turned. It was Tilda, head of Casper's forensics. She was dressed in a Tyvek suit. "We're ready for you."

Rita nodded, following her towards an area covered by a large white tent. It was stifling inside.

"You haven't melted yet?" Rita asked.

"I'm sticking ice cubes down my back every ten minutes."

Rita wasn't sure if she was kidding or not.

The three skeletons were laid out on a tarp. "I can tell you they are all male. Two shot in the frontal bone, the third shot through the occipital bone."

Rita leaned forward, catching a glimpse of light reflecting in one of the skeletons. "What the fuck is that?"

"Mirror."

"Mirror?"

Tilda nodded. "I found a piece lodged beneath each of their hyoid bones."

Rita unconsciously touched her throat. "Antemortem or postmortem?"

Tilda shook her head. "Unknown. We'll know more once they've been examined."

"You think they've been here for four years?"

"That's an oddly specific date, Sheriff."

"I've got a missing poster with three men on it back at the SCSO. They were thought to have been lost in the mountains. Just vanished, no trace of them."

"This is not the mountains," Tilda said.

"No, it is not." Rita wiped the sweat from her brow. "You need me to get DNA?"

Tilda nodded. "I've called a forensic anthropologist from Cheyenne University to do an osteological analysis. But DNA would certainly be a help in confirming ID."

"I'll get on it."

Tilda jerked her head and led Rita over to a 30-gallon plastic storage container on the ground.

"This is everything we've collected so far, but we've only begun sifting through the dirt. We'll be here all night."

Both women squatted down to look inside: a barrette, a wine bottle, some scraps of cloth, coins, an Apex ID card.

"You find any shell casings to match those bullet holes?" Rita asked.

Tilda shook her head.

Rita gestured to the ID. "Don't suppose I could see that?"

Tilda reached in and flipped the card over. It had an APEX GLOBAL logo. And a photo of the employee and a name. Ethan Harris.

Rita blew out a breath.

"That one of your missing?"

"Yep." Rita got to her feet. "I'll put Walter on containment tonight. But call if you get lonely. I'll come back, keep you company."

"Thanks." Tilda gestured towards the full parking lot at the Rancher's Pantry. "But I don't think company's gonna be a problem."

Rita laughed.

"Besides, I've got my guys." Tilda indicated the other forensics officers. "They'll be working alongside me tonight."

Rita nodded. Walter's truck pulled up the street, searching for a parking spot. "I'll check back with you later."

Tilda gave her a wave, no doubt already distracted by the job at hand.

Rita walked down to the street and waited for Walter.

He finally found a parking spot and made his way over to her. "Mary Lou called me on my way back from Court. Heard it was the Apex Three."

"Most likely."

"Jesus. They were supposed to have been lost in the mountains."

"What do you remember from the case?"

Walter shook his head. "Not much. Otto kept a tight grip on it. Worked it with Pants."

Right. Ricky "Pants" Pantalano, who had ultimately been replaced by Jason when he moved west. Something about his wife's father being ill. She wasn't the only one crossing the country for their parent.

"Well, saddle up. I need you on containment. And it's going to be a long night."

"Overtime?"

"Overtime."

He grinned. It was the happiest he'd looked on the job since she'd taken over as sheriff.

Chapter Twelve

By the time Jason dropped Rita off at her apartment, it was close to midnight. She was exhausted.

He was heading home for a shower and a few hours of shuteye before going back to Moses' property to relieve Walter. Both seemed eager for the overtime, so she let them take it.

Soon as she got in, she showered. Then hit the kitchen and drank all the water in the fridge. After which, she managed to at least make herself a peanut butter and jam sandwich, before plugging her phone into the charger and crawling to bed. Not even seeing that Cash had called her back and left a message was enough to keep her awake.

She was out as soon as her head hit the pillow.

Rita stirred once in the night, having to go to the bathroom. Then she drank more water, after which she fell back to sleep right away. When she woke the next morning, she checked her phone.

There was a text from Jason at 4 a.m. *I'm onsite.*

She sent him a thumbs up.

Her fingered hovered over voicemail. But she needed

to get moving. First on the agenda today was Apex. And she didn't want to be rattled by anything Cash may or may not have said to her.

She rolled out of bed and hit the shower again. It was cold enough to wake her up. After she got dressed, she texted Abigail. *Hot water?*

I'm sorry! Henry was at the SCSO fixing the dishwasher yesterday.

As long as it was fixed by winter. Otherwise, she might as well be back in Otto's camper. Or maybe not.

She went downstairs and got into the Honda, driving it over to the station. Mary Lou wasn't in yet. And Ted let her know how disappointed he was by that, meowing at her.

She eyed the cat. "No welcome home yet?"

Ted turned his back.

She walked to the entrance and pulled the missing poster of the three men. Studying their faces. Ethan Harris, Scott Macdonald, Patrick Russell. A set of three white faces looked back at her.

They almost looked interchangeable. Except for the grin on the last man. Scott Macdonald. He wore asshole like a coat.

She walked to Mary Lou's desk and got a manila inter-office envelope. Then she slid the missing poster inside. She grabbed the keys to the cruiser from the peg board and walked outside.

Mary Lou arrived just as she unlocked the car. She slid off her motorcycle, removing her helmet. And didn't look the least bit hot. How was that possible? It was 9 a.m., and Rita already felt rumpled and sticky. "Your boyfriend is waiting."

"Ha ha," Mary Lou said.

Rita held up the car keys. "I'm off to Apex. Walter's sleeping, Jason's on site."

"You get an official ID yet?"

Rita shook her head. "Casper found Ethan's ID in the pit, and although I hate guessing, I think it's a reasonable hypothesis that this is the Apex Three."

Mary Lou cradled her helmet. "It's so bizarre. The town was so certain they were lost in the mountains. We had search and rescue out there combing the mountains for three days."

"I want to hear more about that when I'm back," Rita said. "But for now, I'm heading out to Apex. Are there any notes not in the file?"

She'd read over the missing person's case two months ago, familiarizing herself with the events. She figured the previous sheriff hadn't reviewed it. Last to make any notes on it was Otto. She'd actually kept it at her desk, meaning to update it. A lot could happen in four years. As she well knew.

But the file had caught up to her before she caught up to it.

"Nope."

"So Frank didn't touch the Apex Three at all while he was sheriff?"

Mary Lou shook her head.

"What about Walter or Jason?"

"It stayed with Frank," Mary Lou said. "I think he took it as a personal affront that Otto left him with that mess."

"Alright, I'll ask if Apex has updated info. Then I'll get you to reach out to local PD for each victim and make a DNA request. It'll be helpful if Casper has something to match."

Mary Lou nodded.

Rita slid into the car, setting the manila envelope on

the passenger seat. Then she started it up and drove out to Apex. A guard she didn't recognize manned the front gate.

"Morning," she said, smiling.

He didn't respond in kind. Instead, he walked back to the guard hut and picked up the phone. He said a few words. Nodded. Then returned to the car.

He pointed to visitor parking. "Park there."

He lifted the gate for her, and she drove in, taking the parking spot she always used. Her hands tightened on the wheel for a moment. She hadn't been back inside the building since Boyd died.

For some reason, that felt odd. Like he should still be here. She switched off the ignition. By the time she got out of the car, envelope in hand, Ken strode towards her.

"Morning, Ken." She tried her best smile.

"Sheriff," he said, eyeing the envelope. "What brings you here?"

"Angela Ruiz."

He blinked. That obviously surprised him. "You got an appointment?"

"No, but in this new era of collaboration and cooperation, I figured she wouldn't mind if I swung by for a brief chat."

"New era of cooperation?"

"Her words, not mine."

He studied her for a moment.

"Little hot to be standing out here," she said. His eyes still hadn't left the envelope.

He flushed, then pulled his phone. "I'll have someone escort you up."

He didn't even have to call Angela? Interesting. Rita headed to the front doors. As soon as she entered, she was hit with a wave of cold air. She refrained from sighing. By the time the doors had closed behind her, Peggy was striding across the marble floor towards her, iPad clutched to her chest.

Rita wondered if she slept with the thing.

She looked worried. "Ms. Ruiz will see you."

"Great." Not that Rita had asked. She would have demanded if necessary. Peggy turned on her heel and led Rita to the bank of elevators.

Once they were both inside, Peggy hit the button for the top floor.

Then she stood in absolute silence, eyes fixed on the closed doors.

"How long have you worked for Angela?" Rita asked.

Peggy looked shocked to be noticed, let alone asked a question. She cleared her throat. "Six years."

"Do you like it?"

"It's a good job."

"That doesn't exactly answer my question."

Peggy bit her lip. "Yes, I like it. Beats working the family farm in Idaho."

"I bet it does."

The elevator doors slid open, and Peggy looked relieved the journey was over. "This way."

Rita half expected to be taken to Boyd's old office. But instead, Peggy led her to what looked to be a conference room that took up the entire rear of the building. There was a long custom-made oak table that easily sat two dozen. But there were only three chairs. One on the long side, one opposite it, and one at the head. A laptop, phone, and a few folders sat before one of the chairs.

Clearly Angela's desk.

Angela was standing before floor to ceiling windows that offered a spectacular view of mountains. She wore a suit that was nearly identical to the one she had on yesterday.

"Hello, Sheriff," she said.

"Ms. Ruiz."

Peggy closed the door behind them, then walked to the chair at the far end of the table, which seemed an absurd distance from the other two.

"I came to see how serious you were about that whole spirit of collaboration and cooperation thing," Rita said.

Angela studied her for a moment. "And here I thought maybe you came to piss on my territory."

Rita winced. "Is that how I sounded?"

Angela laughed, then gestured to the chair "Please, have a seat."

Rita did.

Angela did the same. "Now what can I help you with?"

Rita took the missing poster from the manila envelope and slid it across the table. "Ethan Harris, Scott Macdonald, Patrick Russell."

"Yes. Tragic story."

"What can you tell me about them?"

"Why?"

Rita hesitated. "I need you to understand this isn't yet confirmed. And anything I tell you is strictly confidential."

"I understand."

Rita glanced over at Peggy. Her eyes were large.

"As does Peggy," Angela said.

"They may have been located yesterday."

Angela raised her eyes from the flyer. "Alive or dead?"

"Skeletal. So quite dead. We'll need DNA from the families to confirm."

"Of course."

"But we found an Apex ID badge for Ethan Harris."

Angela looked back at the flyer, her expression shifting between sad and something else. "I see."

"Don't suppose you'd have recent contact details for the men's families?"

"Isn't that information you should have? I believe this is still an open missing person's case."

"It seems my predecessor didn't bother with file maintenance."

Maybe if Angela thought they were both cleaning up after prior administrations, it might help establish a bond.

Except Angela had ungodly amounts of money at her disposal, while Rita had two deputies and an overworked Mary Lou. Plus a cat. And an Edith Mae.

So if she had to throw former sheriff Frank Parsons under the bus to make friends of one Angela Ruiz at Apex Global, she was going to do it.

And it seemed to work.

"Ah," Angela said.

She glanced over at Peggy. "HR records for Ethan Harris, Scott Macdonald, and Patrick Russell."

Peggy nodded. And Rita half expected her to salute. Instead, she disappeared out the office.

Angela returned her attention to the flyer. "I don't know why I'm disappointed."

Disappointed. That was the expression on Angela's face.

"It was obvious they were dead," she continued. "After all, it's been three years."

"Four," Rita said.

"Four. But then the Bighorn Mountains are more than a million acres. Who found them?"

Rita tapped her thigh. The news was going to land sooner rather than later. She'd rather Angela hear it from her. "They weren't found in the Bighorn Mountains."

Angela looked up at her. And the surprise in her eyes seemed genuine. "They weren't?"

Rita shook her head. "They were found in town. Less than eight miles from here."

A look of confusion replaced the surprise. "What?"

Rita nodded. "Buried in a vacant lot across from the Rancher's Pantry."

"That doesn't make sense. They were reported lost in the mountains. How did their bodies wind up in town?"

"You sure you don't want to wait for your note taker to get back?"

Angela's eyes flashed. "I'm confident I'll remember this conversation."

"Well, unfortunately, you're asking questions I don't know the answer to yet. Anything you can tell me about what the men were doing here at Apex?"

Angela looked down at the flyer yet again. She remained quiet for so long that Rita began to feel irritated. She had a feeling the spirit of collaboration and cooperation was about to get taken off the table.

But then Angela placed the poster on the table. "Four years ago, Apex had just opened."

Rita knew that much. Otto saw the writing on the wall then and announced his intention to retire.

"The company was considering a secondary site in Still, so the men were scouting locations. There was lots of land to choose from. At the time, everyone seemed eager to sell." She leaned back in her chair, turning to look out at the mountains. "We flew the men in as part of that endeavor. Ethan was an engineer, Scott, an architect, and Patrick headed up the commercial real estate division of Apex. They were here two months, I think."

"Two months?"

"Lots of factors come into play when you're thinking of building a research laboratory, Sheriff."

"If you say so. Where did they stay?"

"Still Haven Inn."

"And yet everyone thought they were lost in the mountains?"

"Yes. It was their last weekend in town. The men had finishing up their work here on Friday. And on Saturday, they went out on their own to explore one of the mines in the mountains."

"So they weren't working when they disappeared?"

She shook her head. "Their trip was purely recreational. I never understood the thrill men have to explore dangerous places. Life is challenging enough."

Rita couldn't argue with that.

"I believe staff at the inn called police to say they hadn't returned by evening. Apex was notified the next morning. The sheriff's office had search parties all over the mountains."

Rita nodded. Mary Lou had said the same thing. "Apex wasn't involved in the search?"

"In a limited capacity. We had volunteers join the search party. But Apex police were just getting up and running, so we had limited manpower. I believe the sheriff found evidence that the men were in the mine. Scott's water bottle and Patrick's sweater. It was ultimately determined they had gotten lost exploring. Searchers experienced a cave-in while looking that resulted in the mine being sealed off."

"And it was assumed they had gotten trapped inside?"

"I suppose. I don't quite remember. It was either in the mine or on the mountain somewhere."

Rita eyed her. "You don't remember? So you were in Still at the time?"

Angela smiled. "Assistant to the COO of the time. Working my way up the corporate ladder."

Rita waved a hand to indicate the large office and view

of the mountains. "Well, congratulations on reaching the apex, pun intended."

Angela gave a tight smile. "Thank you. And to you as well. I understand that before your stint as sheriff, you were a detective in New York."

Rita wondered just how big that file Apex had on her was. "Yeah."

"Jonas. Otto Jonas. He led the previous investigation. You share a name."

Rita nodded. "My father." When Otto had let her know the position was open, she'd assumed he'd put in a good word for her to the governor. But she didn't know. Direct communication was never an element of their rocky relationship.

She hadn't acted on the news at first. But she had a sneaking suspicion that Dale was angling for a conversation about marriage. And she didn't want to leave a second man at the altar. Bad enough that she had nightmares about abandoning Cash there.

She had felt like she should be doing more for Otto, given his cancer. So she'd thrown her hat in for the job. She sometimes wondered if the people who had voted for her had simply done so because they saw the name Jonas. Didn't bother to read the small print: Rita. Not Otto.

She didn't know who was more surprised that she got the job. Herself, or the rest of Still.

Now she was closer than ever to her father in terms of distance, but further apart than ever in terms of their strained relationship.

"I worked with him at the time," Angela said. "Helping to coordinate the search for the missing men. Perhaps he will recall salient details I'm not privy to."

"Yeah." Rita knew she would have to speak to Otto

sooner or later. His body might be dying, but his mind was as sharp as ever.

Angela slid the flyer back into the envelope. Rita had a feeling that as soon as Peggy returned from her mission, the interview would be drawing to a close.

"Any reason you might know as to why someone would want the men dead?"

"What do you mean, want them dead?"

"Well, three men don't die of natural causes in the middle of town."

Angela frowned. "No, I suppose not."

"They each had a bullet in the head."

A flicker of nervousness crossed Angela's face, and she adjusted the collar of her shirt, as though it and the room had suddenly grown too small. When Peggy appeared in the doorway, relief shone in the CEO's face.

Chapter Thirteen

Peggy crossed the room to Rita and handed her an envelope which closely resembled the one she had brought the missing flyer in. "This is everything HR has on the missing men."

Rita peered inside to see a few sheets of papers. "Thank you."

Angela stood. But Rita wasn't ready to end the interview quite yet. "Are the men still considered employees?"

Angela was far too polite to sigh. But it was implied as she sat again. "Technically. Although they are no longer on the payroll."

Rita fingered her envelopes. "You said the men were investigating secondary sites for Apex."

"Yes."

"Was the property across from the Rancher's Pantry one of them?"

Angela pursed her lips. "I'm not sure."

"Find out and let me know?"

Angela raised her brows.

Rita grinned. "Please."

Angela glanced over at Peggy. She was making notes. Rita figured Angela wasn't even going to have to ask her assistant. It would simply be taken care of.

"And if Peggy could get me a list of all employees working for Apex at the time, I'd appreciate it. I'd like to talk to anyone who knew the men."

"I believe your father interviewed everyone at the time."

"Sometimes hindsight is a healthy mirror. What didn't strike someone as odd at the time might now seem important."

"True."

"How well did you and Peggy know them?"

Peggy stiffened, as though uncertain if she should answer.

"Not well. Ethan and Patrick operated out of our New York office, and Scott, Vancouver. We were in completely different departments. You'd be surprised how seldom we crossed paths. Even out here in Still."

Actually, it wasn't that hard to imagine. There only seemed to be a few offices on this floor. Most likely the lab rats didn't have access. And she couldn't imagine Angela or Peggy intermingling with the workers in their lab coats.

Angela stood again. "Now, if there's nothing else, I have a conference call to prepare for."

Rita doubted that. Angela was probably going to make a call to Apex PR in New York. Prep the company for the eventual media circus.

"One last question."

Angela stiffened. Rita could tell she was done with being interviewed. But she was far too polite to say so. "Go ahead, Sheriff."

"Why didn't Apex go ahead with the second site?"

"Pardon?"

"You said they were scouting a second site. And yet this is the only Apex location in Still."

"The company chose to build the lab in Brazil instead."

"More leniency with the environmental agency there?"

Angela's mouth tightened into a grim smile. Perhaps it was best not to poke the bear when it was cooperating, but Rita couldn't help herself.

"What environmental agency?" Angela asked.

Rita almost laughed. Maybe Angela wasn't as corporate-loyal as Rita suspected. "Who decided the site shouldn't be built here?"

"I did. Based on feedback from multiple parties, including the three Apex employees."

"Ethan, Patrick, and Scott recommended Brazil?"

"I believe it was Scott. The team had previously been there and Scotland."

"And were almost on their way out of town?"

"Almost."

Rita stood. "Thank you again."

Angela smiled. "You're welcome, sheriff. Please keep in touch."

Rita nodded. "I will. Soon as we get confirmed identification, I'll let you know."

"I'd appreciate that. We'll have some administration on this end to finalize the men's employment."

No doubt. She wondered what would go on the work record. *Murdered?*

God, Apex was going to find it even harder to find employees if they kept up with this rate of attrition.

Peggy darted across the office and opened the door. Rita turned back to Angela, but she already had her phone to her ear. Not that Rita believed she'd dialed anyone. She obviously didn't want any more questions.

Rita raised her hand. "Nice to see you again, Ms. Ruiz. Wish the circumstances were better."

Angela inclined her head.

Then Rita followed Peggy out. They walked down to the elevator in silence. Rita stepped inside and Peggy pressed the button for the ground floor. "I trust you know the way out?"

That surprised Rita. She expected to have Peggy escort her. "I do."

"Have a good day, Sheriff."

Rita rode down alone. When she got to the lobby, she pulled out the papers Peggy had brought her, flicking through them. Lots of information had been redacted. But there were contact names and numbers for each of the men.

It looked like they had been kept fairly up to date. Which was more than Frank had done.

Rita walked to the cruiser and got in. She lay the documents on her lap, snapping photos of the contact information. Then she texted them to Mary Lou. Might as well get the ball rolling on ID.

When she finished, she started the engine and pulled around to the guard hut. Ken stood in the shadows, hands on his belt, watching.

She wondered if he had been waiting there for her to leave the whole time.

She waved as she drove past.

He did not wave back.

Chapter Fourteen

Rita parked at the Rancher's Pantry.

There were still lots of folks milling about. But there were considerably fewer people than yesterday, now that the bodies had been removed.

The canvas tent, however, still remained. Casper forensics continued to process the scene.

Rita went inside the store and made her way to the cold freezer by the first cashier. She opened it up, retrieving three Drumstick ice cream cones. She paid for them, then walked out, carrying them across the street.

Walter looked hot and dusty. Before he could utter a word, she handed him a cone.

"Thanks. Hot as balls out here."

"I'll take your word for that. Where's Jason?"

Soon as she said his name, he appeared from around the side of the tent, looking chagrined. "Bit of shade back there."

She held out the cone. "Smart."

"Thanks." He smiled. "I used to love these when I was a kid."

Walter laughed, taking a bite of ice cream. "When you *were* a kid?"

"Don't mind him." Rita tore into her own cone. "He's just jealous of your youth."

"You're not wrong there. Youth is wasted on the young. God, if I could know then what I know now…" Walter trailed off.

"You wouldn't have become a cop?" Rita asked.

"Don't know about that," he said. "But I might have tried out for sheriff."

She couldn't tell if he was kidding.

"So, what's the latest?" Rita asked.

"They're bringing in ground-penetrating radar tomorrow," Jason said. Then in case Walter didn't understand, he added, "To make sure there are no more bodies."

Walter grunted, took another bite of ice cream.

"They had K9 here earlier," Jason said, "but the dogs didn't find anything new."

Rita tipped her head. "Anything else?"

But Jason was looking over her shoulder. "Not again."

Rita turned to see a curly-haired man in his late twenties approach the yellow tape. He had a camera with a very long lens. He snapped a few photos of the crime scene, then spotted Rita.

"Who's that?"

Walter licked ice cream from his fingers. "Blaze Wright. Reporter from the *Casper Chronicle*."

"Blaze Wright?" Rita said. "That cannot be his actual name."

"Yep. Major pain in the ass. Don't trust him."

"He already tried to get access to the tents once," Jason said.

Blaze made a beeline towards them.

"Say the word, I'll toss him out," Walter said.

Rita finished her cone, then balled up the wrapper. "I'll take care of him."

She walked over to the man.

He stopped just outside the yellow tape, hand extended. "Blaze Wright, *Casper Chronicle*. Good to meet you, Sheriff Jonas."

She held up her ice cream wrapper. "Might not wanna shake. I've got sticky fingers."

He retracted his hand. "Care to make a statement about the dead men?"

Rita looked him up and down. "No."

"Are they the Apex Three?"

"No comment."

"But there were three bodies?"

"No comment."

"So if it's not the Apex Three, are you saying it's a serial killer?"

Rita resisted the urge to laugh. "Where the hell do you get an idea like that?"

He glowered at her. "Well, if it's not the men from Apex, it seems the next logical conclusion."

"I neither confirmed nor denied it was the men from Apex."

"But it was murder?"

She studied him. Sweat coated his brow, leaking down his face to stain the collar of his shirt. He was nothing if not persistent. "I neither confirmed nor denied that."

"Come on. Give me some kind of hint. This is my livelihood."

Rita gestured to the scene behind her. "And this is mine. Only ones that need to know what happened here at the moment are the police and the family of the deceased." And Apex. But she wasn't about to send Blaze in Angela's direction.

Although maybe she should. Might be entertaining to watch. "Have a good day, Blaze."

"Come on, Sheriff."

Walter appeared at her side, nostrils flaring. "She's done talking. Now fuck off."

Rita blinked. Walter coming to her rescue? Would wonders never cease?

Blaze glared at him. "Just doing my job, man. No need to get all Gestapo."

Walter bared his teeth.

Blaze shuffled off.

Rita patted Walter on the shoulder. "Down, boy."

"Christ, I'm hot," Walter said. That explained it. He was probably about a half an hour away from heat stroke.

"Go get cooled down," Rita said. "Be back this evening to relieve Jason. I don't imagine they're finishing anytime soon."

"Overtime?" Walter asked.

"Overtime."

He grinned, then ducked under the yellow tape and headed for his truck.

Rita walked over to Jason. "Walter's gone home for some shuteye. How are you doing?"

"Better now that I've had some ice cream."

"Why don't you head home as well. I'll cover until Walter comes back."

"No." He shook his head. "You have Otto's birthday party tonight."

Goddamn. Mary Lou must have told him.

"Mary Lou told me," he said, as though reading her mind.

"I'm not going. I'm needed here."

"You're not," he said. "I've got it handled."

"Seriously, go take a nap. I can cover."

Jason hesitated.

"Go," Rita said.

"I just gotta get my water," he said, stepping around the side of the tent.

She watched Blaze working his way through the crowd as though trying to glean additional information from anyone who was watching. Seconds later, her phone rang. Mary Lou.

"Hey."

"You're going to the damned party."

"What? How did—"

She stepped around the side of the tent. Jason had his phone out and was texting.

"You snitch."

He startled, and his face flushed red like a little boy caught with his hand in the cookie jar. "Um, I'm gonna see if Tilda needs any help."

"Yeah, you better," Rita said.

"Don't yell at Jason," Mary Lou said. "I told him to make sure you go."

"Otto won't want me there. I need to work."

"We both know that's bullshit. It's his seventieth, and he's probably not going to see seventy-one. And I don't want to listen to you bitching and moaning after he dies about the fact that you skipped his party because you were holding onto a grudge."

"It's not a grudge. I've got three dead bodies."

"That haven't moved in four years. I think the DA will understand if you attend your dying father's birthday party. So if I need to drive over there myself and get you, I will."

Rita sighed. "Fine. I'll go, but I'm driving myself."

"If you don't stay at least an hour, I'll slash your tires."

"You wouldn't dare."

But Mary Lou had already hung up. Rita tucked her phone away and went to find Tilda. She was seated on the ground, hood off, completely soaked in sweat. And sucking on ice cubes.

Maybe she wasn't kidding about slipping them down her back.

Jason wasn't with her, though. Probably off hiding.

"Hey." Tilda didn't even have the energy to wave. "I'll be wrapping up in an hour. I've got students from the Cheyenne Archaeological Program coming in the morning, so I wanna be rested. They'll help excavate the rest of the grounds."

"You headed back to Casper tonight?"

"No fucking way. Too far."

"Where you staying?"

"At the 'Fuck the Rich' Inn."

Rita laughed. "It does make for a nice addition to the sign. Wanna get some supper at The Shaft?"

Tilda pursed her lips. "I've been instructed by someone named Mary Lou that it's your father's birthday party tonight and you're not allowed to do anything else."

"What the fuck?" Rita tossed her ice cream wrapper in a garbage bag. "Did she call everybody?"

"I don't know, but I certainly want to stay on her good side."

"Yeah," Rita sighed. "So do I."

Which meant, for the first time in over a month, she'd be seeing Otto.

Chapter Fifteen

RITA TURNED DOWN MINER'S WAY. IT WAS CLOSE TO eight, but still light out. As she drove past the inn, she found herself slowing. Cars lined the road.

Had the entire damned county come out to celebrate him? Was she the only one who would rather be anywhere else tonight?

She drove past the property, parking far enough in front of another vehicle so that she didn't get boxed in. She had no intention of staying beyond the hour mandated by Mary Lou.

But once the Honda was off, she felt frozen. She was still angry at Otto. For lying about his affair with Helen. For failing to tell her that she had a sister. A sister who was now dead and she'd never get a chance to know.

She would have loved a sibling when she was younger. Maybe she wouldn't have felt so lonely. So scared of her own damn mother. But Carol didn't want any more kids. She figured Otto didn't either. Apparently, that was incorrect.

Maybe if she had found out about Lisa, she wouldn't

have wanted to know her. It was hard to say. But she wasn't given the chance. Before she knew she had a sister, Lisa's life had been reduced to burning waste in an oil barrel.

She didn't really know anything about Lisa. Only what others had told her. If she wanted to know more, she could read the goddamn letters being held captive in her safe.

A tightness squeezed Rita's chest. A sudden claustrophobia that could only be relieved by getting the hell out of here.

She turned the Honda back on, hit the indicator, and checked the rear-view mirror. A single bright headlight shone on the road. A motorcycle. Mary Lou.

Goddamnit. Her timing was shit.

Mary Lou drove around her, parking in front. Rita switched the Honda off and extracted the keys. Then she opened the door and got out.

Mary Lou removed her helmet and slid off the bike. She was wearing a low-cut sparkly dress that would've made Elvis blush.

She eyed Rita's jeans and t-shirt. "Really?"

Rita glared at her. "I had a shower."

"So glad you made an effort." Mary Lou tucked her key down the front of her dress.

"Well, why are you so dressed up?"

Mary Lou looked affronted. "I might get lucky."

Rita blinked.

"Sixty is the new sexy."

"That's one way to put it."

"You getting ageist on me, Rita?"

"I wouldn't dare. Besides, I'm here, aren't I?"

"You were trying to leave."

"Was not."

"Wasn't a question," Mary Lou said. Then she studied her. "What's going on?"

"Just feeling a lot of things."

"Good."

Rita blinked. "What does that mean?"

"You have a habit of stuffing your feelings down. Probably do you some good to let them rip."

Did Mary Lou have to know her that well?

"Come on," Mary Lou said.

Rita followed her down the road towards Otto's. When they hit the driveway, the sound of laughter and music floated towards them.

Rita stopped, looking at the house. The front porch was adorned with hundreds of twinkling lights. It'd look magical once it was fully dark. Warm light poured from the front windows and the open front door of the house.

"Last time the house had this many people in it, Carol still lived here."

"Your mother did like to party," Mary Lou said.

"I remember she got shit-faced and fell down the stairs. Broke her collarbone."

"But then in true Carol fashion, she stood up, insisted she was fine, and the drinking resumed."

"Yeah." But hours later, when the party was over and the drinking had stopped and Carol had started to hurt, it had been Rita's fault that she'd fallen. Which was stupid, because she'd been tucked up in bed at the time.

"Whatever memory you're ruminating on, stop," Mary Lou said.

"You just told me not to repress my feelings."

"It ain't feelings you're ruminating on," Mary Lou said. "It's a nightmare."

That was for damn sure. It had been the first night Rita ever spent in the camper. She'd run outside, trying to get away from the beating Carol's wooden spoon was delivering. Otto had been passed out. And Carol had locked her out.

Rita took shelter in the camper, blocking the door with her teddy bear. As if a stuffed animal would have kept her mother out.

"Fuck Carol," Mary Lou said, retrieving a small, wrapped parcel from her saddlebag. Jesus. Some daughter Rita was. She hadn't even got Otto a present. Mary Lou held out a hand. "Now, let's go see your old man."

Rita grunted but gave her arm to Mary Lou, and they made their way up the drive.

The sound of conversation and the tinkling of ice-filled glasses played like a track beneath the music, mostly stuff from the Seventies.

She stepped up onto the porch, following Mary Lou inside. Familiar faces greeted her. God, there must have been close to a hundred people here. The town really did come out to celebrate Otto.

The house looked better than it had in years. Gone was the acrid stench of decades of cigarettes. Fresh-cut flowers graced every tabletop. The wallpaper looked almost white — almost.

Otto hadn't done the cleaning, that was for damn sure, so it must have been Helen. Well, good for her. It wasn't anything Rita wanted to do. She imagined when Otto died and the house sold, the thing would have to be torn down anyway.

As she made her way through the crowd, several people stopped her. Mainly to ask about the bodies that had been found. She was met with small murmurs of disappointment when she declined to answer any questions.

She passed a staggeringly high pile of presents on the sideboard, just inside the front door. What the hell were people buying him? What did they think he needed? He was seventy years old and near death.

The dining room table was piled with food. Hamburgers, fries, hot dogs, nachos. All provided by Ruby Joe. She must have closed The Shaft, because she'd commandeered Otto's bar and was pouring out drinks.

"Where's Otto?" Rita asked.

She'd seen everyone else in town, but Otto was still missing in action.

"Try the living room," Mary Lou said, heading for the bar.

Rita nodded, then circled around. The room was packed. But then she spotted him. Seated in his favorite chair, whiskey in hand, talking to Cash. Otto looked better than he had in months. He had a sparkle in his eyes.

Maybe the party was doing him some good.

Otto hadn't seen her yet. Nor had Cash. And then she got that tightness in her chest again. The room felt stuffy, even though the front and back doors of the house were open.

She felt a pressing need to get out.

Now.

She retreated to the back door, trying to do so as gracefully as possible, so as not to call attention to herself.

She stepped past a few people who were seated on the back steps drinking. Someone said her name, but she kept walking. She passed an open cooler filled with ice and beer.

She grabbed one and walked directly to the one place she never thought she'd step foot in again.

Chapter Sixteen

THE CAMPER HAD GOTTEN MUSTIER SINCE SHE LEFT. Obviously, Otto hadn't been airing it out. It was also stiflingly hot.

She opened the kitchen window, then turned on the kitchen light and sat. She opened a beer, tossing the cap on the table.

She caught sight of the tomato-sauce stain on the floor from weeks ago. Okay, she didn't want to think about that. So she got out her phone. Pulled up her voicemail. Hit play. Cash hadn't left a message at all.

Only listening long enough that the option presented itself.

She took a long swallow of cold beer, then rested the bottle against her forehead. Someone knocked on the door. She didn't bother to answer. There was no one here she was interested in talking to.

Except Mary Lou. And Rita didn't want to interfere with her attempt to "get lucky."

The door opened.

Rita sighed.

Helen stood there. "Thought I saw you duck out."

Shit.

There was only one door. Retreat was out of the question.

"Bit warm in here," Helen said.

"I suppose." Rita took another swallow of beer. When Helen didn't leave, she added, "Came out here to be alone."

But Helen did the opposite of what Rita wanted. She came inside, closing the door behind her. She sat on the brown cushioned seat opposite Rita.

"Otto appreciates that you came."

"He saw me?"

She nodded.

Which meant that Cash probably also saw her.

Rita picked at the bottle label. "How's Arnold?"

"Staying with his grandparents in Casper for the summer. George's parents. He's having a hard time, his father being in prison."

"I can imagine." Rita met Helen's eyes. "Guess he knows about you and Otto then?"

"Yes, I told him."

"And Lisa?"

Helen nodded. "Yes, he knows she was his half-sister."

An awkward silence filled the tiny space. Rita glanced at her phone. She still had forty minutes until she filled Mary Lou's mandatory hour. But she sure as shit wasn't going to spend it with Helen.

"What do you want?" It came out colder than Rita intended. Or had it?

Helen hesitated. "I'd like you to talk to George for me."

Rita blinked. "About what?"

"Visiting him at Rawlins. I've tried, but he won't see me."

"No shit. You lied to him about Lisa for twenty years. Plus you had an ongoing affair with my father."

"It's not for my sake, it's for Arnold."

"Please. You don't give a shit about Arnold. You just feel guilty."

Helen's cheeks reddened. "I love my son."

"I'm sure you do. But this is a shitstorm of your own making, Helen. And even if I could help you — and I can't because George hasn't had his trial yet — I wouldn't."

"Why's that?"

"Time has given me perspective, Helen."

"Which means?"

Rita pointed her finger at Helen. "The night I arrested George. You told me he was the one that rammed the Chevy. Shot at me."

"And?"

Rita shook her head. "George wasn't the one who was angry that I didn't save Lisa in time. You were. So I've been thinking…"

"About what?"

"That it was you who chased me around back of this trailer, pulling the trigger. Trying to fucking scare me. Or kill me. I haven't figured it out yet. And that it was you who borrowed Lydia's truck and tried to drive me off the road."

Helen said nothing, her teeth clenching.

"I wonder how Otto would feel knowing the woman who currently shares his bed tried to kill his only daughter. We might not always see eye to eye, but he loves me."

Helen raised her chin. "You have no evidence."

"No, but last time I checked, it was Otto's lungs that were shit, not his brain. I'm pretty sure he'd agree with theory."

Helen stiffened and rose from her seat. "I'll tell Otto you said happy birthday."

"You do that," Rita said.

Helen walked out, letting the door slam shut behind her.

Rita looked at her hand. It was shaking a little. She drained the rest of her beer. Then she got up and closed the kitchen window. She exited and turned down the drive. She was halfway to her car when her phone buzzed.

She shouldn't have looked.

Mary Lou. *Get back to the house, now.*

No.

Rita Marie Jonas.

Jesus. As a kid, she'd often wished Mary Lou was her mom, not Carol. But maybe that wouldn't have been any better.

No.

That wasn't true.

Anyone would have been better than Carol.

I'm coming.

Whatever. If she had to deal with Otto and Cash tonight, she could do it. She made her way back to the house, pushing her way through the folks gathered on the porch as though hoping it would be cooler outside. It wasn't.

She made her way to the living room. Mary Lou was seated in a chair.

Otto spotted her and gestured. She walked over to him. "Dad."

He stood, giving her a big hug. A couple of people clapped. Jesus, did everyone know they were currently estranged? Probably.

He reeked of alcohol but was in good spirits. He wasn't ever as bad a drunk as her mother had been. Usually, he just got a bit sappy.

"Thank you."

Rita stepped back. "For what?"

He held up the key to the Chevy, which was currently rusting in some auto wrecker's yard. Rita glanced at the card on the present wrapping. *To Dad, Love Rita.*

"Good gift," he said, with a grin.

She eyed Mary Lou, who shrugged.

Rita looked her father up and down. "You look better."

"I feel better. Helen got me to give up smoking."

Rita froze. "What? When?"

"I celebrate one month tomorrow."

Rita felt a hit of jealousy. She'd tried for years to get him to stop, to no avail. Then George goes to prison and Helen starts hanging around, and suddenly he plays ball? What the fuck?

He formed a fist and banged his chest. "Still got some life in these old lungs yet." Then he nudged her. "And a few other parts as well."

"Eww, Dad."

He laughed. "Hell, I'm feeling so good, I'm thinking about coming back to work next week."

"God, I hope you're kidding."

"Mostly." Then he lowered his voice. "I heard you found the Apex Three."

Helen appeared, snaking her arm through his, as though staking her claim. "No shop talk tonight, Otto Jonas. It's your birthday."

"Aww, you're no fun," Otto said.

"Actually, Dad." Rita said, more to piss Helen off than anything, "I'll need to talk to you about that."

His eyes looked alert.

"Monday morning?"

"Sounds good, Honeybee."

She almost corrected him, but his eyes were sparkling and he had a smile on his face that seemed was far brighter than she'd ever seen. Who was she to take that away from him?

"Come on." Helen tugged on his arm. "Time to light your cake."

"Be careful you don't start a fire," one of the guests said.

"Fuck you." Otto grinned.

She watched Helen lead him away, and then everyone else began to drift towards the dining room.

"Go on," Mary Lou said, getting up from her chair. "Get out of here."

Rita kissed her cheek. "Thanks for his present. May you be the luckiest woman in the room tonight."

Mary Lou eyed a man on the far side of the room. "I intend to be. You know what they say about electricians."

Rita had no idea what "they" said about electricians. And she had no intention of asking. She slipped out of the room and through the hallway, out into the night. She'd been right. The strings of twinkling lights around the porch did make the place look magical.

She tried not to run as she made her way down the dark driveway.

She'd almost reached her car when she heard a shoe scrape behind her. Before she could turn, his voice filled the dark.

"It's me."

Chapter Seventeen

DAMN IT. RITA HAD ALMOST BEEN HOME-FREE.

She stopped, turning back to face Cash. There were no lights at this end of the drive, so both of them were swallowed in the night.

"You weren't running from me, were you?" he asked.

"Of course not."

She could sense his disbelief even in the dark.

"I was running from Otto. And Helen."

He laughed. "At least I ranked third this time."

She glared at him, even though he couldn't see it. Then she turned and resumed walking to the car. He followed.

When they arrived at the Honda, she stopped. Now what? She felt more awkward than she had in Otto's house. "This is me."

"You never called me back," he said.

At least he was getting straight to the point. "I did."

"At six in the morning. I was asleep. You didn't think to leave a message?"

"I didn't have anything to say. Besides, you didn't leave a message either."

"I figured you would just delete it without listening."

"I would never do that." Well, maybe old Rita would have. But she had turned a new leaf since coming to Still. Or at least she kept telling herself that. She tugged her shirt away from her belly and unlocked the Honda. "It's too hot to talk outside."

"You're right."

Thank God. Besides, she was tired.

He walked around the side of the Honda and climbed in the passenger seat.

She flung the driver's door open. "That's not what I meant."

He grinned. "I know."

"So get out."

"Nope. If I do, we might never talk. And then you'll go back to New York, and I'll have a bucket of words weighing me down that I never got to spill."

"You're awfully poetic. How much did you drink?"

"I didn't. I wanted to be sober for this conversation."

Or more likely because the last time they drank together, there wasn't a whole lot of talking.

"Get in the car," he said. "You're letting all the hot air in."

She did, slamming the door behind her and turning the Honda on, letting the cold air cool them both. After a minute, she switched it off.

"That's it?"

"You gotta earn the air-con," she said.

"You're still angry?"

"No, not really."

"No?"

"Maybe a little. You could have told me you had a date. I would have understood." She probably wouldn't have. But it sounded good. Mature.

"It wasn't a date."

"Friends with benefits?"

"Jesus. Not that either. You didn't recognize her?"

"Should I have?"

"Heather."

"Heather Bannister?" His ex-wife. Jesus. Rita didn't know if that made things better or worse. Her chest felt tight. Were they reconciling? She didn't want to ask. "She looks good."

"Yeah." But he sounded deflated.

"Is Heather being back a good thing?"

"I don't know. She got a job at Chattum Real Estate and will be helping to sell the designer homes on Moses' land — once they get built. *If* they ever get built."

"Yeah, Still is always going to know that site as the graveyard of the—"

"Apex Three?"

"I can neither confirm nor deny that."

He laughed. "Don't worry. The whole town knows it was them."

Rita changed the subject. Last thing she wanted to think about at the moment was work. "I thought Heather hated Still. Wasn't that the whole reason you divorced?"

"Amongst other things."

Rita wondered what the other things were.

"She's separated from husband number two. And because her mom's here, she can get help with the kids. So she's moved back."

Rita didn't like this news. Not that she really knew Heather, not since high school. But she knew she liked her more when she'd lived in Casper.

"Why did you lie to me about seeing Dale?"

She turned to him. "How do you know?"

Cash shrugged. "He's a good guy. We still text."

"What the hell do you have to text Dale about?"

"We've got stuff in common."

"You have nothing in common."

"We've got you."

"I don't think I like that."

He grinned, nudging her. "Come on, spill."

She was silent. Fighting the urge to get out of the Honda and run. But then how would she get back to her apartment?

"Rita?" His voice had changed. He sounded serious.

She shrugged. "He wanted to get back together. And I didn't want to. And I didn't want to have to tell anyone that."

"Why not?"

"Because everyone in Still thinks I should go back to New York and stay there."

"Not everyone."

She waggled her fingers. "I can count on one hand the number of people who have welcomed me back to Still. Besides—"

She broke off.

"Besides what?"

"I don't love Dale. He's not—"

She stopped, letting him fill in the blank.

"Me?"

She glanced over at him. Could tell he was smiling.

"I can neither confirm nor deny that."

He laughed, then reached out and tugged her hair. "Why don't we get out of this heat and make some of our own?"

"That sounds terrible."

"You mean fun?"

She didn't answer. Last thing she wanted in this

temperature was to be skin to skin with another human being. Even the thought of it made her hot.

He sighed and released his hold on her hair, then reached for the door handle. "Alright. Another time."

Only it also made her hot in all the right places. "Wait. I think I changed my mind."

"You *think*?"

She leaned forward and kissed him.

Chapter Eighteen

RITA ROLLED OVER IN BED, EYES ADJUSTING TO THE LIGHT. Cash was gone. She'd heard him leave about two hours earlier.

They'd gone at it pretty hard in the Honda. But when Mary Lou almost caught them, Rita had driven Cash to his truck. And he'd followed her back to the apartment.

It had been hot all right.

She reached for her phone. Then remembered it was Sunday. But she rarely slept in anymore.

Two text messages. One from Walter, around two in the morning, saying he was heading home and was being relieved by Casper PD. That surprised her — he seemed dead set on getting any second of overtime.

The second was from Mary Lou: *I hope you used a condom this time.*

Jesus. Maybe it was a good thing Mary Lou wasn't her mother.

She typed out: *yes, mom.*

And hit send.

Rita got up and went to the shower, turning the knob.

And within seconds, steam filled the small room. She stuck her hand in the water. Hot.

It was a goddamn miracle.

She showered a long, long time. Then toweled off. Got dressed in shorts and a t-shirt, and grabbed a leather cross-body. It doubled as a purse but allowed her quick access to her service weapon, which she retrieved from her safe. She tended to carry it off duty now as well. Ever since that night in the reservoir, when she'd been attacked.

Then she headed downstairs into the Bighorn Bean.

A few locals glanced at her as they sipped on coffee and ate their breakfasts. She felt a bit exposed not being in uniform, looking more like a college girl in shorts, baggy shirt, and a ponytail.

She approached the counter, where Skyler rang up a customer's muffins. Skyler's pink hair now had streaks of purple in it. Another girl circulated behind her, making the coffee.

When it was her turn to order, Rita gestured to Skyler's head. "I like the hair."

Skyler grinned. "I was torn between going platinum or back to natural, but couldn't make up my mind, so I just added some purple for the time being."

"Suits you."

"I heard you were back."

Rita raised a brow.

"Footsteps." She gestured to the ceiling.

"You bet against me coming back as well?"

Skyler snorted. "Course not. I knew you'd be back."

"And why's that?"

"Because you belong here, Sheriff. You're Still through and through. Despite the fact that these lot"—she gestured to the customers at the tables—"call you a flatlander behind your back."

Rita smiled. Why was the teen the one that saw her best? "Two iced coffees."

While her coworker made the drinks, Skyler leaned on the counter, lowering her voice. "So, I heard they found like five bodies at Moses'."

"More like fifty," Rita said.

Skyler's jaw fell open. "Really?"

"No, sorry. I'm just messing with you."

Skyler laughed. "You want any food this morning? Abigail made her gram's famous walnut banana bread recipe."

"No, just the drinks for now. Thank you. You hear anything else about the bodies?" Rita asked. You never knew where, or from whom, you might pick up useful information, especially in a small-town coffee shop where people talk.

"A few people thinking it's those Apex guys that disappeared four years ago. A couple people wondering if it was a serial killer." Her face grew serious. "It's not that, is it?"

"I don't think so, Skyler. But be careful out there, okay?"

Skyler smiled. "Yes, Sheriff. No charge on the coffee."

"You sure?"

"Yeah."

Rita dug into her bag, pulled out a ten, and put it in the tip jar. Considering the volume of folks at the tables, it was lacking in heft.

"Thank you," Skyler said.

Rita grabbed the iced coffees and headed to the back door. She exited and reviewed her terrible parking job. God, Skyler must have thought her an idiot. She hadn't been focused on parking between the lines last night. She'd barely gotten out of the Honda before Cash had arrived.

And soon as he did, she hadn't exactly been thinking with her brain.

She unlocked the Honda, slid the coffees into the cup holders, and turned on the ignition.

Then she drove down to the Rancher's Pantry and parked. Then she walked across the street. There were a few more folks watching today. Plus a whole host of university students gathered under the tent, consulting what looked like maps.

Tilda was seated in the passenger seat of a Casper PD car, door open. She'd lost the Tyvek suit. And looked much happier for it.

Rita walked up to her.

"Casual day?" Tilda asked. "I wish my boss would let us wear shorts."

"Off-duty, but thought I'd check in." She spotted Tilda eyeing the iced coffee. "And bring you this."

Tilda practically snatched it from her hand. "Oh, my God. I could kiss you." She sucked down several mouthfuls before coming up for air.

Rita leaned against the car, watching a man in khaki slacks and a long-sleeved white shirt. He pushed what looked like a lawnmower slowly along the ground.

"That the ground-penetrating radar?" Rita asked.

Tilda swallowed. "Yeah."

"How does it work?" Rita asked.

Tilda gestured with her free hand. "He goes over the land in a grid pattern, then coordinates with the students, who will dig up anything he considers remarkable. Incredibly slow process. You're welcome to hang out."

Rita took a drink of her own coffee. "As enticing as that offer is, I'm going to swing by the office."

"So even on your day off, you work?"

"I guess the only distinguishing difference is I can wear shorts."

Tilda chuckled. "Thanks for the coffee."

"Call me if you find anything."

Tilda nodded. "Will do."

Rita walked back to the Honda, got in, and drove to the SCSO. She parked in the back, in the spot closest to the building. It would get a little shade come late afternoon. Jason's Kia and Walter's truck were already there. Only Mary Lou's motorcycle was absent. Two could play this game.

She pulled out her phone. *You get lucky?*

She got an emoji lightbulb in return.

Probably more than Rita wanted to know. She shouldn't have asked. She grabbed her iced coffee and got out, walking to the back door. She unlocked it and entered.

Jason was eating breakfast at his desk. By the looks of it, he had been to the Bighorn Bean himself.

Ted hopped onto the filing cabinet next to Jason and meowed. Jason peeled a piece of bacon from his sandwich and offered it to the cat.

Ted snatched it and took off running to the cat tower.

"You keep feeding him bacon, and he's going to think mice are beneath him."

Ted yowled.

Jason looked chagrined. "Sorry, Rita."

Rita grinned, squeezed his shoulder.

Walter emerged from the break room with a hot mug of coffee. "I already told him that."

"What are you doing in?"

Walter paled a little. "I thought it'd be overtime."

Rita hesitated. Then nodded. "Yeah. Alright. I'll sign off."

He blew out a breath, relieved.

"How was Otto's party?" Jason asked.

Rita shrugged.

"You did go?"

"I did," Rita said. "And even stayed the requisite hour, as per Mary Lou's instruction."

"Mary Lou instructed you?" Walter asked.

Rita ignored him. "Do either of you know what 'they' say about electricians?" They both looked at her. Blank.

"Electricians?" Jason said.

Rita nodded.

He shook his head.

"Yeah, me either."

She gestured to her office. "I'm grabbing the missing persons file. You want to review it with me?"

Jason nodded.

Rita went to her office and retrieved the file from her desk drawer.

Then she returned to the bullpen, snagged Mary Lou's chair, and pulled it around to join the two of them.

The missing men were reported by Milly Toole, owner of the Still Haven Inn, at 8 p.m. on Saturday, August 4. Ethan, Scott, and Patrick had left that morning at 9, saying they were going to High Peak Mine for the day. Milly had packed them a lunch. They left in Patrick's rental.

It was a one-hour drive there, and a two-hour hike into the mountains. They were planning to have lunch, hike, visit the mine, then head back. They told her to expect them for supper. They never showed.

According to Otto's interview with Milly, she hadn't initially been worried. Not at first. She knew it would be a long day and had recommended they get supper at one of the places along the highway. She figured they did; they just forgot to let her know.

But by 9:45 p.m., that had changed. Couldn't get ahold

of any of the three men on their phones. So she called it in. But there was nothing anyone could do that evening.

The next morning, Otto and Pants drove out to High Peak. There was no sign of Scott's car, so they figured the men had left. But it wasn't at the inn. Or at Apex. Nor had it been returned to the rental agency at the airport.

High Peak Mine hadn't been functional in some time. But it was open as an explore at your own risk place, located in a popular hiking area for both locals and tourists.

Rita couldn't imagine Otto climbing up to the mine with his lungs, but apparently, he'd made it. They found evidence the three men had been there, including Scott's sweater and a water bottle located deep in the mine. They figured the men were lost inside. They sent for experienced cavers.

"Why did they think they were still on the mountain if Scott's car was gone?" Rita asked.

Her voice shattered the silence, and everyone jumped.

Walter cleared his throat. "We had a spate of car thefts at the time. Anything worth a damn was being stolen and taken for a joyride. I think we all figured Scott's Porsche rental would have been a prime target."

"Porsches easy to steal?" Rita asked.

"I don't fucking know," Walter said.

"Can you find out?"

He grunted.

"Is that a yes?"

"Yes."

Rita returned to the file. The cavers had come out and mapped the line.

And discovered a section where there had been a recent cave-in. They tried to excavate it, but as they did, more of the mine began to collapse. It was deemed too dangerous to continue. The three were considered to have lost their lives. Then the mine was closed and sealed.

But the case remained open as missing persons.

"So, everybody just gave up?" Rita asked.

Walter shrugged. "What were they going to do, spend millions, maybe lose more people, to find three guys that shouldn't have been fucking down there to begin with? Still County didn't have that kind of money."

"Why didn't Apex foot the bill?"

He shrugged. "Dunno. But there were signs plastered all over the mine that said 'ENTER AT YOUR OWN RISK.' People round here take that shit seriously. If you're dumb enough to ignore it, that's on you."

Rita raised her brows.

Walter eyed her. "My ten-year-old cousin lost his life in a mine when I was a kid."

"Jesus." She didn't know that.

He grunted. "Little prick shouldn't have gone in. I tried to talk him out of it, but he wouldn't listen. Last thing he ever said to me was, *fucking coward*. Then I got shit for letting him do it. Not that you could tell Burt to do anything. Even his mother knew was a goddamn hellion." He wiped his nose against the back of his hand. "A ton of rock fell on him."

Rita grimaced. "I'm sorry, Walter. Anything else you remember about the search?"

"We did our damned jobs. Some people thought they deserved it. Bunch of flatlanders thinking they could conquer the mountains and the mines."

Jason cleared his throat. "I got more information on the car."

"Go on," Rita said, throwing her file down on the desk.

Jason gestured to the statement he was reading. "It was a Porsche 911."

"Okay."

"And it was found in town the next evening."

Rita straightened. "Where?"

"The Rancher's Pantry."

They were all silent.

Walter rubbed his brow. "I didn't remember that. I think I was off that day. I just heard they found it."

"Well, how the hell did it get there?" Rita asked.

Jason read further, then tapped a finger on the file. "Looks like Otto figured some kids found it out on the highway near the mine, took it for a joyride, and ditched it."

"And no one thought to check across the street?"

"Why would they?" Walter asked.

"I don't know," Rita said. "But wouldn't someone have seen it?"

"Whole damn town was practically out searching the mountain," Walter said.

The phone rang, causing all of them to jump. Rita rolled around Mary Lou's desk and picked up the line. "Still County Sheriff's Office. Sheriff Jonas."

Silence.

"Anyone there?"

Still nothing. Was this a prank call? She was about to hang up when a voice came across the line.

"It's Ken Saunders. From Apex."

Chapter Nineteen

RITA BLINKED.

Then she put on her least interested voice. "Hiya Ken, what can the SCSO do for you?"

Walter and Jason looked at each other and then at her.

"Apex just had a truck vandalized."

"And?"

She could almost imagine him gritting his teeth. "Your jurisdiction. Chester's Gas and Go. I need to make a report for insurance purposes."

"You there now?"

"Yes."

"I'll be there shortly." She hung up. "Apex. I'll go. Jason, you're with me."

He nodded, then glanced at Walter. "You should head home. Be with Adrian."

Rita glanced at him. "You got your kid with you?"

Walter glared at Jason. "Yeah, Adrian's staying the summer."

"Jesus, Walter. Go spend some time with him."

"He's fucking around with friends today," Walter said. "He won't be home."

"Alright, but half-day overtime that's it. We get back at noon and you're still here, consider yourself fired. Got it?"

Walter grumbled something under his breath, then nodded.

"Meet me at the Bean," Rita said to Jason. "I need to go home and change." As much as she wanted to stay in shorts, last thing she needed was to be caught in a shootout and be dressed like she was going to the beach.

Besides, she was meeting Ken. She was going to meet authority with authority. And they'd be on her turf.

It didn't take her long to return to the apartment and get changed. By the time she went back downstairs to the parking lot, Jason was waiting. He had an iced coffee for her.

God, being overly caffeinated and having to deal with Ken might not be a good idea either. But she smiled at him. "Lifesaver."

Jason raised his iced tea, and they touched paper cups.

They drove in relative silence out to Chester's Gas and Go, enjoying their drinks. Chester's was a gleaming new facility located on the bypass. It had more than twenty pumps, diesel, and a giant convenience store that included a diner that served any artery clogging fried items one desired.

Rita had never eaten here. She imagined it didn't hold a candle to The Shaft.

They spotted the Apex van immediately. It was parked near the air pumps.

Ken stood next to it, dressed in a wrinkled suit, mirrored shades planted firmly on his face. He looked pissed, his mouth flapping, his arms waving. Two male Apex employees — one with a Yankees cap and the other with a long braid — stood off to the side, looking bored with his rant.

Jason parked, and they got out.

Rita walked over to them. "Hey Ken. Having a good day?"

"Yeah, this is exactly how I love to spend my Sundays."

"Me too." Rita pulled her notepad out of her vest pocket. "So, why don't you tell me what happened and then we can both get back to shorts and shades. Although" —she gestured to his glasses—"you're halfway there."

Ken glowered at the two employees. "They stopped for a meal, which is explicitly against Apex regulations."

One of the Apex men glanced over at her.

Rita studied him. "You don't look like you're paid enough to skip meals."

"No ma'am," he grinned.

Ken looked like he might explode. But he contained himself. "When they finally got back on the road, the vehicle stalled. They pulled over, noticed the gas cap had been tampered with. Managed to limp back to the gas station."

"You see anyone near the van?"

"No, ma'am," Braid said.

"They were too busy stuffing their faces inside," Ken said.

The man with the Yankees cap belched as though to underline that fact.

Ken's face turned an unhealthy shade of red. It was clear these two did not view him as an authority figure.

"Where was the van parked?" Rita asked.

Ken pointed to a spot near the convenience store's main entrance. "Right there."

"Any CCTV?"

"I don't fucking know."

Rita glanced at Jason. He nodded and walked to the store.

"How long were you both inside?"

"An hour," the man with the braid said. "Just long enough to order and eat."

"Seems reasonable," she said.

They both grinned at her.

"You gonna take prints?" Ken asked, gesturing to the vehicle.

Rita blinked at him. "Hell no."

"Why not?"

She turned back to the men. "Either of you touch the gas cap when the vehicle stalled?"

"Of course," Braid said. "That's how we knew it had been tampered with."

"There we go," Rita said.

Ken clenched his jaw.

"Don't give them shit," Rita said. "It's a natural reaction to check the problem before calling in the boss; they were simply doing their job."

Ken seemed to relax a little. "I guess you're right."

Jesus.

Hell must have frozen over.

"I checked with the clerk," Ken said. "She reported seeing a silver pickup truck idling nearby."

"Either of you get plates?"

They both shook their heads.

"You know how many silver pickup trucks are in Wyoming?"

"No," Ken said.

"780,000 vehicles registered in the state, half of which are pickups, and twenty-seven thousand of them are bound to be silver."

"Is that true?"

"No, total bullshit, but there's a lot. I had to run black ones before, so I know of what I speak. So unless you have any other identifying marks for the vehicle—"

No one responded.

"—then it's not going to be much of a help. We need more."

And as if to prove her point, two silver pickup trucks pulled up to the pumps. Rita jotted down the file number in her notebook and tore it out, handing it to Ken. "Your case number for the insurance company."

"Thanks."

If he kept up with the gratitude, it was about to start snowing.

"Have a good Sunday, gentlemen." She didn't include Ken in her well-wish. His Sunday could stink, far as she was concerned.

Rita turned and walked toward the store to meet up with Jason.

Ken cleared his throat. "Hey, do you have a moment?"

She looked around and pointed to herself.

He nodded, gesturing to a spot a few steps away. She walked over and joined him there. Just out of earshot of the Apex employees.

He looked nervous. "I wanted to apologize for the misunderstanding."

"Misunderstanding?"

He looked down as if he couldn't say the words. He gestured to her.

"You couldn't possibly be talking about the time you and your partner beat the shit out of me?"

He flinched. "It was Boyd's orders. I know it's not an excuse, but it is what it is."

She studied him for a moment. "Boyd order you to rape me as well?"

119

"Jesus, no."

"Clyde seemed to think different."

"I never would've let that happen."

"Glad to see you draw a line somewhere. Assault, okay. Sexual assault, not okay."

His face was red. "My sister—" He broke off. Tried again. "My sister was raped in college. It fucked her up."

"But beating me was acceptable."

He rubbed his head. "I said I'm sorry."

"I'm not dropping the charges."

"I know." He sniffed. "But I still wanted to apologize."

There was something about his body language, his tone, the way he was forcing himself to meet her eyes—

Someone had pressured him into this. And then she got it. Angela.

"Ruiz order you to make nice?" Rita asked.

He hesitated, then nodded.

"So I guess she does take this cooperation seriously."

"Can I show you something?" He didn't wait for her to answer. He reached into his pants pocket and pulled out his phone, the latest and largest iPhone.

He swiped open Instagram.

"Are you going to show me funny cat videos? Because Mary Lou's already started sending me some, and I'm not sure I can take—"

He held out his phone. The account looked a lot like Apex's branding, except that the A in Apex was replaced with an anarchy symbol.

Beneath it were photos and videos of each of the acts of vandalism that had occurred in Still.

"Fuck me," Rita said. Then she glanced at him. "Not literally, please."

Ken flushed.

She scrolled through the photos. Some were taken in

daylight, but most taken at night. Probably when the vandalism had been done. The last post was a copy of the document Lisa had stolen. The letter written by Victor Price.

The tagline on that photo read: "Apex: Killing America One Town at a Time."

She peered at letter closer, blowing it up to full size. The hairs on her arm stood up. This was the original letter. Before it had been stolen from Apex by Lisa. She took a screenshot of the account and texted it to herself.

"Where did they get a copy of the letter?" Rita asked.

He shrugged. "Thought you might have given it to these assholes."

She shook her head. "Our letter had been torn into pieces and reassembled. There is no sign this letter has been destroyed."

"Photocopied?"

"Not by the SCSO."

She checked the time on the Instagram post. An hour earlier.

"Our PR people are on it, saying it's clearly fake."

"Which we both know is bullshit."

He didn't say anything.

"You know who is behind the account?"

"Dunno. We've not been able to get shit from Meta."

Rita laughed. "Finally found a company bigger than you? How's it feel to be pushed around by a giant corporate monolith?"

He scowled but refrained from arguing. "Maybe we can meet and discuss suspects?"

"I dunno. I find myself downright giddy that they seem to have set their sights on Apex."

"I'm trying to extend an olive branch here."

"On one condition."

"What's that?"

"Who shot my deputy?"

Ken looked like a deer caught in headlights. "It wasn't me or Clyde. I swear."

"I know that, you idiot. You were both locked up in Natrona County. But you can find out."

"That information might be above my pay grade."

"Not if you get that promotion."

His eyes widened. "You'd help me with that?"

Rita shrugged. "I might consider it."

"Then I'll see what I can do."

He held out his hand. And as much as it might disgust her, Rita took it. And they shook.

Chapter Twenty

RITA WALKED OVER AND MET JASON EMERGING FROM THE convenience store. He eyed Ken, who was overseeing Bighorn Towing who had just arrived to tow the van.

"What was that about?" Jason asked.

Rita wiped her hand against her pants. "New era of cooperation."

Jason looked doubtful.

"CCTV?" she asked

"Cameras cover the entrances and exits, plus the hidden corners."

"But not right out front?"

Jason shook his head. They walked back to the cruiser.

"I'll drive," Rita said. "I want to show you something."

Jason tossed her the keys. She unlocked the vehicle and got in. When Jason was seated in the passenger seat, she pulled up the screenshot she had taken of the Apex letter and handed him her phone. "Notice anything?"

He studied it for a moment. "It's not the same letter. Or it might be. But this one's not torn up."

She turned on the car and drove out of the Gas and Go. "Yeah. Appeared on Instagram."

"What?"

"Apparently our vandals are media savvy."

"Instagram account name?"

She told him. He handed her phone back, then pulled up his own. Opening the app and finding the account. He hit follow.

"The SCSO has Instagram?"

He flushed. "Not really." He showed her his phone. She squinted. TedTalks. He hit play on a video. Ted's yowl filled the car.

She braked. "Jesus. The cat has an Instagram account?"

"It was Mary Lou's idea." He scrolled through the rest of the posts. "Looks like they were taken when the vandalism was occurring. This video is missing the word *pigs*."

"Yeah, that's what I thought," Rita said.

His phone rang. "Hey, Walter. Yeah. I will. Thanks."

"He still at work?" she asked when he disconnected.

"Just leaving now. Tilda called. They're finished with the site, so they're packing up shortly."

Rita nodded. When they hit Still, she drove past the office and pulled into a spot at the Rancher's Pantry. "Peter's gonna start charging us for parking soon."

Jason laughed.

They both got out of the car and walked across the street. Blaze Wright stood on the periphery of the crime scene, camera out, taking photos.

Most of the Still regulars who had been watching had packed up and gone home. Evidently, the idea that there would be no more bodies had made them lose interest.

Rita walked past Blaze. "No news in Casper today?"

He turned the camera on her and snapped a photo. Then grinned.

Rita turned back to Jason. "Keep an eye on him?"

He nodded.

She ducked beneath the yellow crime scene tape and made her way to the tent. The students were gone, as was the man who had been running the ground-penetrating radar.

She found Tilda zipping up a gear bag. Two other forensics officers were talking about dismantling the tent.

Tilda spotted her and smiled. "Walk me to my car?"

Rita nodded and grabbed one of the kits.

Tilda grabbed her gear bag and walked across the lot, then up the road to where a Casper PD car waited.

"No more bodies?" Rita asked.

"Nope." Tilda unlocked the vehicle. Rita opened the trunk for her. Placed the kit inside. "And I can't wait to sleep in my own bed tonight."

Rita spotted Moses over at the Pantry. He was pacing. "He looks happy."

"Yeah. He wasn't pleased he can't continue digging. We still need to process the evidence for you. Might be we find something we overlooked."

"I'll have a chat with him," Rita said. She needed to talk to Moses anyway. Find out how long he owned the land. And what it was like four years ago.

Tilda yawned. She looked exhausted. "We'll have the evidence and reports ready to review Tuesday. And the forensic anthropologist and medical examiner are scheduled for Wednesday."

"I'll be there."

She nodded. "We've assigned rotating shifts of deputies to watch the site for you this week. I believe there's an email about it."

"Thanks. Now go home and get some rest."

"Aye, aye, Captain."

Rita laughed. Then she walked over to the Rancher's Pantry.

Moses was off the phone. He looked at her glumly. "Every day I can't dig, I'm losing money."

"I get it."

He grunted.

"You own the land four years ago?"

He nodded. "Been in the family a generation."

"And you didn't notice it had been disturbed the morning after the men went missing?"

"Nope."

She waited, expecting more. But he didn't offer anything. So she asked. "Why not?"

Moses wiped his forehead. "'Cause Apex had been digging the land, taking samples. Whole lot was churned up." He shrugged. "Sat fallow until I found a developer wanting to build Still Shadows homes with me."

That made sense.

"I got some photos of the land from back then."

Rita perked up. "Can I get copies?"

"Yeah. But I need to go to Casper today. Gotta meet with my business partner."

Rita nodded. "Tomorrow afternoon?"

He rubbed his jaw. "Yeah, I'll try and be back by then."

"What's your address?"

He gestured to the road. "Just head that way. Last house on the right. Can't miss it."

Rita nodded, then walked to the car where she found Jason waiting for her. "Any trouble with Blaze?"

He shook his head. "No. He seems nice enough."

Rita raised her brows.

He flushed.

She grinned, tossed him the car keys. "Drop me at the apartment?"

Within a few minutes, he'd pulled up at Bighorn Bean. "Go home," she said. "We've got a hell of a busy week coming up. So enjoy what's left of the day."

He nodded.

Rita walked around back and made her way upstairs. She stripped off her uniform, then had a shower. After which she was back in her shirt and shorts.

It was almost dinner time. God, how had the day flown past so quick?

She walked to the fridge. It held nothing of interest.

She blew out a breath.

The Bighorn Bean would be closing any moment. And she didn't have any desire to drive out to The Shaft.

She pulled out her phone and texted Cash: *I'm hungry.*

A minute later he texted back: *Be there in ten.*

He arrived in nine minutes.

But he didn't bring any food.

She let him in anyway.

Chapter Twenty-One

THIS TIME CASH HAD SPENT THE NIGHT.

But it was worth it, because he made her breakfast in bed. Scrambled eggs and toast. "See what living with me would be like?" he asked.

"Is that an invitation?"

"Open ended."

She'd turned back to her eggs, shoveling them into her mouth. And then she couldn't continue the conversation because it was rude to talk with your mouth full. At least that's what Mary Lou told her.

Cash had laughed and kissed her, then he left for work.

Once her belly was full and he'd gone, she'd showered and dressed. And was already sticky by the time she crossed the road and arrived at the SCSO.

She walked through the front door, the first to arrive. Ted yowled at her. She glanced over at his bowl. It still had kibble.

Mary Lou liked to be the one to give him his wet food. Apparently, the ritual involved a special dish, spoon, and a specific amount of water to be mixed in. She had tried explaining it to Rita. But she'd stopped listening when Mary Lou mentioned the number of seconds of mixing required to create the perfect thickness of sauce Ted liked.

"You'll have to wait," Rita said to the cat.

Ted didn't look impressed.

She went to her office and turned on her computer. Then she pulled up her email. She found the one Tilda had mentioned. Casper PD was organizing a rotating shift of officers to help with containment.

It was cheaper to pay Casper for their assistance than have the three officers at the SCSO pulling overtime.

She also had an email from Peggy. Looks like she had worked the weekend as well.

Her email said that of everyone working at Apex at the time the men went missing, fifteen were still onsite. She'd scheduled the meetings for Thursday. Starting at nine, twenty minutes apart.

She also stated that Angela had sent out a company memo instructing everyone to fully cooperate with the SCSO investigation.

Rita wondered if that was actually true, or if Peggy was just so good at carrying the company water that she lied with ease. Because Rita didn't trust anyone who worked at Apex. Not that she believed the company specifically hired villains.

She figured it had started small. They got you with little infractions of your moral compass. Little things that didn't mean much in the grand scheme of things. And then as you gave a little, they took more and more, until suddenly you were doing things you never thought you'd do and felt stuck. That's how they — whether it be politicians, companies, or militaries — got you to give up your soul. Then you had no choice but to keep doing what you were doing. You were compromised, and you were no longer qualified to do anything else. Rita had seen it with several colleagues in New York.

Hell, she'd seen it with Walter.

Rita printed off the list Peggy sent. Eighty workers. The fifteen currently remaining had been highlighted in yellow.

It didn't surprise her that turnover was so high. Flat-landers never wanted to remain in Still County longer than necessary. What was there to do? If you didn't like mountain or prairie, you were shit out of luck when it came to entertainment. Unless you enjoyed hours spent on the road to Casper or Cheyenne.

She walked to the bullpen. Jason was at his desk.

She hadn't heard him come in at all. "Did you sneak in?"

"You looked engrossed. Didn't want to disturb you."

She held up the list. "I'm going to head out and talk to Milly. When Walter gets in, you and he can start going through this list."

Jason nodded.

"Find out what people remember about the men. Did they have any conflict with anyone, that kind of thing."

"Whether they murdered the Apex three?" Walter asked, walking in.

"Sure, if you think that will get you anywhere, Walter."

He grinned.

Rita grabbed the cruiser's keys from the board at Mary Lou's desk. Then she turned back to him. "You call Tammie Mitchell's mother? Let her know her daughter wasn't amongst the dead?"

Walter nodded.

"She a Still case?" Rita asked. She didn't want any more missing persons cases falling through her fingers.

He shook his head. "Cheyenne."

"Any reason to think she could have gone missing in Still?"

"Don't know," he said.

Rita pursed her lips. "Let's check out Cheyenne's list. Not today. But once we wrap this one."

"It's not ours," Walter said.

"I know," Rita said. "But humor me."

Then she headed down the hallway and out the back door. Mary Lou had just arrived. Rita kept the door open for her. "You're late."

Mary Lou tapped her wristwatch. "I'm right on time."

"Which for you is late." As soon as she took the door, Rita headed towards the cruiser.

"Aren't you going to ask me about my weekend?" Mary Lou asked.

"Hell no," Rita said. "I take it you got lucky?"

Mary Lou grinned.

"Then that's all I need to know."

Rita opened the car and got inside before Mary Lou could elaborate.

Chapter Twenty-Two

RITA DREW TO A STOP IN FRONT OF THE BIGHORN MINING Building. She recognized the black pickup crossing in front of her. Quick Cash.

She waved.

Cash slowed. Nodded.

Seated next to him was Arbuckle. And the back of the truck was filled with black garbage bags.

So that's who Arbuckle got to take him into Casper to redeem his cans. She always wondered.

Rita continued on to Miner's Way, then pulled up the main drive to Still Haven Inn. There was a cleaning crew tending to the vandalized sign.

Rita parked, then pulled out her phone. She texted Cash. *Opened a bank account for Arbuckle. He needs to sign some paperwork. Can you do that with him when you get back?*

She didn't wait for an answer. Instead, she got out and headed for the glass front doors. A young man stood behind a lectern that read *Valet*.

He looked bored.

The front doors flew open. Milly strode out. The valet immediately straightened.

Milly had a scowl the size of a thunderstorm on her face. "Can you not park around back in the staff lot?"

"As I said last time, I'm not staff."

"You know what I mean."

"I don't, actually."

"Having cop cars in front of the inn isn't good for business."

"I don't know why not," Rita said. "I'd think it appeals to safety and well-being."

"No one thinks that."

The valet stood watching them, his head going back and forth as though he were at a tennis match.

"Well, usually the only inns and motels that mind a patrol car out front are the ones with sex workers. You haven't taken up a side business, have you?"

The valet barely stifled a laugh.

Milly bristled, turning to him. "Don't you have something to do?"

He looked confused, gesturing to his lectern. "Uh—"

"Never mind." Milly grabbed Rita's arm and dragged her out of earshot. "Have you found the assholes who destroyed my sign? They can't get the paint out. I'll have to replace it."

"I'm not here about your sign."

"Then what?"

"The Apex Three."

"What about them?"

"You didn't hear that we've most likely found the bodies?"

That seemed to take the wind out of her. "You found them? Ethan, Patrick, Scott?"

Rita nodded. "Can we talk inside?"

"Does this mean you're not parking out back?"

Rita worked hard not to scowl. "No, I'm not parking out back."

"Fine." It obviously wasn't, because she threw up her hands and marched to the front doors. The valet lunged for the doors, opening them so that they could sail through. Rita winked at him as she passed.

She'd never been inside the Still Haven Inn before. The lobby had a huge stone fireplace, glass windows, and leather couches and chairs, scattered with throws with a distinctive checked pattern. It was much nicer and cozier than she would've guessed from the outside.

"You got an office?" Rita asked. One guest was sitting by the fireplace (not that it was on in this heat) reading. Another was engrossed in her phone. She wondered if they were Apex clients.

"This way," Milly said.

Milly's office had wood walls as well. Another fireplace. Native American rugs on the floor. A large wood desk held a state-of-the-art computer, which made Rita a bit envious.

Milly sat behind her desk. Rita took the leather chair opposite. It was much nicer than the guest chair in her office. "I reviewed Otto's report. You were the one that called the SCSO to report the men missing."

"Yes."

"The inn's fairly new, yes?" Rita asked.

Milly nodded. "Built five years ago."

"And have you been the owner the whole time?"

Milly pressed her lips together. "And manager. Yes, five years.

"And your main clientele?"

"Honeymooners, wedding parties, tourists."

"Apex."

Milly tightened her jaw. "Yes, Apex."

"Would I be correct in saying they are now the bulk of your business?"

Milly said nothing.

Rita changed her tactic. "What can you tell me about the Apex Three?"

Milly ignored her. "I didn't think High Peak Mine was ever going to be excavated. Too dangerous."

"They weren't found there."

"No?"

Rita shook her head. "No."

Cash was right. There was no point in hiding the details anymore. Everyone knew who the deceased were. DNA testing was just going to confirm it. "They were found buried in the vacant lot across from the Rancher's Pantry."

Milly's jaw fell open. "What?"

"You hadn't heard?"

She shook her head.

"How is it that nearly everybody else in town knows, but you haven't heard a peep?"

Milly sniffed. "I don't have much to do with Still. I keep pretty busy here."

In other words, the town was beneath her. Probably one of those that did her shopping in Casper.

"Yeah, but you have employees. You didn't hear them talking about it?"

Milly shook her head. "Like I said, I'm busy. What happened to them?"

"Murdered."

Milly stiffened. "Murdered?"

"That surprise you?"

"Of course. I thought they died in a mine shaft. The whole town did." Now she was claiming her community. Probably didn't want to be seen as standing out. "Although

135

—" Her voice trailed off.

Rita raised her brows. "Go on."

"One of them — God, which one…Scott, I think."

Rita nodded.

"Yeah, he seemed to be a bit of a ladies' man. Wouldn't surprise me if he hit on the wrong woman, and some good ol' boy decided to let his gun do the talking."

"He did that a lot, did he?"

She shrugged. "Just something I heard."

"From who?"

"A server in our restaurant at the time, Hannah. He'd hit on her and a few other women at the bar."

"Does she still work here?"

Milly shook her head. "Gone to Casper for university."

"You have her contact info?"

Milly nodded. Tapped on her keyboard for a minute. Then wrote down a phone number and slid it across her desk.

Rita slid the paper into her pocket. "He ever hit on you?"

"No!" She seemed affronted. Though Rita wasn't sure if it was because he didn't hit on her, or because he had and was now lying about it.

"What did you think of the three men?" Rita asked.

"I liked Ethan. He was the kind of man that would stack the dishes at the table when everyone finished eating. He talked a lot about his family. Even attended church while he was here. Scott, I already told you. Never mentioned family, although he wore a wedding ring."

"And what about the other man, Patrick?"

"He didn't talk much. Seemed to hang on Scott's every word."

"You think Patrick was interested in Scott?"

"Not like that. Neither of them was gay. It was more

like he idolized him, wanted to be like him. Scott held himself very well, very confident. I could tell that Patrick was insecure."

"What can you tell me about their stay? Did anything ever seem amiss?"

"No." But then she pursed her lips. "I remember once Ethan came back in a mood. There'd obviously been an argument between the three of them. He told Scott to fuck off right there in the lobby. Then he didn't come out of his room the entire weekend."

"When was this?"

She leaned back in her chair. "I don't remember, it was four years ago."

"Try," Rita said.

"Maybe the third week of their stay. But then things seemed to smooth over. I don't recall another disagreement."

"You know what it was about?"

"No."

"Can you tell me everything you remember of the day they went missing?"

Milly sighed. "I went over this with the Sheriff at the time."

"Just want to see if you recall something you might not have thought important back then."

"You mean you want to see if I lied?"

"Not at all."

Milly sniffed. "I don't remember times."

"That's fine." Rita had those in her prior witness statement.

"They had breakfast, the chef prepared them a packed lunch, they said they'd be back for dinner. But it was also a long drive, and I knew they'd be hungry after hiking all day. So that's why I didn't worry when they didn't show for dinner. Just figured they changed their minds and no one bothered to inform me. But as it grew later, I knew Ethan would have called to update their arrival time. He was cautious. By the time it started to get dark, I began to worry. So I called the SCSO."

"You knew their rental car had been found in town?"

Milly nodded. "Figured some kids found the car parked at the bottom of the mountain and stole it."

"Why'd you think that?"

She pinched her lips together. "My own car was stolen at the time. Stupid kids ran it into the reservoir."

The hairs on Rita's arms stood up. She hadn't known Lisa's car wasn't the first to be lost to that water. "They catch who did it?"

She shook her head.

"Anyone from Apex ever visit the men here?"

Milly nodded. "There was a woman from Apex. She used to come here for meetings. They'd use the board-room. Angel something."

"Angela Ruiz."

"That's her. Although we were never formally introduced."

"How many times did she visit?"

"I'm not sure. A few times."

"And the men's possessions?

Milly shrugged. "I packed them up, put them in stor-age. After about a week, someone was sent from Apex to pick them up."

"Angela?"

She shook her head. "Some other woman."

"Peggy?"

"I'm sorry, I don't know. I was in Casper at the time."

"Is there anything else you can remember? Something I haven't asked you about?"

138

Milly shook her head.

Rita flipped her notebook closed and tucked it and her pen in her pocket. "Thank you for your time."

Milly looked relieved. She jumped up from her chair, heading for the door. She walked the carpeted hallway ahead of Rita.

As they reached the lobby, Rita had another thought. "Why did the men want to go to the mine?"

Milly shrugged. "I think they heard about it from someone in town. I certainly didn't recommend it. I don't think they planned on it being a big thing. Just a hike and a lunch to celebrate the fact that they were leaving Still on Monday morning. I offered to hire a guide for them, but they declined."

Rita had celebrated the first time she'd left Still too. Her first night in New York, she'd downed enough beer to give her a three-day hangover. Although maybe that was because she didn't want to think about who she'd left behind. And what was next to come.

When she approached the front doors, the valet opened them.

"Take care," Rita said. Milly hadn't balked at answering any questions, so Rita threw her a bone. "Next time I'll park in the back."

"Hopefully there won't be a next time," Milly said with a stiff smile.

"There's always a next time."

Milly grunted, then made a beeline back down the hallway towards her office. Rita wondered if she was off to call Apex.

She stepped outside in the heat.

The valet shut the door behind her. "*Pleeeeease* don't park in the back next time. That was the most entertainment I've had in a long while."

Rita laughed. "Don't suppose you were working here four years ago?"

He shook his head. "Three months. Probably won't last another."

Rita gestured to the inn. "You know if Apex owns a share of this place?"

He shook his head. "Dunno."

Rita pulled ten bucks out of her wallet and handed it to him. He grinned and snapped the bill, tucking it in his pocket. Then she walked over to her car and got inside.

Time to talk to Otto.

Chapter Twenty-Three

RITA APPROACHED OTTO'S HOUSE SLOWLY.

The driveway was empty.

Helen wasn't there.

She pulled in, parking outside the camper.

Otto opened the door before she even reached the porch. "I was wondering when you'd show. Come on in."

But she needed to make sure. "Helen not here?"

He shook his head. "She's working at the Pantry."

He led her to the living room and sat down in his chair, adjusting his nasal cannula. She took the sofa and sniffed.

The house still smelled fresh. The party was all cleaned up except for the pile of presents, which had been moved to the coffee table.

"You didn't open them yet?"

"Going to do it on my actual birthday. You should come by. Three of us can have supper together."

Nope.

"I'll have to see. This week's going to be busy."

He grunted. "Wished you would've stayed longer on Saturday."

"Parties aren't my thing."

"Parties, or Helen?"

"Both."

He reached into the pocket of his flannel shirt, searching for his cigarettes, then realized they weren't there.

"Old habits," he said, putting his hands on his lap like he didn't know what to do with them. So he fiddled with the cannula instead.

"You really quit?"

"Yeah. Helen's been a godsend."

Rita considered sharing her suspicions about Helen, partly because she felt like he should know, but also because she was jealous. "She try and convince you to change your will as well?"

"Jesus Christ, Rita."

"Just curious."

"No. And I wouldn't. Everything I have goes to you."

That should make her feel better. But it didn't. Although, if he did die and Helen inherited his life insurance policy, Rita would personally see to it that she rotted in a cell alongside her husband.

"Helen getting a divorce?"

He eyed her. "You come to inquire about my relationship, or the Apex Three? I'm guessing the latter, since you're in uniform."

She sighed. "Yeah. I wanted to see what you remembered. Walter wasn't able to add much."

"Because he was on administrative leave."

"For what?"

Otto nodded, coughed. "His gambling addiction. I gave him a choice. Get help, or get fired."

"He didn't tell me that."

"You blame him?" No. Probably not. "I take it the bodies belonged to Apex."

"Just waiting on DNA."

He grunted in acknowledgment, reaching for a cigarette. "Goddamn it."

"What do you remember about the case?"

"How'd they die?"

She hesitated. Then decided to tell him. It had been his case originally. Maybe knowing more about it would put the past into perspective. "Won't have final cause of death until later in the week, but they each had gunshot wounds to the head. Two in the front, one in the back." She didn't tell him about the mirrors. She wanted to keep that tidbit to the SCSO for now.

"Jesus." He pressed his fingertips together, thinking. And then he went over the case. He remembered the details fairly well. His version of events was nearly identical to what he'd written in his report.

"They had food and water and had filed their plan for the day with Milly. Everything you were supposed to do when heading into the mountains. We figured they got lost coming back down. Or left it too late and sought shelter in the mine. We were fairly confident we'd find them the next morning."

"But you didn't."

"Nah. We spotted fresh tracks leading deep into the mine. And found a sweater that belonged to one of them."

"Scott."

Otto nodded. "And a water bottle. The chef from Still Haven Inn confirmed it had been part of the lunch he'd made for them."

"Any chance that they never made it to the mine and someone planted the items to make you think they'd been there?"

143

He coughed. "Nah, they were definitely there. A pair of honeymooners spotted them from a distance earlier. Had even caught one of them in the background on a photo. Ethan, I think."

"What did you think when you didn't find the car?"

He hesitated. "This was bad policing on my part."

"What do you mean?"

"I made an assumption. We had some little shits out of Casper stealing cars and joyriding at the time. I figured that's what happened to the Porsche. They spotted it at the bottom of the mountain, thought it was abandoned, and took off."

"When was it found at the Pantry?"

"Next evening, I think. Put out a BOLO. But I'd spent all day out at the mountain. That's why I didn't see it."

"You think you made a mistake when the vehicle was discovered?"

"I felt relief. Maybe they weren't in the mine at all and had come back to town. But there was zero sighting of them. We searched Apex, the grounds around the property, downtown. The reservoir. All the spots we thought they might be."

"Moses's lot?"

He nodded. "Yeah, we even looked there. But we were searching above ground, not six fucking feet under."

"And no one thought it odd the soil was all churned up?"

"Apex had been digging there for a week, doing soil tests, same as they'd done at half a dozen other properties in town. Far as we knew, they put the dirt back where it belonged."

"You ever hear about the men having any issues while they were in town?"

"One of them spent the night in the cells for drunk and disorderly."

"I didn't see that in a report."

"Guy got black-out drunk at The Shaft, and Ruby Joe kicked him out. One and done. No charges. Just kept him until he slept it off."

"Was it Scott?"

"No, Ethan."

That surprised her. "Looking back, can you think of any reason someone might have wanted to murder them?"

He thought for a long moment, staring at the wallpaper. Then he reached for his ghost cigarettes again. "Goddamn, I could use a cigarette. Helps me think."

"But keeps you from breathing."

He glared at her. "I never heard nothing. Maybe one of them killed the other two, then himself?"

"We didn't find a gun. Besides, if that was the case, who the fuck buried them?"

"Hell if I know."

"Yeah."

They were silent for a moment. Her phone buzzed. She pulled it out. Text from Cash in response to her request regarding Arbuckle.

On our way now.

She typed out: *Thanks.*

Then she got up and stretched. "I should get back to the office."

Otto got up as well, dragging his oxygen machine behind them as they walked to the door. "This has been nice, Rita. If you got more questions, I can get Helen to bring me to the station. Kinda miss the old place."

"That won't be necessary."

"Anything to keep the old man away, eh?" He laughed, but it turned into a cough.

She stopped at the front door. "Who owns High Peak Mine now that Bighorn Mining has gone under?"

"Oh, it was never owned by them."

"What?"

"Bighorn Mining leased it from the landowner."

"And who was that?"

"The Grant family."

Rita stared at him. "Moses Grant?"

"Yeah."

Seconds later, Rita was on her way back to the SCSO.

Chapter Twenty-Four

RITA PARKED AT THE FRONT OF THE STATION AND MADE HER way inside. Jason was on the phone.

Rita glanced at Mary Lou. "I need to make a call, then let's review."

Mary Lou nodded as Rita walked to her office and closed the door behind her. She pulled out the number for Hannah and dialed. There was no answer, so she left a voicemail. A second later, she received a text from the same number.

Who is this?

Rita typed: *Still County Sheriff's Office. Milly gave me your number. Said you worked at Still Haven Inn four years ago. I wanted to ask you a few questions about some former guests.*

Her phone rang. Rita answered. "Hannah?"

"This is about Scott, isn't it? You finally find the asshole's body?"

Rita pursed her lips. "We did."

"Should have left him in the mine. I hated him."

"He wasn't found in the mine. He was found in a vacant lot in Still," Rita said. "Murdered."

Silence. And then, "Holy shit."

"I just need to confirm," Rita said. "This is Hannah…"

"Hannah Collins, yeah. Scott was murdered?"

"Along with Patrick and Ethan."

"Weird," Hannah said. "We all thought they were in the mine."

"Yeah. What can you tell me about them?"

"Ethan was okay. Patrick was a creep. But Scott was pure asshole. Always leering at the staff. I didn't trust that prick as far as I could throw him. Warned the other girls to stay away from him."

"He harassed you?"

"Put his hand where it wasn't wanted, so I almost broke his finger. He reported me to Milly."

"And what she'd do?"

"What d'you think? She fucking fired me."

"I'm sorry," Rita said.

"Milly only cares about Milly," Hannah said. "She wasn't about to allow a little sexual harassment to cost her business."

"Scott ever try anything with Milly?"

Hannah made a few clicking sounds as she thought. "Not that I saw. But Milly didn't interact with staff much. Except to yell."

Rita almost laughed. That she could imagine. "Were you still working there when the men went missing?"

"Nah. I'd moved to Cheyenne in May. I was starting college in the fall, so I got a place with some friends. Started working at Chirps."

"Chirps?"

"Local bar. Tips were a hell of a lot better than at Still Haven. Rich people ain't as generous as you'd think."

"I suppose that's how they stay rich."

Hannah snorted.

"Who told you the men had gone missing?"

She made more of those clicking sounds. "I think it was Taylor? Yeah, probably Taylor. Although everyone called me at some point. Knew how much I hated him. Is that gonna make me a suspect?"

"You got witnesses who saw you the weekend they went missing?"

"Probably a whole bar full."

"Then I think you're good." Although, she'd double check with Chirps. "Is there anything else you can tell me about the men?"

Hannah thought for a moment, but nothing came of it. Rita thanked her and rang off.

She looked up Chirps online. Found a general email address. She composed a quick email identifying herself and asking for confirmation of Hannah's employment at the time the men went missing.

Then she got up and walked out to the bullpen, dragging her chair behind her.

"I've got some information on Patrick," Mary Lou said. "He was an only child. Both parents died when he was six. He grew up in foster care. There's absolutely no next of kin for him. But we did have his dental records on the missing persons file, so I sent those to Casper."

"Great, thank you." She dropped into her chair.

"I also reached Melinda Harris, Ethan's wife, using the information from Apex. She's coming to Still and will be in touch when she arrives."

Rita nodded. "Anything on Scott?"

"Nothing yet. The number I tried from Apex was out of service. And it wasn't for a wife, but a sister. In fact, I can't find anything that suggests Scott was married."

"Except he wore a ring."

Mary Lou nodded. "I'll keep looking."

Her phone rang. Mary Lou answered. "Still County Sheriff's Office."

Rita turned to Jason and Walter. "How are the Apex calls going?"

"Almost finished," Walter said.

Jason glanced at him. "We have twenty left to go."

He shrugged. "As I said, almost finished."

"Get any intel?"

"Well, most everyone I've talked to," Jason said, "seems to know the men have been found."

That didn't surprise Rita. She figured the phone lines between Apex and employees, regardless of their office or employment history, had been burning up.

"But it seems Ethan, Scott, and Patrick didn't really spend much time at the office," Walter said. "They were usually out on location. And if they did come by the office, it was usually for a meeting with Angela."

"Alright."

Mary Lou hung up the phone. "That was Tilda. She's confirmed evidence review for tomorrow morning. I'll get two rooms booked at the Casper Best Western."

Rita glanced at Walter. "Meet me at the office tomorrow morning at 7 and we'll drive out together."

Walter blinked. "Me? Not Jason?"

Rita shook her head. "Nope, I need Jason here." Then she got to her feet. "Now, guess who owns High Peak?"

Walter didn't look interested. Obviously still processing the early start tomorrow.

"Who?" Mary Lou asked.

"Moses Grant. Shall we go have that conversation with him, Jason?"

He nodded and got to his feet.

"I'm gonna go to the Bean," Walter said. "Get some

lunch and see what I can find out about these three assholes from townsfolk. I'm tired of talking to flatlanders." He looked at her as though expecting her to disapprove.

She didn't oblige. "Good idea. Let me know what you find out."

He grunted.

Jason followed her out to the car. Seconds later, she'd pulled onto Main. "There's a reason I'm not taking you to Casper."

He glanced at her. "Not enough seniority."

She snorted. "He might have more seniority. But you have more sense. No, it's 'cause I can't leave Walter in charge of Still for forty-eight hours. What if actual police work needs doing?"

Jason's mouth turned up in a smile. "In charge?"

"Told you I want you to have the badge one day."

He straightened. "I won't disappoint you."

"You could never do that, Jason. Just keep doing what you're doing."

Rita turned left, passing Moses' lot. It was vacant now. Still surrounded in yellow police tape. A single Casper PD car sat in front of it. An officer in the front seat. Obviously on his phone.

She drove past and honked.

He raised his head.

She waved.

But was gone before he could respond.

Moses' house was located at the very end of the road. And he was right. She couldn't miss it. The house was falling apart, and the yard was full of old junkers and garbage.

"The town ever ask him to clean up the place?" Rita asked.

Jason shook his head. "Not that I know."

Rita parked on the grass in front of the house. They got out and walked to the front door. Jason knocked.

Moses answered, opening the door wide. Rita was hit by the smell of engine oil and dust. He gestured for them to enter. "Cooler inside."

Rita entered. Jason, following in her footsteps. The inside of the house was even worse than the outside, and that was no small feat. She'd only been in one hoarded space before. An apartment in New York that had been so full of garbage they'd had to wear masks to enter.

Moses' living room was filled with boxes, shopping bags, newspapers, magazines, books, unopened cereal boxes, clothes (many of them still with their tags), and boxes upon boxes of tools, car parts, and electronics.

His belongings were piled from floor to ceiling with a narrow path carved through the center. The couch and chairs were stacked with more boxes. She glanced at Jason. Where the hell were they supposed to sit?

She supposed it could be worse. It wasn't filthy. No roaches, dirty food containers, or horrible smells beyond the mustiness and the scent of oil from the car parts. It smelled more like an old garage than a house.

"You'll have to mind the mess," Moses said. "Doing some rearranging."

"I see," she said.

"This way." He led them along the narrow passage that cut through the boxes to the kitchen which was, by comparison, far more spacious. The table only had a few boxes on it. And there were four chairs that were accessible. "My daughter's been cleaning in here," he said.

That made Rita feel better. At least he had someone looking after him.

"Have a seat, " Moses said on his way to the fridge. "Want something to drink? Got water, beer, pop."

"No, thanks," she said. "You, Jason?"

He shook his head.

Moses grabbed a beer. He popped the top, then sat across from her at the kitchen table.

"How'd your meeting in Casper go? You get your business partner up to speed?"

Moses took a sip of beer. "Sure did. Now what do you wanna know about the property?"

"Actually," Rita said. "I want to know about the mine first."

"High Peak?" Moses asked and when she nodded he continued. "Been in the family for generations."

"You didn't think to tell us this earlier?"

He shrugged. "Figured you knew. Ain't a secret."

"Bighorn leased it from you?"

"Yep."

"Did they pay well?"

"Sure did, though Pa ran off with most of it."

"Were you the one to tell the men about High Peak?"

He took another swallow of beer. "Guess so. Yeah."

"How'd it come up?"

"Patrick asked if I owned any other property in the area. I mentioned the mine. Not what they were looking for in terms of a new site, but he seemed interested in checking it out."

"Why didn't they choose the Still Shadows property to build on?"

"Underground water table. Not what you want when you're building sub-basements. I think they considered rerouting it, but it came down to cost. Not worth the investment."

"You said you had photos of the property at the time?"

"Yeah." He took another drink of his beer, then got up. "Let me find them." Moses left the kitchen, disappearing back into the living room. They heard him shuffling boxes about.

"You know his daughter?" Rita asked.

Jason shook his head.

It was about five minutes later that Moses returned with a dusty 8-by-10 white envelope. He gave it to Rita. She reached inside and pulled out some photos, documents, and promotional material that Apex Global must've given him at the time.

Thank God he was a hoarder. Anyone else would have chucked the lot.

For the most part, the promotional materials were general PR for the company. Saying how great Apex was without actually saying what they did. She found a folded newspaper clipping from the *Casper Chronicle*.

It boasted the headline: "Apex Global Scouts Second Site in Still."

Beneath it was a photo of Moses, Angela, Peggy, and another man standing in front of a bulldozer.

Rita looked at the caption, which didn't name anyone other than Moses and Angela. The others were referred to as Apex employees. She pointed to the man. "Who's that?"

"Patrick."

She eyed Peggy. She looked like a deer in headlights, clutching a red jacket to her chest. Probably more exposure than she was used to.

"Can I take these?"

Moses hesitated. "I'll get 'em back?"

"When we're done the investigation."

"Yeah, I guess." He didn't look happy about it.

"What do you remember about the men?"

He shrugged. "Not much. Thought they were gonna buy the land."

"But they didn't."

"Nope."

"That bother you?"

"No. Plenty of it around."

Rita tucked the papers back in the envelope. "What do you remember of the day they went missing?"

He took a sip of beer. "Not much. Just knew they were headed out there. Next morning, your pappy knocks on the door and asks me to guide them out there. Thought they might have got lost in it." He shrugged. "So I went."

"But you didn't find them?"

"Found a sweater. And then all sorts of complications. It was unstable. Damn near came down on our heads."

Rita couldn't imagine a worse way to die. Trapped underground in the dark. The thought of it made her skin scrawl.

"And you didn't think it odd, the holes were filled in on your lot?"

Moses shook his head. "Nope. Was part of the deal. Whatever they dug up, they had to fill back in. Whether they bought the lot or not."

Rita nodded. "Did I miss anything, Jason?"

He shook his head.

Rita got to her feet. "Jason and I would like to take a look at High Peak. Can you take us out there?"

Moses fingered his beer. "The entrance was boarded up after the cave-in. Didn't want anyone else getting lost in there. But sure, I can take you in."

"How's Friday?" Rita asked.

"Friday works. Just make sure you wear boots and jeans, and prepare to get dirty."

Chapter Twenty-Five

RITA AND JASON GOT INTO THE CRUISER.

"You think he killed them?" Jason asked.

"I don't know," Rita said, turning on the vehicle. "Can you imagine Moses getting angry about anything?"

Jason glanced at the house as they passed. "Not really."

"Yeah, me neither."

She slowed as the neared the Rancher's Pantry. It was almost 5 p.m. She glanced at Jason. "You in a hurry to get home? 'Cause we haven't talked to Peter yet. And the car was found in his lot."

"I don't have anywhere to be," Jason said.

"Esther not waiting on you for dinner?"

He shook his head. "Nope."

Rita hit the indicator and turned left. "What do you think about Edith Mae working out of the office?"

He shrugged. "It's okay. Keeps her out of trouble."

That it did. There hadn't been a single report of her shoplifting in the past two months.

"Besides," Jason said. "It's only until she goes back to school in September."

"Okay. But if you change your mind, let me know. I'll find somewhere else for her to work."

Rita parked in the spot she had been using the past few days, although she could have had her choice of spaces. The parking lot was nearly empty. It seemed the Pantry had returned to its previous low number of clientele.

Rita hoped that would change. It would be a shame if the town were to lose its only grocery store.

She and Jason got out of the car and walked to the front doors.

Peter must have spotted them in the parking lot, because he was already making his way towards them. "What now?"

"Can we talk in your office?"

He glanced over at the clerk Rita had bought her groceries from the other day. She was watching with interest. Peter jerked his head. They followed him to a narrow set of linoleum stairs that headed up to the second floor.

His office was small and cramped. Desk, filing cabinet, stacks of papers. Manifests, receipts, tax forms.

He gestured to two vintage yellow kitchen chairs. The vinyl was cracked and faded. Peter's own chair wasn't much newer.

Rita sat. It was surprisingly sturdy.

Jason took the chair beside her.

"How's business?" Rita asked.

He grunted. "Best month in ages. Thinking maybe I should bury some more bodies across the way."

Jason cleared his throat. "Please don't."

Peter looked at him as though assessing an idiot.

Rita said, "We were hoping you could tell us about a Porsche found in your parking lot four years ago."

Peter looked surprised. "I thought you were gonna ask me about the bodies."

"We'll get to that," Rita said.

Peter shrugged. "I came into work. Found it in the lot. Didn't think much of it. People often used the lot without coming into the store." He gave her a pointed look. "Still do."

"Why was that?"

He gestured towards Main Street. "Proximity to the movie theater. When it was open, we'd often get overflow. A lot of mornings I'd find vehicles parked out front. People would hit up one of the bars after a movie. Walk home or get a lift. Pick up their car in the morning."

He took a sip of his coffee. Made a face. Glanced at her. "Cold."

"What can you tell me about the day the men went missing?"

"It was quiet. Most of the town had volunteered to search the mountains. Wasn't until evening when I heard the radio. That cops were looking for the Porsche. Sure enough, I go down and check the plate. Figured your lot were idiots. Searching the mountains, when they'd been in town all along."

"But there was no sign of them here."

He shook his head. "I figured the car had been stolen and dumped. Windows were left down."

"You ever meet Ethan Harris, Scott Macdonald, or Patrick Russell?"

He ignored her question, taking a sip of cold coffee. "I wasn't happy about it, you know."

"About what?"

"Apex building one of their poison sites across from my business."

"You let them know?"

He inclined his head. "I wrote letters."

"You argue with the men about that?" She stood. Sure

enough, the window looked out over the parking lot and Moses' land. "You would have had a prime view of the work they were doing."

He opened his mouth, then closed it again and shrugged. "You're probably going to find out anyway. I had some choice words for them. But I didn't kill them. Seems a little extreme, don't you think?"

Rita didn't comment.

"What did you do when you realized the Porsche was the one the police were looking for?" Jason asked.

Peter eyed him. "Called it in, of course. And then wished I hadn't. Cops crawled all over the Pantry looking for any sign of those ass — those guys. Didn't find a single thing."

"No CCTV?"

Peter shook his head. "Not at the time. Got it installed right after. Cops made a fucking mess of the store. Didn't bother to help clean up neither."

"What can you tell me about Moses' property at the time?" Rita asked. "Did it strike you as odd that it had been filled in?"

"Nah. We all knew the Apex boys were leaving. Just figured they were putting the soil right again. They'd been looking at Greg Harper's place out of the highway as well. Did some digging there. Put it all back when they rejected it."

Rita made a note to check with Greg if that was the case.

Then she turned to Jason. "Jason?"

He shook his head. No questions.

"Thank you for your time."

Jason stood.

Peter didn't bother. "You know the way out."

The two of them made their way down the stairs and out to the car. It was almost 5:30 now.

"Want me to take you home?" Rita asked.

Jason shook his head. "Kia's at the office."

"I can pick you up in the morning."

"You're heading to Casper with Walter."

"Right. Office it is."

She drove back to the office and parked.

Mary Lou and Walter had both gone for the day. She texted Walter: *7 am tomorrow.*

He didn't respond.

She'd be leaving with or without him.

Jason walked over to the back door of the SCSO. "I'm just gonna check on Ted."

"Don't stay long. And I'll check in tomorrow. See how it's going."

He smiled. "Thanks, Rita."

"And do me a favor?"

"Yep."

"Get us prepped for Friday's hike? Water and the like. Use petty cash."

He gave her a salute.

She waved, then walked home. After which, she showered and changed into shorts and a t-shirt. She looked in her pantry, trying to decide between SpaghettiOs or calling Cash to see if he wanted to grab a bite at The Shaft.

Ten minutes later, she was sitting on her couch, watching an old *Friends* episode, and eating pasta out of her favorite bowl. After all, she had to be up early tomorrow, and she needed rest.

Chapter Twenty-Six

Rita woke early, dressed for work, and took the stairs down to her back door. She stepped outside. Shards of broken mirror glittered on the ground. She kicked them aside. Goddamn kids.

She made her way across the street. Walter was waiting by the Honda, much to her surprise. Jason's Kia was already in the parking lot.

Walter pointed to the Kia. "You work that kid too hard." And then his eyes narrowed. "Or is he getting overtime?"

"I didn't tell him to come in this early," Rita said. She'd talk to him about it when she got back.

They climbed into the Honda, and Rita drove out to the highway. "You know Greg Harper?" she asked.

"We were at school together."

"Peter told me Apex was looking at his property as a potential site as well."

"Yeah, that sounds right."

"Find out if they did any digging. And how they left the site when they rejected it."

Walter nodded, pulled out his phone. Did some typing. "Anything else?"

"What was it like when Apex arrived? How'd the town feel?" She knew Otto's view. And even Mary Lou's ("if it's too good to be true, it probably is."). But was that the majority opinion?

He shrugged, settling back in his seat while she merged onto the highway. "Folk seemed happy enough when they first arrived. Fire, medical, and police services. Although Otto fought tooth and nail against the SCSO being taken over."

"What did you think about that?"

"Dunno. Thought we might all get raises if they did."

So Walter was probably in favor.

"So they backed off."

"Yeah, Otto made sure of it."

"But then they did their own little deal with the Governor."

"Most thought it would mean more employment, you know?"

"But it didn't."

"Nah, they built Apex Hills. Brought most of their staff in from outside. Made 'em sign contracts not to talk about what they did there."

"You pick up any gossip at the Bean yesterday?"

He pulled his notebook from his pocket and flipped it open. "Seems most folk remember Scott and Patrick."

"Not Ethan?"

He shook his head. "No, but the other two were joined at the hip."

"Anything in particular stand out about them?"

"It's not like they were rock stars or anything, they were men looking at land. They stayed at the inn, didn't stray into town much. If they did, they were mainly seen at The

Shaft. They were flatlanders. Nobody was exactly striking up friendships with them."

Of course not. Rita was born and raised here and got labelled as a flatlander. Although, she had been gone fifteen years. Maybe Still had a point.

She pulled out and passed a large semi. "How's Adrian's visit going?"

He shrugged. "His mama's been soft on him."

Rita had no idea what that meant.

"But he's made it to eighteen without getting arrested or knocking anyone up. So he did better than me."

God, was that Walter's measure of what made a successful adult? And considering he'd passed a background check to get hired, she figured it was the ex that he'd knocked up. And not that he'd been arrested. "When's the last time you saw him?"

"Three years ago, when Winona took him with her to Beaumont."

"Three years!"

He glared at her. "Not for lack of trying. Winona kept him from me."

"Why was that?"

"None of your damn business."

She held up a hand. But he was right. Probably his gambling addiction. "He's eighteen now. He can make his own decisions."

"And he wanted to spend summer in Still?" Rita asked.

Walter nodded. "He's headed to Cheyenne for college in September. Last chance for some time with the old man."

"You're not that old, Walter."

He flashed her a grateful glance. She wasn't used to him looking at her like that.

His phone buzzed. He pulled it out. "Greg."

"What's he say?"

He scrolled through what looked like a long block of text. "Apex screwed him around. Made him think they were gonna buy the property, so he bought a place in Cheyenne." He looked at her. "Greg always put the cart before the horse."

Rita nodded.

"But then they stopped calling. Eventually, some engineer returned and filled in all the holes they'd dug. Said they'd found a more desirable property. That's how he found out they weren't buying his land."

"You think he got pissed enough to kill anyone?"

Walter laughed. "Greg? Nah. He was always brains over brawn. He sold the property to his brother-in-law for twice its value. Then sold the Cheyenne house to the city, which wanted to knock it over to widen the boulevard. He made out okay. Moved him and Gwen to Florida. And they ain't never been back."

Rita pursed her lips. So maybe it wasn't that odd that Moses' property had been filled.

They continued the drive, mostly in silence. Walter had his eyes closed, but Rita didn't imagine he was sleeping.

Eventually, they arrived in Casper. The police department looked like someone slapped a giant brown box on the street. But at least it had windows. And large ones, which was more than she had in Still.

They checked in at the front desk, where they were given visitor passes and asked to wait.

Five minutes later, a secured door next to the reception desk opened. Tilda poked her head out. "Good to see you, Rita."

Rita and Walter made their way over and passed through.

Tilda led them into an institutional-looking stairwell

and up to the second floor. She took them down a hallway to a boardroom, where she had set up muffins and a coffee station.

"Have a seat."

Walter went and got a couple of muffins. But they looked nothing like what the Bighorn Bean provided, and Rita could acknowledge that she was spoiled. However, she did pour out coffee and hand it around.

Knowing full well that it would be bitter.

It was.

But at least it was hot.

Tilda had a PowerPoint projected onto a screen. "We're going to go through all the evidence we found. Then I'll take your questions. And we can review it in person as well."

Rita nodded.

Tilda clicked through her first few slides. They were photos of the bodies as Rita had found them.

Then things got more detailed.

"They were buried at seven feet," Tilda said. "Two were buried together, with the third a few feet away. The anthropologist will probably be able to tell us more about the positions they were buried in. We were very lucky that there was very little damage to the skeletons from the excavator."

She clicked through to close-ups of three skulls. "One shot in the occipital bone. Two in the frontal bone."

Rita frowned.

"Annoying, isn't it?" Tilda asked.

Rita nodded. "Why the different head shots?"

Tilda grinned. "Glad it's not my job to figure it out. But I've got more bad news."

"What?"

"Ballistics is working on it now, but they believe two different weapons were involved."

Rita blinked. "What?"

Tilda nodded.

Rita glanced over at Walter. He seemed invested in picking apart the paper wrapping on his muffin. "Alright, what else do you have for me?"

Tilda pulled up her next slides. Beer bottles and caps (no fingerprints), a used condom (no DNA), some chicken bones, ID for Ethan Harris, three unused condoms, an Apex business card for Patrick, a bottle of aspirin, a barrette, three pennies (all pre-2000), and a necklace with a charm and the letter "M."

Rita studied the necklace. It seemed more feminine than masculine. But it was rather hard to tell. It was simply a letter.

"The necklace," Tilda said. "It was twisted in Scott's hand. However, I can't say if that was deliberate, or it simply wound up there due to the excavation."

Rita nodded.

"We're checking it for DNA."

"What about the glass shards?"

"Definitely mirror," Tilda said. "No fingerprints. But we're checking to see if we can find the type of mirror."

Rita pursed her lips. There had been broken mirror on the ground outside her door that morning. Coincidence? In her world, coincidences were rare.

She texted Jason: *there's some broken mirror outside my back door. Bag and tag it for me?*

He returned a thumbs up emoji.

They spent some time discussing the property they had found, all agreeing that the necklace was probably the most substantial lead.

Around noon, they broke for lunch. Tilda took them to

a sandwich place down the street where Rita tried Greek chicken. It was good, but still not as tasty as the Bighorn Bean. After lunch, they returned to the department.

Tilda then took them down to the property room. They donned protective gear and gloves and reviewed all the evidence in person. Rita took a photo of the "M" charm on her phone.

It was close to dinner when they finished up.

"Tomorrow, bodies," Tilda said. "Bring all your questions for the forensic anthropologist."

Rita nodded. They said goodbye to her at the front doors and walked out to the Honda.

Rita drove the truck to the Best Western hotel that Mary Lou had booked for them. Thankfully, their rooms weren't quite side by side.

"You wanna eat together?" Walter asked. He looked like he'd swallowed acid.

"Nah," Rita said. Instant relief crossed his face. "I got a couple errands to run. I'll meet you for breakfast in the morning."

He nodded.

Rita went to her room and dropped her bag. She resisted the urge to lie down on the bed. If that happened, no way in hell was she going to get up again.

Instead she texted Mary Lou. "I need you to get an address for me."

Chapter Twenty-Seven

By the time Rita had a shower, changed into jeans and a t-shirt, and grabbed her leather crossbody, Mary Lou was calling her back. "Stephanie Szabo stopped by."

Stephanie Szabo? "Who is she?"

"Used to run the movie theater before it closed. She claims to have seen the three men just last week, so clearly they can't be dead. She's cuckoo."

"Is that an official diagnosis?"

"Far as I'm concerned. I got the address for George's parents. I'm texting it over now."

"Thank you, Mary Lou."

She disconnected. But not before Rita heard Ted yowl.

Rita plugged the address Mary Lou gave her into the phone's GPS. Then she headed out to her Honda.

Within ten minutes, she was pulling onto a beautiful tree-lined street filled with sprawling houses and lush green lawns. She slowed as she approached a rambling Queen Anne with a copper roof, matching brick chimneys, and a turret with bay windows.

That couldn't possibly be the address, could it?

She double checked the number. Yep. That was the one. She had no idea George's family had this kind of money. No wonder Arnold wanted to stay for the summer. Probably had a giant pool in the back yard.

She drove onto the stone driveway and parked next to a BMW.

She got out, walked up the front stairs, and knocked on the front door. Within a few seconds, a woman answered. Her appearance (apron, rubber gloves) suggested that she was a maid. She looked Rita up and down. "Yes?"

Rita pulled out her badge. "Sheriff Jonas, Still County. Is this the Myers residence?"

"Yes." She immediately looked worried.

"I've come to see Arnold."

"Oh." She stepped back. "Please come in."

Rita stepped inside the air-conditioned house. It might look old-fashioned, but at least someone thought it should have a modern convenience.

The maid led Rita to a sitting room.

"Please wait here," she said, then disappeared.

Rita looked around. Everything looked old. And expensive. Antique couches and chairs. Nope, she'd rather stand. She walked over and studied a large oil painting. Appeared to be a gathering of hounds. And then she realized the dogs were tearing a fox to pieces.

Jeez. Imagine looking at that every day.

Although maybe nobody used the room. Maybe somewhere in this house was a living room that had a couch with shot springs and a coffee table with water stains.

She avoided looking at any of the other paintings, listening to the sound of a grandfather clock ticking away the hours. It was the only noise Rita heard.

For all its beauty and expensive furnishings, the house lacked the one thing a home needed most — warmth. She couldn't imagine George growing up here. Hell, she couldn't imagine anyone growing up here.

A woman cleared her throat.

Rita jumped and turned.

A woman wearing a black dress and pearl necklace and earrings stood in the doorway. Her gray hair was styled in such a way as not to be out of place on the Titanic. She almost looked like a specter. Moving in silence through the house.

"Mrs. Myers?"

"Is my son all right, Sheriff?"

"As far as I know. And please call me Rita."

Her shoulders relaxed a little.

"I'm sorry," Rita said. "I didn't mean to frighten you."

She shook her head. "It's been a long few months."

"I can imagine."

George's mother collected herself and remembered her etiquette. She walked over, hand outstretched. "Eleanor."

Rita took her hand. Cold but strong.

"Please have a seat." She gestured to one of the chairs.

Rita sat. And it was a hell of a lot more comfortable than she figured it would be. "Nice chair."

Eleanor smiled. "George and I bought them on our honeymoon in France. George, my husband. Not my son." Her mouth slipped into a frown. Then she studied Rita a moment. "You're the sheriff?"

"Yes."

Eleanor folded her hands on her lap, her eyes growing cold.

Rita continued, "I only found out Lisa was my half-sister after she was murdered."

Eleanor's mouth fell open. "After?"

Rita nodded.

Eleanor reached out and squeezed her hand. "You

poor lamb. I can't imagine what that must have been like for you."

She said it with such warmth that Rita felt tears spring to her eyes. Crap. She didn't want to cry. Not in front of a stranger. Rita forced a smile on her face. "It must have been hard for you as well. Learning your granddaughter wasn't yours."

"It was shocking," Eleanor said. "Although not as shocking as hearing that George confessed to murder."

She said it with such disdain that it caught Rita off guard. "You don't believe George killed Matt Kirkland?"

Eleanor pressed her lips together and shook her head. "I do not. I believe it was Helen."

Rita dropped back against the chair, a chill running over her. Had she got it wrong? Had Helen been the killer all along, and George was just covering for her? After all, he'd taken the fall for the assault charges on Rita when it came to the black pickup.

"Sheriff?"

Rita met her eyes. "Just thinking."

"My son would never hurt a fly."

Rita pursed her lips. "Did you know Helen accused him of domestic violence?"

Eleanor's eyes flashed. "Lies. That woman is nothing more than a self-serving, manipulative gold digger."

No love lost between them then. "You didn't get along?"

"We did not. George Senior and I didn't agree with Junior marrying that woman, but she got her claws in him and he ... settled."

"That's how he ended up in Still as a firefighter."

Eleanor nodded. "We cut him off, kicked him out, thinking she'd leave once she realized we weren't going to fund her lifestyle. But I guess she was in it for the long game."

Or else Helen really loved George.

"Guess he showed us. They got married, moved to Still, and he took that job. He had so much promise, and she destroyed him." Tears welled up in the woman's eyes. "And even if George was the one with his foot on the gas pedal, I'm certain that Helen put him up to killing that man. And now he rots in prison while she's still out free."

"Have you talked to George about this?"

She sniffed. "He won't see us."

Or Helen. Interesting. She wondered if he was agreeing to see Arnold. Which brought her back to her reason for being here. "I'm actually not here to bring up bad memories," Rita said.

Eleanor shook her head. "It's all right. When you have a murderer for a child, no one wants to talk to you about him anymore. But he's still my son. I love him."

"I understand," Rita said. "And I'm glad Arnold has you."

Eleanor smiled. "Such a sweet boy."

"I actually came by to check in on him. See how he's doing with the transition to Casper."

"Arnold isn't here. He only stayed for two weeks before returning home."

Rita blinked. "Helen said he was spending the summer here."

"That was the plan, but he wanted to go back to Still. We tried to talk him out of it. Stubborn, just like his father."

Rita felt cold. Praying to God Arnold wasn't missing as well. "When's the last time you talked to him?"

"Saturday night. He and Helen were having a quiet night in."

Saturday night? The night of Otto's party? Helen was most certainly not spending a quiet night at home with her son.

Jesus, Arnold wasn't even living at Otto's house. What the hell was going on?

"Has something happened to him?" Eleanor asked.

Last thing she wanted to do was alarm her. "I think what's happened," Rita said, "is that I've misunderstood Helen."

Might as well blame her.

"She was always duplicitous."

Rita laughed. "You've that got right."

Eleanor smiled. And it seemed genuine.

"I won't keep you any longer," Rita said.

"I'll walk you to the door."

Eleanor escorted her, and Rita tried to walk as silently as possible. But her boots still echoed. She wondered if it took practice to walk as quietly as Eleanor. Or if she was born with that skill.

Rita arrived at the door first and opened it.

"Sheriff," Eleanor said. Rita paused. "Thank you for checking in on Arnold. That means a lot to me."

"You're welcome, Eleanor. And if you ever need me, or you just want to talk about George, please let me know."

Tears sparkled in Eleanor's eyes. She couldn't answer, so she just nodded.

Rita patted her arm, then turned and walked out to the Honda. When she arrived at the vehicle, she glanced back, surprised that the front door was already closed. She hadn't even heard it shut.

She climbed into the Honda, thinking.

Interesting that Eleanor didn't think George capable of violence. But now that she thought about it, Helen hadn't ever said George hit her. She just inferred it. And Rita had run with it.

Was it possible she kidnapped Matt? Then ran him over with the fire truck, not once but twice? She couldn't see Helen doing that. Not alone. Maybe the two of them had been working together?

Or maybe it was exactly what the evidence showed. And it was all George. She could understand Eleanor not wanting to believe it. That must be a hell of a thing — having your child murder someone.

She glanced up at the house. Spotted a curtain twitch.

She started up the Honda, then reversed out of the driveway. It didn't take her long to get back to the hotel.

By now, she was starving. Lunch had long since worn off.

She didn't feel like eating in her room. And she didn't want to risk running into Walter in the restaurant. So she walked out to the street, spotting a bar further up the road.

She had almost reached it when the hairs on the back of her neck prickled. She turned around. But no one was behind her. Regardless, she fingered her cross-body, feeling the comforting weight of her service weapon.

Chapter Twenty-Eight

O'MALLEY'S PUB WAS DARK, AND LARGER THAN ANYTHING in Still County. Wanting to avoid the pool tables, the dart league, and the random drunks dancing near the jukebox, Rita found a table in the corner and sat with her back to the wall.

As she waited for a server, she pulled up the image she had taken of the necklace earlier that day. It was definitely an *M* and not a *W*.

A shadow passed over her.

She looked up, expecting it to be the server.

It was Angela Ruiz. Although Rita almost didn't recognize her. She'd changed from business attire to a low-cut black dress. Still expensive though.

Rita flicked off her phone. "You following me?"

Angela laughed. "Heaven's, no. If I needed you followed, I'd pay people for that."

"You just happened to be in the city?"

"Yes."

"Not sure I believe that."

The server approached, a tired-looking dirty blonde in

her late 40s, sleeves of tattoos riding up both arms and creeping onto her neck. She had a pad and pen in hand. "What can I get you ladies?"

"Frozen Margarita," Rita said. "And the more frozen the better."

The server didn't even crack a smile. She glanced over at Angela.

"Old Fashioned."

Rita looked up at her. "We drinking buddies now?"

"Seems like it."

Rita gestured to the chair across from her. "Then you may as well have a seat."

Angela sat down, leaning back in the chair.

Garth Brooks started singing about friends in low places on the jukebox and a table full of drunk women started singing, or rather yelling, along with him. Angela glanced over at them.

"Not your usual haunt, Ms. Ruiz?"

"Is it that obvious?"

"Well, now you can cross it off your bucket list."

Angela laughed.

The server brought their drinks and sat them on the table. "How about something to eat?"

Rita reached for the menu. But Angela placed her hand over it. "What do you recommend?"

The server perked up. "The potato skins. Best in the state."

"That's a bold statement," Angela said.

The server pointed to a bunch of plaques on the wall. Sure enough, O'Malley's potato skins were best in the state. Four years running.

"And the jalapeño poppers."

"We'll take a plate of both," Angela said. The server jotted down the information and disappeared.

Rita took a sip of her margarita. Just the right amount of sweet, sour, and frozen. She sighed.

"Good?"

"Maybe I can get one of these babies for the office."

"Drinking on duty a regular habit at the SCSO?"

"Sometimes I feel like it should be."

Angela laughed again and took a sip of her drink. "Not bad."

"So, Ms. Ruiz—"

"Honestly, Rita. Call me Angela."

"All right. Angela." It felt strange on her tongue. Or maybe that was the drink. And while she'd never have let Boyd call her Rita, it was interesting that she didn't feel the same about Angela. "What are you doing in town, other than completely not following me?"

"Taking a meeting with the bank."

"Yeah? Elk Mountain Equity no longer in the running for payroll?" By the reaction on Angela's face, she knew she'd hit pay dirt.

"Who has been talking?"

Rita felt bad for Margot. It would hurt losing a client like Apex. "Just a guess."

"I was asked by the board to consider it."

"Don't."

Angela looked at Rita, appraising.

Rita shrugged. "They could use the business."

"Then I shall reconsider."

"Just like that?"

"Just like that."

"Must be nice to have that kind of power," Rita said, taking a sip.

"Oh, it's not all a bed of roses," Angela said. "I deal with my share of pricks."

This time it was Rita's turn to laugh. God, Angela might be the devil, but she liked her. "I'm sure you do."

Angela smiled, took another swallow of her Old Fashioned. Then she leaned forward. "You want to know the real reason I'm here?"

Rita leaned forward as well. "Sure."

Angela grinned. "I don't like to eat where I shit. And when I want a little fun, I leave Still and come to Casper."

"And you just happened to want fun in this particular bar tonight?"

She shrugged. "Like I said, I happened to be in town."

Rita finished her drink. Angela signaled to the server for another round. Seconds later, they had their refills. Apparently, Rita wasn't the only one who had noticed the quality of Angela's clothing. Their server had noticed too, and she was working her ass off tonight for a good tip.

The food arrived shortly after their drinks.

Rita pulled a potato skin onto her plate. It smelled delicious. But it almost burned her fingers. She left it to cool. "So how long have you been with Apex?"

"Seventeen years."

"And you like it?"

"The company has been good to me."

"And what exactly does the company do?"

Angela eyed her. "Is this an interrogation?"

"Of course."

Angela laughed and selected a jalapeño popper. "We contract with companies for research and development."

"I think I know less than I used to," Rita said. "And I didn't know much before."

"It's really not that exciting." Angela bit down on the jalapeño.

Rita took a bite out of one of the potato skins. It was crispy. Salty. And fucking delicious.

"Worthy of the plaques?" Angela asked.

Rita nodded. "All four of them."

They ate in silence for a few minutes. Rita had a jalapeño. It was good. But not as good as the potato skins.

"Why didn't Apex pay for the mine to be excavated?"

Angela shrugged. "Not my call. That would have been Victor's decision."

"And he chose not to."

"Apparently. But I can't imagine the board would have approved."

"Too much money?"

Angela nodded.

"So what do you think happened to the Apex Three?" Rita asked.

Angela drained the last of her Old Fashioned. Signaled for another. "I honestly don't know. I can't imagine who would've wanted them dead. They didn't really know anyone in Still."

"Perhaps it was someone from the company. Seems to me the ability to murder might be a requirement of employment."

The corners of Angela's mouth turned down. Fuck. Rita felt like she might have crossed a line.

"I'm sorry. I've had a few bad experiences with Apex."

"I understand." Angela smiled as their server brought more drinks. "And I know you won't believe me, but I can assure you that not all employees are like Boyd. Or Ken. Or Clyde. But morale is low. And part of the reason I'm here is to improve it. So I hope you'll see by my actions that we are not the enemy."

Rita tipped her head in acknowledgement. Then took a drink.

"So why did you leave New York?" Angela asked.

"It wasn't in my Apex file?"

"Who said we had a file on you?"

Rita grinned. "Just how big is it?"

Angela indicated an inch with her thumb and forefinger.

Rita laughed. "My father is dying."

Angela's mouth turned down. "I'm sorry."

Rita shrugged, rubbing the stem of her glass between her fingers. "He's been dying for years now. Lung cancer."

"He smoke?"

"Pack a day."

"Jesus."

"Yeah."

"You must have a good relationship then? Following him into policing?"

"Now, that's where your file has got it wrong."

"You don't?"

"We're getting a little personal."

Angela smiled. "Simply returning the favor."

"I didn't ask about your parents."

Angela raised a hand and ticked off her fingers. "Lawyer father, lawyer mother, lawyer brother."

"Jesus. You didn't have a chance."

Angela laughed. "Waitress sister."

"How does that go down at family dinner?"

"She works at The Park."

"In Manhattan?"

Angela nodded. "She makes more per annum in tips than I do in wage."

"Lucky her."

"So…" Angela took a sip of her drink. "Your mother?"

Rita shrugged. "Don't fucking know. She disappeared out of my life years ago."

"She doesn't live in Still?"

"No, she does not."

"And you don't speak to her?"

"Don't even think of her." Liar.

"Interesting."

Rita raised her brows.

"So what will you do when your father passes? Stay in Still?"

Rita swallowed the last of her margarita. "I haven't given it much thought."

Angela took a drink, met her eyes. "And why do you think the Apex Three were murdered?"

Rita laughed. "Trying to catch me off guard? You'll need to buy me a lot more of these to get that information."

Angela's eyes flashed. "Done."

She signaled the server.

"Jesus, I was just kidding," Rita said. But their server was already returning with another Margarita and Old Fashioned.

As she left, a man approached their table. Late twenties, backwards hat, and a faded Wyoming Cowboys jersey. "Hey, ladies. Buy you a drink?"

Angela looked him up and down. "We've already bought them."

He stared at her.

She made a shooing motion with her hand.

"Fucking dykes." He hit the palm of his hand against their table and shuffled off.

"Charming," Angela said.

"I thought you were here to 'eat.'"

Angela laughed. "Eat, not get heartburn. I might be desperate, but I'm not going home with a drunk man-child."

"I hope you don't think you're coming home with me."

Angela gave her an appraising look. "Would you say yes if I asked?"

Rita flushed a little. "Nope. I've got a rule."

"Only one?"

"No fraternizing with the enemy."

"Ah. Yes. Well, I hope I one day I can convince you that we're sharing the same foxhole."

Rita reached into her crossbody and found her wallet. "I should get going. I've got an early day tomorrow."

"No, no," Angela said. "My treat."

Rita hesitated.

"I promise this isn't a bribe."

Rita slid her wallet back in her purse. "All right. I'll accept in the spirit of greater cooperation."

Angela smiled.

"You're not driving back tonight, are you?" Rita asked.

"No. I'm staying at the Marriott. But I think I'll have another drink or two."

"Have a good evening. Beware of drunk man-children."

Angela laughed.

Rita headed to the door and exited. But she didn't leave. She slipped over to the front window and peered through the glass.

Angela wasn't staying either. She pulled out a black credit card and paid their tab. Then she got up and walked towards the door, pulling out her phone and making a call.

Rita ducked around the corner of the building.

A black Mercedes Benz with tinted windows pulled up and parked in front of the bar. Seconds later, Angela exited.

Ken got out of the driver's seat and opened the rear

door. Angela got inside. He closed the door. And returned to the driver's seat. Moments later, they drove off.

Rita immediately felt icky. As though she had spent the evening drinking with the enemy.

Chapter Twenty-Nine

RITA WOKE.

Light filtered in through a gap in the curtains. She hadn't pulled them all the way closed last night. Probably because after she got back to the room, she'd texted Jason to see how the day had gone, then fallen into bed.

Which was a mistake.

At least she had the foresight to put a glass of water on the bedside table. She sat, drinking it down.

Crap. She had a headache. Too many margaritas.

She'd have to bum aspirin from Tilda. She pulled her phone and checked her messages.

There was one from Jason: *Apex vehicle full of lab equipment and supplies was stolen last night.*

Rita dialed his number. He answered right away. "Don't you sleep in?"

"Don't you?" he asked.

She laughed.

"How's it going? Tilda sent a copy of her PowerPoint."

"Good. We see the bodies today. What are you up to?"

"Dealing with the stolen vehicle. Following up with the last of the Apex employees. Only a handful left to call."

"Sounds good."

"What was with the broken mirror you had me collect from your apartment? You think it's related to the Apex Three?"

"I dunno. Just struck me as odd, after finding broken mirror in the grave."

"Yeah."

She was about to hang up when she said, "Listen, have you seen Arnold Myers around?"

"No. I thought he was in Casper."

"Apparently not."

"Is he missing?"

"I don't think so. He's been in contact with both his mother and grandmother."

"I can reach out to Helen for you."

"No. Not yet." She rubbed her head. "I don't want to alarm her. But if you see him, tell him I want to chat."

"Will do, Rita."

Rita hung up and stretched. Then she showered, got dressed, and packed her bag. She made her way downstairs and spotted Walter in the restaurant.

She walked over and joined him. He had a plate full of eggs, bacon, and toast. A continental breakfast had been set up on a table. Rita walked over and got a bowl of oatmeal and a glass of orange juice.

Rita sat across from him. "Hungry?"

"Just figured I'd get my money's worth on this trip."

She swallowed a mouthful of oatmeal. "What'd you get up to last night?"

"Early bed." He sounded defensive. She wondered if he had gone to the casino. "You get your errand done?"

"Yeah."

He didn't ask any more questions. If he had gone to the casino, he must have lost, because his mood was foul. She decided not to ask and left him alone.

They finished their meal in silence. Each on their phone.

A text came in from Angela. Rita pursed her lips, trying to remember if she had given her the number.

Nice chatting with you. Let's do it again.

Rita had the oddest feeling that she was being courted. It didn't hurt to play along. She sent a thumbs up.

After she and Walter finished breakfast, they checked out, then made their way to the Honda. Rita drove them back to Casper PD, and they parked. Once again, they were greeted in the lobby by Tilda.

Only today, they followed her out to a forensic van and climbed in. Tilda drove them to Casper General Hospital. They entered, taking the elevator to the bottom floor. There they donned protective gear before entering the morgue.

"Tilda." A man dressed similarly strode towards them. He was tall, in his fifties, with a thick Swedish accent.

"This is Edvin Blum," Tilda said. "Forensic anthropologist from Cheyenne. Edvin, this is Sheriff Jonas and her deputy."

"Nice to meet you," he said. "Please follow me."

He took them through to another room. The three skeletons each had their own metal exam table. Rita walked over and studied them. Three human lives, now nothing more than bones.

"All male," Blum said, joining her. "Dead of GSWs. The two frontal shots are confirmed to be from a .38. The third occipital shot from a .22. Remains have been in the ground four to five years. Looks like they were laid to rest and immediately buried. No signs that scavengers got to them. No indication that any of them struggled prior to death, though it can't be completely ruled out."

"What about the mirror?" Rita asked.

"Yes, Tilda showed me where the glass was found. But I agree with her assessment. Impossible to tell if it was placed there before or after death."

Rita nodded. "DNA?"

"We received DNA from the Harris and Macdonald families," Tilda said. "It's been couriered to the lab to check against our deceased."

"Nothing for Patrick?"

Tilda shook her head. "We'll be going on dental records for him."

Dr. Blum nodded. "And I've sent soil samples from the gravesite to a colleague at the university. She'll be getting those processed shortly. We'll see if we can match them to High Peak."

He led them over to the first skeleton. "Skeleton one is the man we believe to be Ethan. We found a gold wedding band, scraps of denim, remnants of a red coat, leather boots, leather belt. Shot in the occipital."

They moved to the second table. "From the man we believe to be Patrick, we found scraps of jeans, a coat, plaid shirt, and boots. No jewelry. Frontal shot."

Finally, they reached the last skeleton. "And lastly, from the man we believe to be Scott, we've got a gold wedding band, scraps of clothing, jeans, boots, shirt, coat. Again, a frontal shot."

When Blum finished, they reviewed each of the skeletons again. Rita wanted to be sure she understood the trajectory of the bullet holes, the positioning of the bodies, the rate of decomposition.

When she ran out of questions, Tilda escorted her and Walter back to the station. Rita still had a headache. But it didn't have anything to do with the margaritas.

Chapter Thirty

RITA DROVE THE TWO OF THEM BACK TO STILL COUNTY.

"Bad night?" Walter asked.

She glanced over at him. "Huh?"

"You're awfully quiet."

"Just wondering why Scott and Patrick were shot with one gun and Ethan with another. It doesn't make sense, unless—"

"He ran out of bullets?"

Rita blinked. "Not what I was thinking."

"There were two killers."

"Maybe."

"Yeah." Walter settled back in his seat. "My question is. Why would three guys just stand there and get shot?"

"We don't know if they were standing there," Rita said. "We don't even know if they were killed there."

"Maybe Ethan interrupted whoever was killing Scott and Patrick?"

"And they used a different gun on him?"

"Okay, maybe he was killing Scott and Patrick. Then someone else killed him."

Rita couldn't argue with that. She hated not knowing. But she also hated guessing. She rubbed her temples. Her headache had not dissipated. And she'd forgotten to ask Tilda for aspirin.

"Except he doesn't sound like the kind of the guy who would do that," she said.

"No."

"But then we don't really know a whole lot about our victims yet."

That was the next step. Talking to the families. Well, at least Ethan and Scott's. Nothing she could do about Patrick's.

She and Walter lapsed into silence again, maintaining it until they reached the office. Soon as they arrived, Walter hopped out of the Honda. "Overtime?"

"Is over," Rita said. "For now."

He grunted, headed for his truck. "Tomorrow."

She glanced at her phone. It was almost five. She could probably go home. But she walked to the back door instead and let herself into the office.

Mary Lou was on the phone.

Jason and Edith Mae were playing cribbage. He jumped to his feet when he spotted her. She waved a hand. "You find your truck?"

He shook his head. "Not yet. I put out a BOLO, drove the town twice." Which for Jason, probably meant ten times. "And got the phone calls all finished. Nothing new."

"Alright," Mary Lou said. "I'll send an officer." Then she hung up.

"More vandalism?" Rita asked.

"Merritt's Drugs. Shoplifting."

Jason and Rita turned to look at Edith Mae. She glared at them, snapped her gum. "I've been here since this morning." She pointed at Mary Lous. "She is my witness."

"She's been here," Mary Lou said.

Rita yawned. "I'll go."

"You're tired," Jason said.

"Yeah, but it's on my way home. I'll see you all tomorrow." She made her way out of the office and down Main Street to Merritt's.

Inside, it smelled of bleach and vitamins. She walked over to the register to find a girl in her late teens. She had jet black hair, a nose ring, and a monotone voice. Her badge said that her name was Luna.

Rita pulled out her notepad. "You had a shoplifting incident?"

Luna nodded. "Well, my manager says so."

"And where's your manager?"

"Gone home." She said it with such vitriol that Rita suspected she drew the short straw and had to stay and make the report.

"What got stolen?"

"Mirrors."

Rita stiffened. "Mirrors?"

"Yeah, compacts."

"Your manager see who took them?" Rita asked.

"Nope."

"Did you see who took them?"

"Nope."

"Do you know when the compacts were stolen?"

"Nope."

Rita tapped a finger against her notebook.

Luna sighed. "Manager said the count is low. And our computer says we didn't sell any. So they must have been stolen."

"How many are we talking?"

Luna walked her down to the makeup aisle and

pointed to a cardboard box full of cute little mirrored compacts. "At least three."

Rita looked around for cameras. "You got CCTV?"

"Nope. Not yet. Edith Mae is getting us some."

Right.

"So can I go home now?" Luna asked.

Rita nodded. "Not yet. I want to buy one of those compacts and some aspirin."

Luna uttered a sigh worthy of any stage performance. She grabbed a contact mirror, then walked to the pain relief aisle and snagged a bottle of aspirin. Rita met her at the register.

Soon as Rita paid, Luna had her coat on and was walking to the door. Rita jogged along behind her so as not to spend the night locked inside Merritt's.

"Thanks, Luna."

"Tell Edith Mae I said hi."

"I will." Rita walked towards her apartment. As soon as she arrived, her phone rang. Mary Lou. "Hey."

"Just got off the phone with Melinda Harris. Ethan's wife. She's in town. She'll be here tomorrow at 9."

"Thanks, Mary Lou."

Rita stopped outside her back door. Jason had done a good job of collecting the mirrored pieces. She wondered if they belonged to the stolen compacts. Or were just random garbage. But it seemed rather coincidental.

But if they were the same, how had they wound up here? And why?

Rita went up to her apartment. She shook out two aspirin and downed them with a bottle of beer. And then realized she really was going to have to do something about the state of her refrigerator.

Chapter Thirty-One

RITA WAS IN THE OFFICE EARLY.

But so were Jason and Mary Lou. He was at his desk. Mary Lou was pacing. As soon as Rita entered, Mary Lou gestured to Rita's office. "She's waiting."

Fuck. Rita had wanted a few minutes to prepare.

She smoothed down her hair and walked to her office. Melinda was seated on the old couch. Thank God, Mary Lou hadn't given her Otto's off-kilter guest chair. Melinda had an unmemorable face, long blonde hair that hadn't been brushed, and wore a cozy-looking sweater with apples all over it. Didn't seem to matter that it was hot out.

Melinda stood as Rita entered. She had a tissue box tucked into her elbow. She gestured to it. "I've been crying lots, so I brought my own."

Rita walked over. "Please sit."

She did and Rita joined her on the couch.

"I heard you found Ethan." Melinda sniffed.

"We're still waiting on the DNA confirmation, but I believe we have."

"I know it's him. I was asked to identify a photo of his

wedding ring." She took a deep breath. "Is it true he was shot?"

Rita nodded.

Melinda brought a handful of tissues to her nose. Tears began to stream down her cheeks. Rita reached out and squeezed her hand.

"I mean," Melinda hiccuped, "I knew he wasn't coming back. But—"

"You'd hoped?"

Melinda nodded. "Do you know who killed him?"

"Not yet. We are working on it." Melinda bunched her tissues into a ball in her palm. Rita got up and fetched her waste basket. Set it on the floor between them. Melinda flashed her a grateful glance.

Rita waited a moment, softening her voice. "What can you tell me about Ethan?"

She smiled. "He was lovely."

"Had you been married long?"

"Five years."

"Kids?"

"Two. Joseph and Sadie. My mom's at home with them now."

"I'm sorry."

"We'd started to talk about him leaving Apex because of all the traveling it required. Or moving to another department."

"Did he like his job?"

"Yeah. But…"

Rita sat a little straighter. "But?"

"It's not the job he disliked so much as Patrick and Scott. He had been trying to get out of working with them for a while."

"Why's that?"

She shrugged. "Different priorities. Scott was a"—she

made air quotes—"ladies' man. So Ethan tolerated him because he had to. But when they got back from their scouting trip in Brazil, he seemed even more deflated than usual. He said Scott had done something he disagreed with."

"What was that?"

"He wouldn't tell me. I told him to report Scott to Human Resources. But he said that wouldn't help. And then the trip to Still County came up, and something else happened. He called crying one night, saying he'd done something terrible."

"When was this?"

Melinda shook her head. "About a week after they had arrived. Sometime in April."

So he hadn't been referring to killing Patrick or Scott.

"What had he done?"

"He wouldn't tell me. He sounded drunk and couldn't really talk at the time. Said he'd tell me when he got home."

Melinda yanked out another handful of tissue. Blew her nose.

"What do you think he'd done?"

The question hung between them for a long moment.

"I dunno. A one-night stand was about the only thing I could think of. But he wasn't really that kind of guy. I suppose in a moment of weakness, if he was drunk, maybe ... but I just can't see it. I tried to convince him to quit and come home. Our son, Joseph, had just been diagnosed with diabetes. My father was dying, and I'd just found out I was pregnant with Sadie."

"That's a lot."

Melinda nodded. "I was having trouble coping."

"But he didn't come?"

She shook her head. "If Ethan had been the only one

killed, I would've believed the other two killed him. The way Ethan described them? They were bullies."

Interesting. The three didn't get along.

"But when they all disappeared, I figured Scott got them lost in the mine. Making them go exploring where they weren't supposed to be."

"I hate to ask you this question," Rita said.

Melinda pressed a handful of tissue to her mouth. "Go ahead." Her words were muffled.

"Was Ethan ever violent? Do you think he could have killed his co-workers?"

Melinda shook her head. "No. Absolutely not."

She sounded confident. Then she tossed the wadded-up tissues into the garbage can and pulled out her phone. "Ethan texted me some photos before they headed out that morning. Can I AirDrop them to you?"

"Yes, please." Rita hadn't remembered seeing any photos from Melinda in the files. "Did you talk to the police at the time?"

She shook her head. "I was having a difficult pregnancy and was hospitalized."

Jesus. She'd been through the ringer.

"Mom did all the talking. I just couldn't..."

"I understand."

Rita got out her phone and accepted the drop. Moments later, she was looking at the last known photos Ethan Harris had taken.

All three men in the lobby of the Still Haven Inn. They all had big smiles. Almost looked like friends if you didn't know better.

Rita tapped Ethan. He wore a bright red coat. "A little hot for that, no?"

She laughed. "He was worried about exposure if they got lost in the mountains. He was always careful."

196

Rita blew up the jacket. It looked a hell of a lot like the one Peggy was holding in the newspaper clipping.

"Did Ethan own a gun?"

"No. He didn't like them."

Rita nodded. "Thank you for coming in. Are you headed back home?"

"No." She yanked more tissues out of the box as she got to her feet. "I'm staying in town at a bed-and-breakfast for a few days. Elm something."

"Wandering Elm."

"That's it."

Rita stood and walked her to the door. "Before you go, have you ever seen this?"

She scrolled to the photo of the "M" charm.

Melinda's brow furrowed. "No."

"It doesn't belong to you?"

She shook her head.

"Thanks, Melinda. I'll be in touch when I have more information."

Melinda nodded, then hesitated. "Ethan's wedding ring. Would I be able to get it?"

"It's evidence right now. But I'll be sure it's returned when it's no longer required."

"Thank you." And then she walked out, tissue box planted firmly in the crook of her arm.

Chapter Thirty-Two

Rita stood at the window, watching Melinda walk back to her bed-and-breakfast. Then there was a quiet knock at the door.

She turned to see Jason.

"How'd it go?"

Rita pointed to the garbage can. Full of tissue.

"So what's next?"

"I want to look at those mirror pieces you collected."

He led the way through the office and downstairs to the evidence room. God, she loved the new door. It made the whole place feel that much more secure.

She unlocked it and they entered, donning latex gloves. Jason fetched a slim, narrow cardboard box from the shelf and placed it on the large table. Then he opened it up. Inside were the loose bits of mirror.

Rita drew out the compact she bought at Merritt's. Laying it on the table. "They seem the same to you?"

Jason fit a couple of the pieces together like a puzzle. "Yeah."

"Me too."

She leaned back against a bank of cupboards.

"You think it has to do with the case?" he asked.

"Seems awfully coincidental that the men were found with mirrored bits in their throats — presumably. And now there are mirrors stolen from Merritt's. And I find this outside my door."

"Why you?"

"Hell if I know."

"Apex?"

Rita laughed. "God, are we always gonna suspect them of every dastardly act?"

Jason rubbed his leg. "We have good reason to."

She scowled. "You got that right."

Rita studied the glass again. Completely smudge-free. No fingerprints. She stored the mirrored pieces back in the box, and they returned to the office.

She glanced over at Walter's empty desk.

"Out looking for the stolen Apex truck," Mary Lou said.

Rita nodded.

"And you've got an email from some place called Chirps, confirming employment for one Hannah Collins."

"Great, thank you. We find a wife for Scott yet?"

Mary Lou shook her head.

"And no response from his family?"

"Nothing."

Rita frowned.

She then went over Tilda's evidence with Jason so that he was up to speed. By the time they'd reviewed it all, it was late afternoon.

But she still had one last task for the day.

She said her goodbyes and headed out to her Honda.

Rita drove in silence. Her chest felt tight. She hadn't been back to the Myers home in months. Last time had been with the search warrant. They'd found George's bloody jeans in the trash. And a pair of work boots in the shed. Also splattered with Matt's blood.

If Helen had been the one to kill Matt, she'd done a bang-up job of framing her husband.

Rita pulled into the driveway and parked.

There was a "FOR SALE" sign on the front lawn.

Rita sat in her car, staring at the house for some time. Then she got out and walked to the front door. It had one of those lock boxes on it, the kind with a punch code interface that allowed Realtors to access the property for potential buyers.

She flicked it. Too bad she didn't know the code.

She tried the doorknob on the off chance it wasn't locked. But it was.

She peered through the front windows. No lights were on, no sign of anybody being in there. The living room had gone from cozy to austere, containing only the basic furniture required to give an impression of a home.

The couch had been replaced.

She wondered if that was Helen or the Realtor.

Rita walked around to the side of the house, peeking in a bathroom window. It was clouded. No shadows moving about.

"Sheriff."

Rita turned around to see Jason's aunt watching her. She had a bag of garbage in her hand. "Lydia."

"Problem?" She walked over to her can and dumped in the bag.

Rita shook her head. "Just checking on the house. You see Helen out here lately?"

Lydia's mouth compressed into a single line. "She no longer comes by now that she has Otto." Her tone indicated displeasure at having been abandoned after all she'd done for Helen.

"How about Arnold?"

"He's at George's parents' for the summer."

"Right."

Lydia turned around and walked back to the house. She disappeared inside and the door banged closed behind her.

Rita went around to the back of the Myers house and tried the rear door.

Locked as well. Not that she expected anything less.

She leaned closer, peering through the door's windowpanes, trying to see anything in the dark house.

Somewhere a phone rang.

Inside the house?

She pressed her ear to the door, but the ringing stopped.

Rita took another look around the house but didn't see any sign that Arnold had been here. As she went back to her car, she caught movement to her right.

A teenage boy walked towards her on the sidewalk. He was tall, gangly, face covered in acne.

He looked up from his phone and spotted her, slowing his gait.

She stood, waiting. "Hey."

He approached, tucking his phone away, and letting his greasy hair fall over his eyes. "Hey."

"You don't happen to know Arnold Myers, do you?"

"Who?"

She jerked her head towards the house. "Kid that lives here."

"No." He shook his head. Kept walking, past the Myers. Pulling his phone out, his attention on the screen.

She refrained from telling him to look both ways when he crossed the road.

She studied the house again. Still dark. A shell of its former self.

She glanced up.

The sky was a beautiful shade of ochre, orange, pink, and violet. For all New York City had over Still County in amenities and architectural wonders, it couldn't hold a candle to a Wyoming sunset.

She headed back to the office and parked in the lot. Jason's Kia was still there. Jesus. She really needed to talk to him about knocking off earlier.

Or maybe he was waiting for Edith Mae.

She walked back to the Bighorn Bean. The backdoor leading to her staircase was open. She stared at it. Had she forgotten to close it all the way when she'd left that morning?

Crap, she couldn't remember.

She drew her weapon and pushed the door open, looking up the stairs. "Hello?"

No response.

"Anyone there? Police."

Still nothing.

She listened, ears straining. Nothing.

She took the stairs slow. When she reached the top, she froze. Her door was ajar. And Rita knew she had locked that.

Chapter Thirty-Three

RITA SWEPT HER APARTMENT.

The front door had been kicked in. It hadn't been the best lock anyway. God, what was with Still and her issue with locks? She'd never had this much trouble in New York. As far as she could tell, only one thing had been touched. Well, maybe two.

The bathroom mirror. Completely shattered. And the pieces were laid out on her bed. Written on them in black Sharpie was: "YOU'RE NEXT."

She went back downstairs and got in the Honda. Then she pulled her phone and called Jason. "You still at work?"

"Yeah."

"My apartment's been broken into."

"I'll bring the kit."

"Good, kid."

She hung up.

Jason was there within minutes, kit in hand. He was dressed in jeans and a t-shirt. That had been a fast change over.

He gestured to his clothes. "I changed at the office. Was taking Edith Mae out for supper."

"Sorry I messed up your evening."

"It's okay. How are you?"

"In one piece. Unlike my mirror."

She led him back up the stairs and into her bedroom.

"Mirror again," he said.

"Yeah."

"What do you make of the writing?" he asked.

"They spelled 'you're' correctly."

He glanced at her.

She shrugged. "Just not sure what I'm next for."

"You think anyone heard the break-in downstairs?"

"Don't know," Rita said. "I'll check with Skyler in the morning."

Jason gestured to a towel on the floor. "Maybe they used that to muffle the sound of the breaking glass."

Rita grimaced. "No, that was probably me."

He laughed.

Then they went back to the bed. Studying the mirror. No smudges. Whoever it was had worn gloves. While Jason boxed up the mirror, Rita texted Abigail.

Door kicked in. Need a new lock. And bathroom mirror.

Seconds later she got a reply. *Oh my God. Are you okay?*

Wasn't home. And then because she didn't want to scare Abigail. *Probably the vandals.*

I'll come by in the morning.

Rita typed out: *thank you.*

"You can't stay here alone tonight," Jason said.

"I'll sleep in one of the cells."

"Not what I meant."

She looked at him. "Then what?"

"If you leave it insecure, they might come back. Do more damage. I can stay with you."

"Don't be silly. I'll call Cash."

"You sure?"

She nodded, picking up the evidence kit and mirror box and handing them to him.

"I can wait 'til he gets here."

"Go home," she said. "You've been at the office too late as it is. I don't want word to get around that I'm working you to death."

"You're not."

She followed him to the broken door, a worried look on his face.

"I'll be fine, Jason."

"Okay."

Rita closed the door after him. As soon as she released it, it started to swing open. She kicked off her boot and used it as a doorstop. Then she pulled out her phone.

Someone broke into my apartment. Her finger hesitated over send. She could stay at the camper if she needed somewhere to crash. Or at the SCSO. But Jason had a point. She didn't want to leave the apartment insecure.

She hit send.

It took him ten minutes to reply. For a minute, she wondered if he was busy with Heather.

And?

Asshole.

She waited.

Nothing.

I don't want to be alone tonight.

So?

Please come over. Happy?

Extremely.

She stuck out her tongue at the phone. Alright, that wasn't very mature of her.

What's the state of your fridge?

Same as before.

I'll get provisions.

Provisions. God. He made it sound like she never ate anything healthy. Maybe she didn't. She couldn't remember the last time there was a vegetable in a fridge.

She threw her phone down next to her on the couch, her eyes on the door.

What the fuck did *you're next* mean?

She was the next to be vandalized? Murdered? Was the Apex Three killer still stalking victims? Only she didn't work for Apex.

Maybe their employment had nothing to do with their deaths. Maybe they had been simply in the wrong place at the wrong time.

She closed her eyes and leaned her head back against the couch cushion. Thinking about Melinda. She'd never come to Still when Ethan was alive. And yet here she was now. What a strange feeling that must be.

A second later, she felt something touch her foot.

She jerked awake.

Cash stood in front of her, a brown paper bag tucked in the crook of his arm. The smell of hamburgers and french fries from The Shaft filled the room. "Really?"

She blinked, getting up. "I wasn't sleeping."

"Uh huh."

He handed her the paper bag, then went over to the door, inspecting it. "Gonna need a whole new door."

"Abigail's dealing with it in the morning."

"I'll stick around and help her."

Rita felt a weight slide off her shoulders. "You will?"

He glanced over at her and nodded.

"Thank you." She set the paper bag on the coffee table and went and got plates from the cupboard.

"Plates?" He walked a chair over to the door and placed it in front to keep it closed.

"I keep telling you I've matured," Rita said. And then she stuffed a handful of fries into her mouth.

Chapter Thirty-Four

RITA WOKE.

This time, Cash hadn't left. He was fast asleep next to her. She rolled over and kissed his bare shoulder. He grunted, reaching for her.

She rolled away.

She didn't have time for shenanigans this morning.

She got up and hit the shower.

They'd cleaned up the broken glass last night. It had felt downright domestic. Rita wasn't sure what she made of that feeling. It was uncomfortable.

It reminded her of the way they had been before she'd run away to New York. She hoped she wasn't cycling through old habits.

She toweled off and dressed in uniform.

Cash was still asleep.

And she didn't want to wake him. She pushed aside the chair to leave. Then did some acrobat movements to pull the chair up to the door as she closed it. There was still a gap. But at least it felt more secure.

She walked down the stairs and into the Bighorn Bean. Skyler was working behind the counter.

"Iced coffee?" Skyler asked.

Rita nodded. Pulled out a five. "You hear anything odd coming from upstairs?"

Skyler waggled her brows. "What do you mean by odd?"

Rita pinned her with her most authoritative look. "Not that. My place was broken into yesterday."

Skyler's mouth dropped open. "No shit?"

Rita nodded.

Skyler shook her head. "Nah. But it gets noisy down here. Sound bounces off the ceiling."

"So no footsteps? Breaking glass?"

Skyler pursed her lips. "I remember hearing a loud bang at one point. But I don't remember when. Sorry."

"Not your fault."

Skyler made up her drink and set it on the counter. Rita handed her the bill, dumped her change into the tip jar.

"Be safe, Sheriff." Skyler looked worried.

"Thanks, appreciate it." She gave her a wave, then headed out the front door. And over to the SCSO.

Mary Lou was drinking water and looked like she'd had a longer night than Rita. "Heard your place was busted into."

"It was. And you look like shit."

"Lucky kept me up all night."

"Who the hell is Lucky?" Rita asked.

Mary Lou looked at her as though she were stupid. "The electrician."

"That's his name?"

"Yes. And you're changing the subject."

"You were robbed?" Walter asked, leaning back in his chair and sipping his coffee.

"No. Someone broke in and broke my mirror."

"And wrote 'you're next,'" Jason said.

"And that."

"Next for what?" Mary Lou asked.

"Hell if I know."

"Speculate."

"I hate guessing," Rita said. She turned to Jason "You ready for today?"

He nodded, hair still wet from the shower. He collected the truck keys from Mary Lou's board while Rita got her manila envelope from her desk.

She stopped at Walter's desk on her way out. "What are you up to today?"

"Tracking gun registrations. Seeing if any of the men had any."

"Keep me updated."

"Uh huh."

Considering he had solitaire up on his screen, she wondered how devoted he was to the cause.

Rita's phone buzzed as she walked out.

Cash. *Be careful.*

Always.

She was sure that gave him a laugh. She tucked her phone away and met Jason out back.

As they got in the vehicle, she eyed Jason. "Everything okay at home?"

"Yeah, why?"

"The late hours."

He shrugged. "I just want to do a good job."

"And I don't want you to get burned out. So keep an eye on it."

"Yes, Sheriff. Rita."

Rita stretched her neck. The long days were getting to all of them. They drove in silence until they reached Apex. The guard must have been told to expect them, because they were waved through without delay.

Jason parked in their usual spot. Peggy met the two of them in the lobby. "I've got the interview room on the second floor set up for you. Please follow me."

She took them up the marble stairs and down a hallway to another boardroom. Not as fancy as the one Angela had met Rita in. And this one did not have a view of the mountains. Instead, it looked out over the parking lot.

A pitcher with ice water and empty glasses sat on the table.

"I can stay and take notes if you'd like," Peggy said. Probably so Rita didn't wonder if they had the meeting room bugged. She wondered who would be listening in. Angela? Ken?

"No, thanks. We've got it."

Peggy frowned ever so slightly. She was obviously not used to her note-taking skills being declined.

"If you need anything, please call." She set her business card on the table. "I'll send in your first interview."

"Actually," Rita said, "we'd like to interview you first."

Peggy looked at her in surprise. "Me?"

"Yes, if you don't mind," Rita said, gesturing. She and Jason took seats on the far side of the table, facing the door, backs to the window.

Peggy consulted her iPad and typed out a few words. Then she walked to the chair and sat, setting the iPad on the table. It was the first time Rita hadn't seen her holding it.

"Where were you that Saturday?"

"In New York with Angela. We'd gone back Friday.

Returned Sunday when she got word some employees were missing."

Rita pulled out the newspaper clipping Moses had supplied them with. She lay it on the table and pushed it towards Peggy.

"The red jacket you're holding. Is it yours?"

Peggy studied the photo. "No. The paper was there taking a bunch of photos. Someone asked me to hold it. So I did. But I don't remember who it belonged to."

Rita pulled the photo of Ethan wearing the red coat that Mary Lou had printed.

Peggy nodded. "Oh, yeah. It was Ethan's."

"He was found buried in that jacket."

"He was?"

Rita nodded. "Do you remember returning it to him?"

"I think I did after the photo."

"When I asked you about the men before, you said you didn't know them. Is that true?"

Peggy fidgeted with her hands, reached for the iPad, then stopped. She was like Otto without his cigarettes. "I don't like to be negative, Sheriff, but I didn't like Still. Not at first."

"Not many do," Rita said.

Peggy flashed her a grateful look.

"Ethan helped me with that. Not in a creepy way. Like a brotherly way." Peggy reached for a glass, poured herself some ice water. The pitcher didn't shake in her hand, but the way she was focused on the pour, it might as well have.

When she finished, she took a drink.

Rita continued, "Were Patrick and Scott creepy?"

"Those two, I didn't know at all. They talked mostly to Angela."

"But Ethan you did?"

Peggy shifted uncomfortably in her chair.

"Peggy?"

She flushed, glancing towards a camera in the corner of the room. Rita pulled out her notebook and pen and slid them across the table. Peggy picked them up and wrote: *We slept together.* Tears gleamed in her eyes. She truly looked upset about it.

"When?"

April. We'd been drinking. I was lonely. It was just the once. We agreed it was a mistake.

April. That was close to the time Ethan had called Melinda, crying that he'd done something awful. Much as she hadn't wanted to believe he'd been unfaithful, he had.

"Thank you," Rita said.

Peggy nodded.

"Did Ethan ever confide in you about his coworkers?"

Peggy shook her head. "No. But I got the impression he didn't like them."

"Why's that?"

"The day of the picture"—she gestured to the news clipping—"the three of them were there. It wasn't anything specific. Just body language. He seemed tenser around them."

"And you didn't talk to the men that day?"

She looked affronted. "Of course not. I was assisting Angela."

"You held Ethan's coat."

"He asked politely."

Rita smiled, looked over at Jason. "Anything else?"

"Not at the moment."

"Okay, Peggy. You can send in our first interview."

Peggy grabbed her iPad and practically bolted from the room.

Chapter Thirty-Five

THEY SPOKE TO APEX STAFF FOR CLOSE TO SIX HOURS.

By mutual agreement, they didn't break for lunch. But Jason had prepared, bringing protein bars.

Ken followed Peggy. He looked nervous throughout. Though whether he was hiding something or because he was worried Rita might say something about their little agreement, it was hard to know.

In the end, he didn't have much to offer. He remembered the men, but he'd been a trainee security guard at the time. So outside of being the designated driver for a trip to Beaumont one night, he didn't have much to report.

And no, he didn't interact much with them that evening. Patrick and Scott sat in the back.

Ethan hadn't gone at all.

One of the lab technicians thought he overheard that one of the men, maybe Patrick — he wasn't sure — was dating a woman in Still.

Another technician had heard Patrick was seeing someone that worked at the bank, but he didn't remember a name. And maybe it wasn't the bank. Maybe it was the drug store?

The receptionist, Ginny, reported that the men were rarely at Apex. They spent most of their time surveying the sites or at the inn. She remembered them coming through a couple times to meet with Angela — but not with any regularity. And they certainly didn't fraternize with anyone.

Aside from Ethan.

He always seemed a friendly sort.

Another employee said the men had asked him and his girlfriend to join them on the trip to High Peak, but he declined, as they had a baptism in Beaumont that weekend.

When Rita asked why they'd been invited, he didn't know. Maybe because he joined them for drinks a couple of times at The Shaft? But he hadn't really cared for them. He thought Scott was a shit and Patrick his toady.

When Jason asked why he met them at The Shaft, he laughed. "Free beer is free beer."

Another staff member recalled Scott asking for something to do in town. She'd gotten the feeling he meant nightlife, so she referred him to Beaumont or Casper.

A researcher was next. She had remembered seeing Scott outside The Shaft one night.

"He'd lost his car keys and was having a fit. Patrick was bugging him, saying he was always losing them, and I thought Scott was gonna deck him. He called the rental service, and it was going to be the next day before someone could get him a new set. He screamed and cursed, accused Ruby Joe of serving thieves. It was fucking obnoxious."

She didn't know if he ever got the replacement set or found the originals.

When she left, Rita turned to Jason. "There could have

been a spare set of keys to Scott's hanging around Apex. Would make taking the car easier."

Jason nodded.

Their last interview was with one of the security guards. He mentioned that Patrick owed money to Ken. They'd argued about it, and Patrick promised to pay him back. He had no idea if he actually had.

When the guard left, Rita drummed her fingers on the table. "No loyalty there, is there?"

"Maybe he wanted Boyd's job and Ken got it."

"Yeah, maybe. Funny, Ken didn't mention Patrick owed him money."

Jason put his finger on Peggy's business card. He pulled it towards him and dialed her. "Can you send Ken back in? Yeah. Thanks."

Jason disconnected. "She'll track him down."

A second later, his phone rang. "Yeah. Where? Thanks."

He turned to Rita.

"Ken's out. The Apex van has been found."

"Where?

"Reservoir."

She looked at him. "Goddamn reservoir."

She hadn't been back since she'd been pummeled there.

"Want me to go?"

"I'll come with you. We're finished here, and we can kill two Kens with one stone."

"I hope you're not being literal."

She grinned. "Don't test me."

Rita called Peggy to let her know they were done with the room. By the time they made their way out the door, Peggy was waiting for them. A chair was placed next to the door. Had she been sitting there the whole time?

"We'll be in touch if we need to make additional interviews."

Peggy nodded. "You know the way out."

"Indeed I do," Rita said.

She and Jason made their way back down to the truck. While Jason drove, Rita called Walter.

He answered with a grunt.

"I got a few things I want you to follow up on."

"Let me get a pen. Mary Lou! A pen!"

His voice blasted into her ear. Rita held the phone away. "Jesus."

"Alright. Shoot."

"Was Scott's car key found with the vehicle? And were there any employees currently at the bank or at Merritt's who dated Patrick?"

"Got it."

"Thanks."

"And you should know," Walter said. "Scott had a gun registered to him. A .38."

Chapter Thirty-Six

THE GATE TO THE RESERVOIR WAS ONCE AGAIN WIDE OPEN, the lock cut off. A billowing cloud of black smoke rose from beyond the trees. Two fire engines were parked beyond the gate.

Jason parked beside an Apex police truck. Probably Ken's.

When they got out of the car, the acrid stench of burning gasoline assaulted Rita's senses. Her stomach flip-flopped. A flash of Lisa's charred necklace. She took a steadying breath.

Jason walked around and patted her back.

She smiled at him.

They made their way down the gravel road. At the bottom right was the missing Apex truck.

The firefighters had cleared the brush around the fire so it wouldn't spread. They'd also created a barrier between the reservoir and the vehicle, no doubt to keep the water from being contaminated. The truck was now a smoking husk.

Ken stood, hands bunched into fists. "Fucking idiots. How the fuck do you lose a goddamned van?"

Rita approached. "Fancy seeing you here, Ken."

He jerked, startled. Turned to face her. "Sheriff."

"Is there a manifest of materials? Anything we need to worry about breathing in or getting into the water supply?"

"It's lab equipment. Expensive."

A black Audi arrived. Angela was in the driver's seat.

She parked, watching for a moment. Then she reversed and left.

"Fuck," Ken said when all that was left of her presence was a cloud of dust on the gravel road.

"Guess she didn't want to stay and enjoy the fireworks," Rita said.

Jason touched her arm and gestured to the firefighters. Rita nodded. He walked over to them, pulling out his phone.

"Walk with me, Ken," Rita said. "I've got some follow-up questions."

"Now?"

"You in a rush to get back to Apex and meet with Angela?"

He hesitated. "No."

She led him back up the gravel road to where Jason had parked. She had no interest in discussing anything with Ken down near the reservoir. Too many memories.

"How come you didn't tell us Patrick owed you money?"

"I did."

"You didn't. You told us about taking the men to Beaumont."

He eyed her for a moment, then his shoulders dropped. "It wasn't Patrick who owed me money. It was Scott."

"Scott?"

"Yeah. He said he lost his credit card. Dumb fucker was always losing shit. So I put the drinks on my card. After that, they asked where they could get some"—he looked her over—"companionship."

"Companionship?"

He shrugged. "Prostitutes."

"That's why you went to Beaumont?"

"Well, there ain't any here in Still, unless you wanna get tugged by Dizzy. And she's old."

"Dizzy Simpson?" Ran the laundromat. Was in her forties.

"Yeah."

Interesting. Rita didn't know Dizzy had a side hustle.

Ken shrugged. "I took 'em to the Rawhide Revue. Told 'em to talk to Dallas. Said I'd be back to get them in the morning."

"And Ethan didn't go?"

"Nope. Just Patrick and Scott."

"And where did you pick them up?"

"At the Economical Knight Inn. Next morning."

"It's closed now, isn't it?"

He nodded. "Shut its doors about a year ago."

"They ever pay you back?"

"No, but I didn't kill them over it." He sounded hostile. "Was just a couple hundred bucks."

"I believe you."

He blinked at her. "Oh. Thanks."

"You didn't like them, did you?"

Ken shook his head. "Assholes. Acting like their shit didn't stink."

Rita almost said, "pot, meet kettle." But she held her tongue. "Speaking of assholes, any leads on who broke into the SCSO?"

He shuffled his feet in the dirt. Shook his head. "It's not that easy getting answers out of Apex."

"You're telling me? Keep asking."

He glowered at her. "How about you? Any leads on who is doing this shit?" He gestured to the van. "Because if I can't figure it out, I ain't getting the job."

She wanted to tell him she didn't give a shit if he got the job. But instead, she said, "You'll be the first to know when we get something."

Her tone must have satisfied, because he gave her a nod.

Chapter Thirty-Seven

IT WAS PAST THE SUPPER HOUR BY THE TIME THE VEHICLE was towed and the scene cleared. Rita and Jason had just driven off from the reservoir when her phone rang.

Tilda.

She answered. "Rita."

"Hey, I've got good news for you. Well, good considering the circumstances. We got DNA confirmations on the bodies. And a dental match for Patrick."

"So it's the Apex Three?" Rita supposed it had never really been in doubt. But it was good to know for certain.

"Yep. I've emailed the results. Let me know if you need anything else."

"I will." Rita disconnected.

"Confirmed?" Jason asked.

"Yeah. Drop me at Wandering Elm."

"What's there?"

"Ethan's wife."

"Want me to wait?" he asked, hitting the indicator and turning left onto Elm.

"No, I'll walk back," Rita said.

"In this heat?"

She grimaced. "I'm getting used to it."

He pulled up in front of the bed-and-breakfast. Rita got out. There was a tiny sign that read *Wandering Elm* and an arrow that pointed around back of the house.

Rita took the path to the back door.

She knocked.

The door opened immediately. Melinda had her phone in one hand, the tissue box in her elbow. Her eyes and nose were red.

"I just got the news. Casper PD called." Her voice was hoarse, and she looked like she wanted to bawl. But she gestured for Rita to enter.

There were a pair of leather chairs by the window. She walked over to them and dropped into one, while Rita took the other.

"I always knew he was dead," Melinda said. "But knowing he was murdered...it's like him dying all over again."

"I'm sorry."

"I don't even know what to tell the kids. He never even got to meet Sadie. They only know Simon as dad."

Rita glanced at Melinda's hand. "You married again?"

She twisted the gold metal band on her ring finger. "No. We live together. I knew after a year that Ethan wasn't coming home. Whether or not he'd died in the mine, he wasn't coming back. Would it be horrible not to tell them what happened to him? Would that make me an awful mother? Would it diminish Ethan's life? He was their father, and I ... I feel like if I don't tell them, I'm erasing part of his history, but if I do tell them—"

She broke down, sobbing.

Rita reached out and took her hand. Melinda grabbed onto it as though it were a lifeline. When the sobs receded, she yanked some more tissues from her box. "I'm sorry, I'm a mess."

"Is there anyone who can come and be with you?"

"Simon wanted to come. But it felt too much like cheating to bring him here. Stupid, right?"

"Not at all."

"But he's going to be on the next flight out."

"Good," Rita said. "In the meantime…" She reached into her pocket and retrieved her card, setting it on the glass coffee table. "If you need anything, please call."

Melinda nodded.

Rita flipped it over and wrote the number for Casper PD. "You'll need to talk to them about how you want to handle the remains."

A moment of panic flickered across her face. "Do I have a funeral? We had a memorial service when we were advised he was considered lost in the mine. Do I have another?"

Rita squeezed her hand again. "You'll figure it out. Simon will help."

Melinda nodded, clutching the card to her chest. "Thank you."

Rita stood.

Melinda walked her to the door. "You'll tell me if you find out who hurt him?"

"I will."

"Thank you, Sheriff Jonas."

Melinda hugged her. Rita held her for a moment, then stepped away. "Call if you need help. Whatever it is."

Melinda nodded.

Rita made her way outside and walked down the street toward Main. She wondered if she was going to be as upset as Melinda when Otto died. Christ, she didn't even know if he wanted to be buried or cremated. She supposed she should ask him. She just wasn't sure how to bring that up in conversation.

Her phone buzzed.

She pulled it out.

Cash.

You have a brand-new door. Pick up the key from Skyler.

She grinned and typed out: *I love you.*

She'd hit send before she realized what she wrote. God. What a stupid thing to say. She wanted to delete it.

Is this Rita?

Ha ha.

Love you too.

Fuck.

Chapter Thirty-Eight

Rita dropped into her chair. Jason was right. She shouldn't have walked. She was soaked with sweat.

Edith Mae had her headphones on and was snapping gum while typing away at her laptop.

"Update?" Rita asked Walter.

"I talked to Margo at the Elk. She checked with all the employees, but nobody recalled anyone dating Patrick or Scott. She thought she heard one of them hooked up with a waitress at The Shaft. But she couldn't remember. I checked with Ruby Joe, but if they did, she didn't know about it."

"What about Scott's .38?"

"Apparently, he kept it in the glove compartment of the rental. But there was no sign of it when the car was recovered."

"So it's missing?"

He nodded.

"Kind of odd we haven't heard from Scott's family yet."

Walter shrugged. "It's been four years."

"Exactly. Look at Melinda. Soon as she could get away, she came. Where's Scott's family? Keep trying."

"Will do. But tomorrow."

Rita glanced at the clock. It was after five. She was hot and most definitely hungry. The front door opened, and a kid entered the SCSO. It was the same one she had seen outside the Myers property.

"Who's that?" Rita asked.

Walter looked at her. "Adrian. My son. We're going to Beaumont for supper."

"That's Adrian?"

He nodded. "Yeah. Why?"

She shook her head. "No reason. Go enjoy your evening. And remember, Jason and I will be at High Peak tomorrow."

He grunted and walked out to his kid. Neither bothered to greet the other.

When the door closed behind them, Rita turned to Mary Lou. "Where does Walter live?"

"Maple."

So not far from the Myers.

"God, I really don't want to leave Walter in charge while we're at High Peak," Rita said.

"I have Casper on speed dial," Mary Lou said.

Rita laughed, then asked Jason, "You ready to go?"

He pointed to two backpacks on a corner desk. "All prepped."

"I'll see you bright and early," she said.

Rita put her chair back in her office, then left the SCSO. She walked across the street to the Bighorn Bean. Skyler was getting ready to lock up.

"I hear you have something for me," Rita said.

Skyler pulled a key from behind the counter and handed it to Rita. "Key to your heart, apparently."

"Ha ha."

Skyler grinned, said goodnight.

But Rita didn't go home. Unless the food fairies had visited, she still had nothing worthy of being called a meal.

She walked back to the SCSO, calling Ruby Joe as she did, placing an order for a burger and fries.

"Not that I don't love your business, Rita," Ruby Joe said. "But I'm getting concerned about your diet."

She hung up before Rita could respond.

Rita arrived at the back lot and walked over to her Honda. And froze. Broken shards of mirrored glass were scattered around her vehicle.

She spotted Victor and Stu play fighting in the abandoned lot.

"Hey!"

They glanced at her, then took off running.

Jesus, she'd only wanted to ask them if they'd seen anything. Although if she were them, she probably wouldn't tell either.

She sighed, crouching down and examining the mirrored splinters. They appeared to be similar to the pieces found outside her door.

She returned to the office.

Mary Lou was tidying up her desk. Jason was feeding Ted. Edith Mae hadn't moved.

"What are you doing back?" Mary Lou asked.

Rita walked to the kitchen and retrieved the broom and dustpan. "More mirror."

Jason set the cat bowl down on the floor. "Where?"

"By my Honda."

"I'll check the cameras."

"Thanks." She headed back out and swept up the shards, dumping them in an outdoor trash bin that was located by the back door. By the time she had finished and walked the broom and dustpan back inside, Jason had consulted the security footage.

"You park in the one area there's no cameras."

"Because it's shady. You didn't see anyone?"

He had a clip on his computer. Tapping it. A figure in baggy black track pants and an equally over-size hoody momentarily came into view. But they were more of a black blob than a human with identifying features.

"Goddamnit," Rita said.

"Next time, park near the cameras," Mary Lou said.

Rita scowled at her.

"Get going. Your dinner is most likely getting cold."

Rita did as instructed, heading back out to the Honda and driving it to The Shaft.

The supper rush was just beginning. Ruby Joe had her burger and fries waiting. "What kept you? You're usually in here ten seconds after I get your order."

"Work," Rita said.

Ruby Joe rang up Rita's order. "How's that overtime going? Am I going to faint when I get the bill?"

"Hopefully not," Rita said, laying a twenty on the counter. "And I have a couple questions for you."

"I might have a couple of answers," Ruby said, handing Rita her change.

She stuffed it into a glass tip jar. "You remember the Apex Three?"

"Those are the bodies you dug up?"

"Yeah. What do you remember about them? I heard they used to frequent The Shaft."

Ruby Joe leaned against the counter. "Two of them were real assholes. Patrick and Scott, I think were their names. One of the cooks caught the real estate guy doing lines of cocaine in the men's room."

"Patrick."

"Yeah, that asshole. He asked if I could score him some. Almost kicked him out on principle alone."

"But you didn't?"

"Not that weekend."

"But another?"

"The following Saturday. Ethan got so shit-faced that I kicked him out."

"You sure it was Ethan?"

"Yep."

"Is that the night Scott lost his car keys?"

"Yeah. Asshole was in here accusing everybody of taking them, asking if they knew who he was, like he was King Fucking Shit."

Rita laughed.

"I got so sick of listening to him. But eventually Marnie came out with a new set of keys. The car, and him, were gone when I closed up."

"Thank you, Ruby Joe."

"You're welcome, Rita Marie."

Rita laughed and walked back to her Honda. When she got inside, she pulled out her phone and googled Keymaster.

She dialed. Getting a recording that said they'd be open at nine in the morning. Or if this was an emergency, she could press "0" and get the dispatcher.

The only emergency was in Rita's stomach.

She was damned hungry.

She left a message, asking Marnie to call her back at her convenience.

Marnie. M. She wondered for a moment if the charm could belong to her. Rita made a mental note to ask. And then she drove home.

She parked in the back lot and took the stairs up. Her

door was ugly. Metal. Solid. And oh so safe looking. She resisted the urge to kiss it.

She unlocked it, then walked inside. There was a new mirror in the bathroom. Written in red lipstick was *you're welcome. XO.*

She laughed. Then went to the fridge to grab a beer to eat with her burger and fries. And was shocked. The fridge was full. Yogurt, tomatoes, carrots, potatoes, celery, lettuce, mayo, ketchup, and more.

The food fairies had indeed arrived. And they were named Cash.

She selected a beer, then collapsed on the couch with her bagged meal.

Then she pulled out her phone.

Thank you again.

You owe me.

I know.

I can think of plenty of ways you can pay me back.

Oh yeah. Name one.

The back of your neck.

Rita got tingly.

Want me to come over?

She hesitated. *I have to be up early.*

Then I better hustle. See you in five.

Rita scarfed down her burger and fries in record time.

Chapter Thirty-Nine

RITA WOKE THE NEXT MORNING FEELING SURPRISINGLY well-rested. She might have worked out some of her tension with Cash.

She rolled over and looked at him.

This was getting to be a habit. Spending nights together. She didn't know if she liked it or not. She almost touched him, but it was early. And she didn't want to wake him.

She slid out of bed and padded to the bathroom, carefully not to make any noise. When she got out of the shower, she was pleased to see he was still asleep. She got dressed. Jeans, shirt, coat, thick socks, hiking boots.

Then she returned to the bathroom and scrubbed the message he'd left her from the glass. Then she wrote her own lipstick message: *stay as long as you want. XO.*

She debated erasing it. Fuck it. She left it.

Rita still had an hour until she had to meet Jason. But she had an errand she wanted to run.

She went downstairs and out to her Honda. Thankfully, Cash hadn't boxed her in. She knew she could call and get the answer to her question. But she was looking forward to getting it in person.

Especially given that it was just gone 5 a.m.

She drove out to Miner's Way and pulled into the driveway. Otto's house was dark. Not even a porch light on. The twinkle lights were still present. But they were dark as well.

She got out of the Honda and crossed to the front door, knocking. Loud. And she kept knocking. Until the porch light came on.

Only then did she stop.

The door was yanked open.

Helen stood there in her nightgown. "Do you know what time it is?"

"No, that's why I drove over here, to ask you the time."

Helen tightened her jaw.

"I need the code to your lockbox."

"Pardon?"

"The code."

"Why?"

"I'm thinking about buying the house. You are trying to sell it, right?"

Helen stared at her. "I don't want you buying my house."

"Got lots of other offers, have you?"

Helen sniffed. The answer to that was probably no. Who wanted to buy the house where a murderer and a murder victim had lived?

"So, you're staying in Still permanently?"

"I'm getting used to the idea." A lie, but she owed Helen no truths.

Helen walked away, leaving Rita standing in the doorway for more than a minute. Finally she returned with a piece of paper. The code 7199 was written on it.

"Thank you." She snagged the paper from Helen and walked off. She was back in her car seconds later, pulling out of Otto's and driving back to Still.

Rita made her way to the Myers' residence. She parked down the street, then got out and walked to the house. When she arrived at the front door, she punched in the lock box code, got the key, and opened the front door.

Rita stepped inside, closing it behind her.

The house was dark. She flicked on her flashlight app. Walked up the carpeted stairs and down the hallway to Arnold's room.

Inside was a sleeping bag, several bags of chips — some opened and some still in a case — cans of pop, and a can of spray paint. It was a vibrant yellow.

She heard a vehicle outside.

She hit the flashlight, turning it off. Then she went to the window and looked outside. A silver pickup truck had pulled up to the curb.

Arnold got out, waved to the unseen driver. Then ran up to the front door.

A moment later, she heard him enter.

Rita crossed the hall into George and Helen's old room.

Seconds later she heard Arnold's footsteps on the stairs. He flicked the light on, and light flooded his room and the hallway.

Rita stepped into the light.

"Arnold."

He screamed, startled. Spun around to face her, swinging a can of paint like a weapon.

She dodged, avoiding the yellow spray.

He sprinted toward the door, making a break for the stairs.

She reached out, grabbed his collar, and yanked him back into his room.

"Jesus. Relax! I'm just here to talk."

His pupils darted all around, as if his brain was still trying to process that she wasn't a threat.

"It's Rita. Sheriff Jonas."

"Right."

She stepped back, put her palms up. "You're not in trouble. I just wanted to check in. Eleanor's worried about you."

"Oh." His shoulders dropped.

"Can you give her a call for me? Let her know you're okay?"

He nodded. "I can do that."

Rita looked around. "Helen know you're staying here?"

"No."

"Lydia?"

His eyes flashed. "I told her not to tell anyone."

"She didn't."

He looked grateful for that. "You're not gonna tell Helen I'm here, are you?"

She hesitated. She really should.

"I'll go back to Nan and Papa's," he added.

"Tomorrow."

He nodded so hard, she thought he might fall over.

"Why'd you leave your grandparents' house anyway?"

He shrugged.

"Come on, Arnold. Give me something."

"They didn't want to talk about Lisa because she wasn't family."

Ah. So Eleanor did have trouble processing that fact.

"But I'm tired of pretending she didn't exist. Helen

won't even say her name anymore." Tears rimmed his eyes. He wiped his nose with the sleeve of his long tee.

"That paint can belong to you?"

He flushed.

"Arnold."

"I hate those fuckers. They killed Lisa. Dad's in prison. Helen is — she's not even a mom anymore. Staying with your dad."

"Helen told you all this?"

"No. But I figured it out. I mean, she's not here."

"She sure ain't."

He sat down on the floor as though he was a balloon that deflated. After a second, Rita sat beside him.

"Where'd you get the paint?"

He shrugged. "Apex. Old stock from one of their garages. Stole it one time when I was visiting Dad out there."

Rita wanted to laugh. How appropriate that they were chasing their own tail.

He picked at the carpet. "Are you gonna arrest me?"

"For what?"

He shrugged. "Vandalism."

She kicked the paint can to the other end of the room. "I don't have any evidence. That could have been brought here by anyone. House has been empty for months."

He gave a half sob, half laugh.

"But I do have one question."

"What?"

"The Rancher's Pantry?"

"Stu bullied me in school. He can suck a dick."

Ah. It was revenge. And some of it was a little petty. Worthy of a teenager.

"You take their truck too?"

"What?" He looked surprised by the accusation. "No!"

"You didn't steal an Apex truck?"

"Hell no!"

"So no grand theft auto?"

"I'm not trying to go to jail with my dad."

"What about breaking into my apartment?"

"Someone broke into your place?"

She nodded.

"It wasn't us."

She raised her brows. "Us?"

"Me."

"I know there are two of you. Who's the accomplice?"

Arnold pressed his lips together. He wasn't going to answer.

"Listen," she said. "I need you to stop with the vandalism."

"Why?"

"Because if Apex catches you, they won't be as nice as me. And I don't want anyone else in your family to get hurt."

"What about Apex? Who's going to make them pay for what they did to Lisa?"

"The man responsible has paid," she said. "And no amount of violence or vengeance will ever bring Lisa back."

"Do you really believe that?"

She rubbed her head. "Fuck no. If it were up to me, I'd buy you another round of paint."

He laughed.

"But Arnold, Apex is a machine. And I really don't you want to get caught in their gears. One last question."

"What?"

"Where'd you get the copy of the Apex letter?"

"Lisa's cloud account."

Jesus, of course. She hadn't even thought to check if Lisa had one.

"I only found it a month ago. I didn't know she had one." He sniffed. "I miss her."

"Me too. And I didn't even know her." She nudged him. "Why don't you tell me about Lisa?"

He blinked at her. "What?"

"Yeah. What's your favorite memory of her?"

He thought for a moment. "Dad bought us ice cream when we went to the Casper Fair, and I dropped mine. She gave me hers."

That was Lisa. Always taking care of other people.

"You got another one?"

That was all it took. He exploded with stories. God, the kid just wanted to talk and have someone listen to him. His parents and grandparents had let him down significantly on that front.

As the hour grew nearer to six, she said goodbye. He promised again to return to Casper the next day.

"I'm going to follow up," Rita said.

"I know."

She left him twenty bucks to buy some healthy food, not that she was a leader in that area, then made her way out to the Honda.

She glanced back at the house. Torn between wanting to burn Apex to the ground herself and crying for the sister she never knew.

Chapter Forty

RITA PULLED UP TO THE STATION.

The Kia was still parked where it had been last night. She got out and walked over to it. A slight sheen of dew covered the vehicle.

So either Jason had left the car here last night.

Or he hadn't left.

Rita entered, quietly.

She stepped downstairs to the cell block and looked around. Both were empty. She pursed her lips, then went to the storage room. Inside was a suitcase. She flipped the lid open. Jason's clothes.

He was staying here.

But why?

Was it the cat?

Or something else?

She went back upstairs, this time making noise. He met her in the hallway, a knapsack slung over his shoulder. Ted weaved between his legs, looking like he wanted to trip him.

"Moses is going to meet us at the site," he said. "He didn't want to drive with us."

"Sounds good."

He patted the knapsack. "I got us water, protein bars, toilet paper, apples and pepperoni sticks, spare socks, flashlights, evidence bags, blankets."

"Jesus." It's more than she would have thought to bring, which was why she'd asked him to do it. "I would hug you, but Ted might take offense."

Ted yowled.

Jason leaned down and patted his head.

They locked up and went out to the police truck. Jason dangled the keys. "You want me to drive?"

She held out her hand. "No, you look tired as hell. I'll do it."

He tossed her the keys.

She climbed in, waiting to see if he'd volunteer any more information. He didn't. "Try and get some shut-eye. We've got a long drive and a longer hike."

"Yeah." He leaned his head back and closed his eyes. But he was restless. And eventually he pulled out his phone and started scrolling. "We got an email from Tilda."

"What's it say?"

He scanned the message. "The pieces of mirror found with the bodies, when reassembled, seem to come from a small mirror. They have all the pieces save one."

"Small mirror as in compact?"

"Yeah."

They were both silent a moment.

"You think our killer is the one breaking mirrors for you?" Jason asked.

"Maybe. Or it's somebody who knows something about the murders. Only thing is why focus on me? Not like we're close to identifying them."

"Maybe we are, and we just don't realize it."

"True."

He studied the email a bit more. "A compact would suggest it's a woman, right?"

"I wouldn't take that bet," Rita said. "Could be a man wanting to throw suspicion on a woman."

"Yeah."

Rita spotted a deer on the side of the road and slowed. It darted into the woods as soon as they neared. She applied the gas again.

He put his phone away.

"I know who the vandal is. Well, one of them anyway."

His jaw fell open. "Who?"

"Arnold."

"Arnold Myers?"

Rita nodded. "Gave him an ultimatum. I'll tell his mother he's in town unless he goes back to his grandparents in Casper tomorrow. Which should put an end to it."

"What about the truck?"

"Swears they didn't steal it."

"You believe him?"

Rita hesitated. "I do. Before the graffiti, Arnold didn't have any kind of record. Stealing a vehicle seems extreme."

"What are you going to tell Apex?"

"Nothing. Their losses are all covered by insurance. It's a victimless crime. Unlike shooting you, which is fucking attempted murder."

Jason looked worried. "Yeah, I guess so."

"Far as I'm concerned, the playing field is only starting to get even."

They rode in silence after that. And then Jason did fall asleep. When she arrived at the base of the mountain,

Moses' battered red pickup was parked on a gravel pullout at the side of the road, waiting for them.

She woke Jason, then they got out and donned their knapsacks.

Moses had a crowbar, a hammer on a loop on his jeans, and a packet of what looked like nails sticking partway out of the pocket of his orange vest.

He rested the crowbar against his shoulder. "You ready?"

Rita looked him over. "Is that all you're taking?"

He grunted.

Jason looked around the area. "Is this where Scott would've parked?"

"Dunno. But it's where I told him to park. Unless someone else was here. And then there's a pullout about fifty yards up the highway."

"Don't get a lot of traffic out here, I'm guessing," Rita said.

"Not anymore." Moses jerked his head for them to follow him. So they did.

Rita glanced over at Jason. "I'm surprised by the joyrider theory. I mean, how would they have found the car all the way out here?"

Moses overheard. "Lots of folk noted how flashy the car was. Didn't have any of its kind in Still at the time. And he drove it like a goddamn bat outta hell. Surprised he didn't kill no one."

She looked at him with surprise. It was the most Moses had ever said.

He shrugged. "Or so I heard." Then he gestured to the steep bank. "Careful here, soil's loose."

Moses didn't look it, but he was surprisingly spry. While she and Jason struggled to keep pace, he scrambled up steep rocky sections with the ease of a mountain goat.

She caught him watching her once and could almost hear the disdain — *flatlander*.

She wondered what he thought Jason's excuse was.

As time wore on, she got hotter, even though the air was cooler. Her shirt and jacket were soaked with sweat.

"How the hell did Otto do this?" Rita asked.

"ATV."

Rita blinked. "ATV? Why didn't we bring one?"

"You didn't ask."

Fucking hell. How was she supposed to know that was an option? She pulled out her water and took a sip. "It's too damned early to be this damned hot."

Jason patted her back and took it as an opportunity to slip past her. Now she was last. She polished off one of her water bottles, then tucked it back in the pack and carried on.

They walked the rest of the way in silence. Mainly because Rita was breathing so hard.

She wondered if the Apex Three had stopped on their way to the mine. Had they considered turning back? Why did they even want to see the bloody thing?

From what she knew about Patrick and Scott, they preferred nightlife, not nature. So why make the trek? Especially when they were about to leave town?

Moses blasted a whistle.

She glanced up at him. Jason was seated on a boulder, drinking water. And Moses was pointing to the rock.

Thank Christ. They had arrived.

She made her way up the slope.

There was a gap in the stone face of the mountain that looked like a gaping maw. But the entrance was covered in old, weathered boards that looked like you could probably kick through them relatively easy if you wanted to get inside. A large red sign on a metal pole warned: "CLOSED. DANGER — DO NOT ENTER."

A small plastic sleeve taped to the boards had a photo of the three men. It was the newspaper article of their deaths at the mine. Bouquets of dead flowers were laid at the entrance. Rita wondered who had placed them here.

Moses pulled a crowbar from his backpack, then hesitated. "Guess I can take this down."

But he didn't move. Rita walked up to him. He had tears in his eyes. She placed a hand on his back.

"Thought my mine had killed them, you know?"

She nodded. "I'm sure you can leave it, if you want."

"You think?"

She nodded. He wiped his eyes and nose with his forearm. Then applied the crowbar to the boards. He pried two away.

Jason dug out his flashlight and Rita did the same.

Moses entered first, then they followed.

Immediately, Rita noticed two things at once. Silence, and a heaviness weighing down on her. But thankfully it was cooler than it was outside.

She shined her light along the ground, the walls, and the ceiling. It was supported by decaying wooden boards. The place smelled strongly of moist rock and dirt.

"You sure this thing won't cave in on us?"

"Can't be certain of anything," Moses said.

"Awesome."

"Follow me." Moses led them through a network of narrow tunnels that were a lot lower than she expected them to be.

"Who mined this place, Lord of the Rings dwarves?"

Jason glanced over at her.

"I'm fine."

"It's not too much farther," Moses said. "I'll show you where we found the water bottle and sweater."

The tunnel narrowed, and Rita felt light-headed. In fact, the deeper into the tunnel they went, the dizzier she got. She started to slow. Her chest was tight, her heart pounding.

She had to stop. She sat.

Jason crouched beside her. "You okay, Rita?"

"I just need a break."

"Wait, Mr. Grant," he said.

Rita settled a hand on her chest. "Don't like small spaces. I need to calm my breathing down."

"You gonna pass out?" Moses asked. "Get your head between your legs."

She did.

"We should go back," Jason said.

"No, no." That was better. "You go with Moses. Report back to me."

Jason looked worried. "You sure?"

She nodded. "Take photos."

"I will."

Moses eyed her. "We'll be back in twenty."

She raised a hand. Keeping her eyes focused on the ground. She felt Jason touch her head and then they were gone, their footsteps receding.

She leaned against the cold stone wall. Crap. She hated that this had happened in front of them.

She wanted to be invincible Rita.

She felt better. Maybe she should follow them. No. She didn't know which way they might have gone. And last thing she was going to do was get lost in a goddamn mine.

Her flashlight flickered.

She stared at it.

It flickered again.

"Don't you dare," she said.

But it did. Flickering off and plunging the mine into a darkness so pure, so black, and so overwhelming, that it felt like she'd been buried alive. *Don't think that. Not true.*

She closed her eyes. There. That was better. *She* was making it dark, not her damn flashlight. She heard a noise. It sounded like falling rocks.

Was it to her right or left?

"Jason?"

No response.

"Moses?"

What if something happened to them? What if they needed her and she couldn't get to them?

Stop.

She got onto her hands and knees. The earth was solid beneath her.

Breathe.

Empty your lungs.

Inhale deeply. 1, 2, 3, 4.

Hold. 1, 2, 3, 4, 5, 6, 7.

Exhale. 1, 2, 3, 4, 5, 6, 7, 8.

She repeated this exercise, focusing on only her breath and the counts. She felt her pulse slow, and the tightness in her chest subsided.

And then she heard footsteps. She opened her eyes.

"Rita?" It was Jason.

"I'm here. My flashlight died."

She saw their light bleeding into her darkness. And then they were with her. She sat. "Hi."

Jason crouched beside her. He wiped her cheeks. Oh God. Had she been crying? He set his light down, then fiddled with hers. It came on. "Sometimes they jiggle off."

"That's a stupid design."

"It really is."

"Did you hear rocks falling?"

Moses nodded. "Ain't safe. We need to go. And you should have told me you were claustrophobic."

"Didn't really know," she said. "What'd you find?"

"More of the tunnel has caved in," Jason said. "We can't get to the spot where the items were found."

Rock fell nearby. Rita jumped to her feet.

"The mine is like a living creature," Moses said. "It shifts."

"And you should have told me that," Rita said.

Jason stood, taking her hand. She clutched it tight. Then they retraced their steps. As soon as Rita saw sunlight, she felt the anxiety slip away.

She squeezed through the entrance first. Not even caring that it was hot. She was out.

She glanced over at Jason. "Sorry."

"I won't tell a soul."

She smiled. He probably wouldn't.

While Moses nailed the boards back over the entrance, she and Jason sat. She had a protein bar and felt better. Then drained another bottle of water. Jason showed her the photos he'd taken on his phone. Rock. It all looked the same.

Moses finished nailing and declined food or water.

They got up and started walking.

"All that was found in the mine was the sweater and water bottle?" Rita asked.

"I think the cops found other litter. It was a popular hiking spot at the time."

"But you don't remember anything specific?"

He shook his head.

"And the whole mountaintop was searched?"

"Yeah. Well, not Low Peak Mine, because it was closed at the time. We were gonna send cavers over. But then we found the sweater and water bottle and the whole dang thing caved in."

"Low Peak Mine?" Rita said.

"Yeah."

"Did the Apex Three know about it?"

"Don't recollect. "

"Where is it?"

He pointed southwest. "About an hour's trek."

She glanced over at Jason. He nodded.

"Can we see that as well?"

Chapter Forty-One

An hour and twenty minutes later, Rita was regretting the detour. She was exhausted. Maybe they should have come a different day.

She could also see why it was originally assumed that the Apex Three had gotten lost on the mountain. Even with Moses, they'd gotten completely turned around more than once. But he quickly realized his error and they backtracked, picked up a different trail and arrived at the mine. Another red sign warned trespassers away.

"What was the weather like on the mountain the day the men went missing?"

Moses stopped to wipe sweat from his brow. "Cool, not cold. But cooler than this damned heat."

He pried the boards away and peered inside. Then he held out his hand. Jason gave him his flashlight.

Then he stepped back. "It's collapsed."

Rita took Jason's flashlight and shone it inside. The tunnel extended back twenty feet. And then a mound of stone and earth blocked whatever tunnel had once been there. There was still a decent amount of space that someone could take shelter in if necessary.

She panned the light across the debris. "Was this mine boarded up at the time?"

"Yeah." But then he scratched his head. "Although, when I checked it, the boards had been pulled away."

Rita looked at him. "When was that?"

He shrugged. "Six months later. Check 'em a couple times a year."

"And it didn't get searched at the time—"

"—because we found their possessions at High Peak."

"Right." She swung the flashlight around to give it back to Jason.

"Wait," he said.

He took it from her. And retraced the path the light had taken. Something yellow jutted out beneath a collapsed beam.

Jason squeezed through the entrance.

"Careful," she said.

He crouched low, crawling over to the item. It was mostly buried in dirt and rocks. He set the flashlight down, took some photos, then pulled it out.

It was a blanket.

"That's a throw from Still Haven Inn," Rita said.

He tossed it to her. Something bright flashed in the light, falling to the ground with a metal clink.

She reached for it. A keychain with the Porsche logo and a fob. She set her pack down and pulled out a plastic bag, collecting it. Then she grabbed the blanket and rolled it up, stuffing it into her backpack.

Jason sifted through the dirt and rocks. "I found a cellphone."

He took more photos, then got out an evidence bag and collected it.

"Anything else?" Rita asked.

Jason crawled around a bit more. Then shook his head. Rita studied the cellphone while Moses boarded the entrance back up.

"You wanna see anything else?" Moses asked. She and Jason were both covered in dirt and sweat. Moses, on the other hand, was a little dusty, but no dirtier than when they had arrived.

"Any more mines?"

"Nope. That'll be them."

"I hope Bighorn paid you well for whatever they took from your earth."

He smiled and nodded. "That they did."

It seemed to take less time to get back to their parking spot than it did to get up the mountain. Probably because it was mostly downhill and they had already made their way partially back when they detoured to Low Peak.

Moses got in his truck, then gave them a wave, and took off.

Rita glanced at Jason. "Guess that's it for Moses."

"You think he had anything to do with it?"

She shook her head. "Those were genuine tears in his eyes when he saw that photo on the boards. He honestly thought they were inside. And I don't think Moses is that good an actor."

And if he was? Then more the fool, she.

Jason unlocked the truck, and they put their packs in the back.

Then Rita surveyed the parking area. Thick rows of pine trees lined the pullover and road.

"Okay, so the Porsche is parked here."

He nodded. "And they go up the mountain."

"Right. And everyone thinks they're stuck up there.

Then kids steal the car and go joyriding. Did Walter ever find out how easy it is to steal a Porsche 911?"

"I think he said hard."

"That doesn't tell me much." She walked around "Somehow the three of them got back to town. And what's the most logical way to do that?"

"Drive."

"Right. How come no one saw them? As Moses said, it was the only one of its kind in Still."

"It was late."

"Right. They got back later. Because they went to both mines. We have evidence of that."

Jason nodded. "So something happened between leaving here and getting back to town that got them killed."

"Yep."

She glanced around the clearing. Wishing like hell she'd been here to search it four years ago. And then she spotted it.

In one of the pines.

A hole.

Too perfectly round to be natural.

"Jason." She pointed.

"Shit."

"That look like a bullet hole to you?"

"Sure does." He got out his phone. Took a photo.

Rita searched the ground for a casing. It probably wasn't there — the odds of it being washed away by rain or snow melts were high. Or tossed away by the plow. Kicked away by a hiker. Picked up as a souvenir. Jesus it was highly improbable it was still around.

Why the hell hadn't Otto searched more diligently? Because no one thought they were looking for murder victims. They were looking for three lost hikers.

Rita pulled out her phone. Dialed Casper. Eventually she got through to Tilda.

"What's up? I'm about to head home."

"May have found my crime scene."

"You're shitting me," Tilda said.

"Nope."

"Where's it at?" Rita told her. "I got a kid's recital tonight."

"It can wait until morning," Rita said.

"You sure?"

"It's waited four years. A few more hours won't hurt. We'll keep continuity. But bring coffee."

"You know I will."

Rita disconnected. "I'm staying until Casper can get here in the morning. You wanna head back? I can call Walter to pick you up."

He shook his head. "Nope, I'm staying with you."

"I'll call Mary Lou. Let her know where we are and that Walter's on call tonight."

Chapter Forty-Two

THE SUN HAD SET, AND IT WAS STILL HOT. THEY WERE BOTH stinky. And dirty. The car windows were down. Rita had her socks and shoes off and her feet out the window. She didn't care what it looked like.

Not as though this was a well-travelled road. They'd only seen a handful of vehicles. Most slowing to stare at them. Wondering if they were there for a speed trap. Or something more sinister.

Every now and then, Jason would turn on the vehicle and run the air conditioning. But as it grew cooler, they gave up. Rita was pretty sure the temperature was going to drop substantially when it became dark.

They ate a dinner of protein bars and beef jerky, washing it down with warm bottles of water.

Rita had examined the cell phone at one point, thinking they could charge it. But it was a Samsung. She and Jason both had iPhones. Different charging cords.

It started getting dark. They rolled up the windows. Rita put her socks back on. Jason got blankets out of the back. God, he really was prepared for everything.

As if he could read her mind, he said, "Me and Edith Mae got lost camping once. Ever since then, I'm prepared."

"Esther took you camping?"

"No, my dad. Before he left."

He sounded sad. So Rita didn't ask. Maybe he'd tell her one day. But there was something else she wanted to know.

"Why are you living at the office, Jason?"

He choked on his water. Started coughing.

"Jesus, I'm sorry."

She patted his back. He waved his hand, indicating he was okay. "How d'you know? Did Edith Mae tell you?"

"I'm a cop, Jason. I notice things. Like how you're there before anyone else, and you stay later than anyone. Besides, you've been dragging ass since I got back. What's going on?"

"Mom kicked me out."

"Why? Because you got shot?"

"No. And I don't really wanna talk about it."

"You can talk to me."

"You'll probably fire me."

"I caught Walter telling tales about SCSO to Apex and didn't fire him, did I?"

"No."

What the hell was he doing that he thought she'd fire him? Maybe she didn't want to know.

"You running drugs or doing murder for hire?"

He managed a slight laugh. "No. But Esther kicked me out when I told her."

A prickle of awareness began to form in Rita's mind. "You know, Jason, you don't get to pick the family you're born into. Hell, I know that better than anyone. But you do get to choose the people you surround yourself with. And I chose you. And Mary Lou. And we're better than fucking family."

He laughed again and nodded.

"So you don't have to tell me anything, but I want you to know I'll be here."

"I'm gay."

She stared at him. She took his hand. Kissed his fingers. "Thank you for telling me."

Tears sprang to his eyes.

"And here I thought you were going to tell me you were sneaking into houses and stealing women's underwear or something."

"No worries about that," he said with a laugh.

She squeezed his hand. "Why would you think I'd fire you?"

He sniffed. "Frank and Walter — they used to say shit."

"Fuck them. Walter's stuck in the 'good old days,' which weren't good to anybody but fucking him. I can talk to him if you'd like."

"No! Please, don't. He's gotten better since Frank left. I don't want anyone else to know. Not yet."

"I promise I won't."

She released his hand. He wiped the tears from his face.

"So what happened?"

"I think I always knew I liked guys, but I tried to tell myself I was just confused. I tried like hell to like girls."

"Me too," Rita said. "It would have saved me so much pain."

Jason laughed.

"After the shooting, when I was seeing the psychiatrist, we talked about all kinds of stuff."

"Including being gay?"

He nodded. "Esther was always throwing girls at me, so I figured I should tell her."

"And she threw you out?"

He nodded. "Said I was an abomination." He looked at her, eyes worried. "I'm not an abomination, am I, Rita?"

She felt rage. Immense, incendiary rage. And a great deal of relief that Esther wasn't here. "No, kid. You're about as far away from being an abomination as we are from New York. Is this why Edith Mae is at the office all the time as well?"

He nodded. "She thinks she's bisexual, so…"

"She's next to get the boot?"

"Probably."

"Well, if your mom doesn't kick her out for shoplifting at Merritt's, I can't imagine she'd kick her out over that."

"Yeah, it's funny the things she draws a line at."

"Well, stay as long as you need to. If we need the cells, my couch isn't comfy, but it's passable."

"Thanks Rita."

"Yeah. You're not still sending Esther money for bills, are you?"

He dropped his eyes.

"That stops now."

"But they're my sisters."

"They're her fucking responsibility, Jason. She's the one that had seven kids. Not you. She can ask your father for money if she needs it. Got it?"

"Yes ma'am. Sheriff. Rita."

"I'll withhold your checks if I find out you're disobeying me."

He laughed. "You wouldn't."

"Probably not. But I'm serious."

"I promise."

She grabbed another protein bar. Split it in half and

handed him some. He accepted. They ate in silence. Then looked out the window.

"Shooting star," Rita pointed.

Jason didn't reply.

She peered over at him. He was fast asleep. She tucked the blanket in around him. Then curled up in her own seat. Before she knew it, she was asleep as well.

Chapter Forty-Three

RITA WOKE IN THE MIDDLE OF THE NIGHT. IT WAS COLD. The blanket had fallen away, so she pulled it up. Checked on Jason. He was still sleeping.

Probably the best damn sleep he'd had in a while, she guessed.

But the cold wasn't enough to keep her awake. She tucked her hands into her coat and was out again.

Later, they both woke, and by the time they had relieved themselves in the bushes, had a protein bar breakfast and some water, Tilda showed up.

She not only brought coffee, she brought donuts.

"You are a fucking saint," Rita said. "Thank you."

"Really, we need to stop meeting like this. Tell your criminals to pipe down."

"I will," Rita said. "Not that they listen to me."

She grabbed a cake donut and shoved it in her mouth. God, that tasted better than a protein bar. She washed it down with hot coffee.

Then Rita walked her over to the tree.

"Yeah, that looks like a bullet hole," Tilda said.

"Would love to find the cartridge."

Tilda nodded to another officer getting out of the van. "Matt's brought the metal detector."

"You want us to wait?" Rita asked.

"No. That the only one you found?"

Rita nodded.

"We'll take another look. But I trust your eye."

"Send me the results."

"Will do."

Rita handed off the evidence they had collected at Low Peak, then they said goodbye. Rita and Jason climbed back into the truck. By nine, they were back at the office. Rita didn't get out of the vehicle. "Get your suitcase."

"I'm not going home."

"I'm not taking you there. I got another idea."

He hesitated.

"Don't you trust me?"

"I trust you."

"Then get the goddamn suitcase."

He still looked worried, but he went to the back door and disappeared inside. God. He certainly put up with a lot from her.

He reappeared moments later, putting his case in the back of the truck. Then he got back in. Rita didn't talk as she drove to Miner's Way. She pulled up the driveway and parked.

Jason looked at her. "The camper?"

"Yeah, why not?"

He turned back to it.

And then Rita had doubts. What the hell was she thinking? It was shit. She didn't even want to stay there.

"Maybe this was a bad idea."

"No! I love it."

She glanced at him. "Really? It's older than you and doesn't have hot water."

He shrugged. "I can shower at work."

Why the hell hadn't she thought of that? "The owner is an asshole."

"What if he doesn't want me living here?"

She eyed the house. "He doesn't get a choice. I'll tell him. Why don't you explore?"

He nodded, getting out and fetching his suitcase, then went inside the camper. Rita got out and walked to the porch.

By the time she arrived, Otto was waiting for her. Holding a cup of coffee and a cigarette.

She glanced at it. "That didn't last long."

"Don't tell Helen."

"I'm sure she can smell it."

He grunted. "What are you doing here so early?"

"Jason needs a place to stay for a bit."

"And the camper is it?"

"You're not using it."

"Maybe I want to start a meth lab. Isn't that the hot thing to do when you get cancer?"

"Jesus. Why are you so ornery?"

"I don't need a goddamn babysitter."

"Is that what you think? I brought him here to watch over you?"

He shrugged.

"You have seriously overestimated our relationship."

He grunted, stubbing out his cigarette. But didn't light another one. Which was a small miracle. "Anything else?"

Ah, to hell with it. "I think Helen is the one who drove me off the road. Shot at me in the yard."

He froze. "What?"

"I think it was Helen."

"You got evidence?"

"No. Just a feeling. George shut down when Lisa died. And then when he thought he knew who was responsible, he took action. But he never directed any of his anger at me. Only one person did that. Helen."

"Get out."

"Dad."

He pushed her towards the steps. "I said get out!"

Rita resisted the urge to cry. "Can Jason stay?"

"He can do what he likes." Otto turned his back on her and banged back into the house. What the fuck was wrong with parents in this town?

Well, she had just accused his girlfriend of attempted murder.

Rita walked back to the truck. Jason was watching. "I guess it was a no?"

She shook her head. "You're welcome to stay. I sure as hell am not."

"What happened?"

"Told him I thought Helen was the one who shot at me."

"Shit."

"Yeah. He didn't like that too much. Fuck." She rubbed her face. "Why the hell did I say that?"

"He needs to know the truth, Rita."

"You think?"

"Wouldn't you?"

"Yeah, I guess so."

"It's himself he's angry at. Or her. You just took the brunt of it."

"Same, kid."

He smiled.

She looked over at him. "I meant what I said earlier, Jason. You're my family."

"Same, kid."

She laughed. "Now you're getting too big for your britches. Get a shower and get changed. I'll pick you up in an hour and we'll go to the office."

"Sounds good. How much is rent?"

She waved her hand. "Cover the electricity and water and he'll be happy. Also do me a favor and let Mary Lou know we're back in town? I'd hate for Walter to put out a BOLO on us because he has to do actual work."

Chapter Forty-Four

Rita drove to the apartment and walked straight into the shower. Stripped off her clothes and let the hot water beat down on her until the tank drained.

She toweled off, dried her hair, and put it up in its requisite bun.

Then she dressed and went and got an iced coffee from Skyler.

She still had twenty minutes before she had to pick up Jason, so she drove out to the Myers residence.

She knocked on the door. No answer.

She retrieved the key from the lockbox and went inside. But she didn't wanna scare the kid. "Arnold, it's me!"

There was no response.

She went upstairs. Arnold's bedroom door was open. The garbage had been tidied. The sleeping bag was gone. It looked like he'd followed her instruction to return to Casper.

She hadn't got Eleanor's phone number. So she texted Mary Lou asking her to track it down.

Then she walked to Lisa's room.

A bit of sticky tape was all that remained of the glitter "Lisa's Room" sign that had hung on the door before Helen had moved the family out.

The room was completely empty. She wondered where Lisa's things were. Had Helen packed them up and taken them to Otto's? Thrown them out? Put them in storage?

If she lost a child, she'd want to hold on to everything.

She walked in, wondering where Helen had found the letters Lisa had written her. She lay down in the center of the room, staring up at the ceiling. Lisa had looked up at this ceiling every night for years.

A few sticky stars remained of a glow-in-the-dark galaxy that she must have placed there once upon a time.

Rita blinked back tears. She really needed to open those letters. She promised herself that she would.

She checked the time.

She needed to get Jason.

She got up and went back downstairs.

She spotted shadows at the front door. She frowned. Had Arnold returned? She opened the door.

Cash stood there.

He blinked, surprised.

And with him was Heather.

Rita looked from one to the other.

"Rita," Cash said.

"Hi."

Heather frowned. "What are you doing in the house?"

"I have the owner's permission."

"That doesn't answer my question."

No, she supposed it didn't. And she wasn't about to. "That would be SCSO business. Why are you here?"

Heather tipped her chin. "I have a viewing."

She looked at Cash. "You're house shopping?"

He held up his hands. "Nope. I'm here for moral support."

Heather gave a tight smile. "More than that, honey."

Rita raised her brows. Honey?

He shook his head.

Rita tossed her the key. "Knock yourself out."

At least Arnold had cleared out before they arrived.

"I'll call you later," Cash said to her back.

She raised a hand. But didn't turn around. Just how much time were the two of them spending together?

Not her business.

Soon as she got in the truck, she got a text.

You're pissed again. I'm just helping her find a house.

That something you do with all your exes?

Helped you find your apartment, didn't I?

She glared at the screen.

And put her phone away. He texted again. She didn't look. Didn't want to keep Jason waiting.

She drove back to Miner's Way.

Jason was waiting for her at the bottom of the drive. "World War III broke out once you left."

"What?"

He nodded. "I never heard Otto yell before."

"Fuck." She glanced at the house. Should she go and talk to him? Smooth things over?

"I wouldn't," Jason said. "This is between them."

"Yeah."

She reversed out of the driveway and hit the road, taking them back to the office. Her phone pinged a few times.

"Cash," she said to Jason.

"You two fighting?"

"I have no fucking idea."

She parked in the back lot. When she finished parking, her phone rang. "I'll be a minute."

He nodded and got out so she could have privacy.

But it wasn't Cash calling.

It was Helen.

She debated. Then answered. "Helen."

"You fucking bitch!"

Rita disconnected and blocked her. Then she blew out a breath and checked her messages.

Don't shut me out, Rita.

Do you love her?

She waited.

I will always love her. I married her. But I'm not in love with her.

Rita didn't know if that made her feel better or not. And she couldn't think of a single thing to say. So she typed: *okay.*

And then she put her phone away and went into the office.

Chapter Forty-Five

WHEN SHE WALKED IN, MARY LOU WAS HOLDING A TREAT over Ted's head. He stood on his hind legs. "Theodore Francois is a hungry boy, isn't he?"

"You're calling him by his full name now?"

Mary Lou glanced at her. "It's what he's used to."

"Uh huh."

"Careful, or I'll put Ted's litter box in your office."

"You wouldn't dare."

"And for the record, I'm just being nice to him because his owner is dead. I'm still a dog person."

"Whatever you say, Mary Lou."

She gave Ted the treat, then turned to Rita. "Is it true, Jason has taken over the camper?"

"Yep."

"Why would you do that to him?"

"He couldn't live in cells forever."

"I was working on him. I have a spare room."

"You knew."

"I may not be a detective, but I sure as shit know when the station water bill goes up."

Rita laughed. "You're a better detective than me. I just figured it out."

"Well, that and he asked me for Brian's number. Said he had some questions. Figured it would be good for him to have a like-minded friend."

Rita gave her a hug.

Walter walked in and eyed the two of them. "Something I should know about?"

"Yeah. We found a Porsche fob at Low Peak mine."

"The hell?"

"The file say anything about the car being found with it?"

"Just a sec." Walter went to his desk and pulled out a file. He skimmed over it, then tapped paperwork. "Found with the car."

"So which one was the replacement?"

Walter shook his head. "But you should know, the Porsche has keyless entry and ignition."

"So why call a locksmith?" Rita said.

"Maybe there was something in the vehicle he didn't want anyone to see."

"Like what?"

Walter shrugged. "A body?"

Rita blew out a breath. "I don't fucking know. Contact the dealership that Scott rented the car at. See what you can find out about that car and the rental agreement in particular. Hell, see if they still have the vehicle."

"Won't be any evidence in it."

"No, but we can still take a look."

"Marnie returned your call," Mary Lou said, waving a pink message slip in the air. "She'll be in Beaumont around eleven if you want to meet her there."

Rita grabbed keys from the peg board. "I'll head there now."

"Little early," Mary Lou said.

"I want to stop by the Rawhide Revue."

Walter glanced up. "How come you get that place and I have to call a rental company about a fucking car?"

Rita looked at Mary Lou. "You want to answer that?"

"Hell, no."

"Neither do I."

Rita glanced at Jason. "Get a hold of Vancouver Police. See if they can find you a number for Scott's family."

"Will do."

Rita went out to the truck and made the drive out to Beaumont. She flipped on the radio, caught a Clint Black song, then switched it off so she could think. The car thing bugged her. And she couldn't figure out if she was focusing on the right thing or the wrong thing.

But damn, it bugged her.

Probably because she hated the idea that Otto had simply accepted the idea that the vehicle had been stolen and taken for a joyride. Okay, they searched in town. But they'd called everything off when they found the men's gear in the mine.

And then the cave-in happened.

It was a logical assumption the men had lost their lives there.

Only it was the wrong one.

And maybe she was worried she would have made the same one.

The men would still have been dead.

But the evidence would have been fresh.

She sighed, driving the rest of the way in silence.

When she arrived in Beaumont, she headed straight for the Rawhide Revue. It was still early. There were only a couple of cars in the lot.

She parked her patrol car right in front of the entrance. When she entered, she was immediately plunged into the darkness of the vestibule.

A bouncer — a different man than the one she'd met before — sat on a stool, blocking the double doors leading into the club. He was the size of a linebacker and wore a snazzy blue suit that hugged his large frame. He looked bored, scrolling on his phone, which looked tiny in his giant hands.

He looked up, eyes blinking as he put his phone screen down on his lap. "Morning, Officer."

"Sheriff." She said it nicely, with a smile even.

"Sheriff. Can I help you?"

"Here to see Jeff."

He jerked his head towards the doors. "Behind the bar."

She raised a hand in thanks.

He grunted, turned back to his phone. Probably not paid enough to argue with the law.

She entered. The place was dark, save for the lights on the main stage. This time, she stopped and took a better look at the place.

Along the left wall were now some private curtained booths with a sign that read "CHAMPAGNE ROOM." The beefy bouncer she met last time stood there. He glared at her. She waved.

On stage, a bleached blonde stripper in a schoolgirl outfit was working the pole. The sound system hadn't been improved. It faded in and out as Warrant's "Cherry Pie" played.

Her eyes tracked over to Jeff, behind the bar. He was still wearing that damned leather jacket like it was a second skin that he never took off.

He poured out a drink for a red-nosed heavyset older man who looked like he was born in a bar.

Rita walked over to him. "Jeff."

"You again?"

"Me again."

The red-nosed man looked over at her, appraising.

"You come to audition?" Jeff asked.

"No. I did not."

"Shame, you already got the uniform."

She bared her teeth. "I need to ask about some guests you had."

"Don't talk about clientele."

"These ones you will." She pulled out her phone, showed him photos of the Apex Three.

He stared at the phone blankly, shook his head. "Can't say I've seen 'em. When were they in here?"

"Four years ago."

"Four years ago? Jesus fuck. I don't remember what I ate last night."

"Probably that shitty barbecue place you always go to," the red-nosed man said.

Jeff glared at him. "I didn't ask you, Al."

Rita glanced over at the woman on the stage. "Maybe I'll ask her."

"Tennessee is new. Four years is a lifetime in strip clubs, Sheriff. Ain't none of my staff been here four years."

"I have," Al said.

"Nobody that's worked here. Drinking ain't working."

"Don't tell my wife," Al said. "She thinks I'm working."

"Alright," Rita said, turning her phone to Al. "You recognize these men?"

Al looked delighted to have been asked. He took his time, diligently studying each photo. He looked almost disappointed when he shook his head. "No."

"Well, thanks, Al. I appreciate it."

He nodded.

Rita turned back to Jeff. "Where's Dallas?"

"She ain't here."

"I can see that. Where can I find her?"

"She ain't gonna remember."

"Well, you can either get me the address or I can radio the SCSO and ask them to look it up for me. And while I wait for them to do that, I'll just keep my car parked out front and ask every guest that comes in if they remember these guys."

Al chuckled. "She got you there, Jeff."

"Fuck you, Al." Jeff grabbed a cocktail napkin, scribbled down an address, and slid it to her.

"Thank you for your cooperation, Jeff."

He grunted.

"Al."

He smiled, sitting taller in his seat.

On the way out, she stopped at the bouncer. "How long have you worked here?"

"Six months."

"You like it?"

"Hell no. But my sister is a dancer and I hated seeing the shit she had to go through. So..." He shrugged. "Jeff don't bother her long as I'm working."

"Anyone been here longer than you?"

"Jeff. Dallas."

"What about your co-worker? The other bouncer?"

He smoothed the lapel of his suit-jacket. "I'm a door-man, Sheriff. Ollie's gone away for a few weeks. Something about his twin aunts dying. Jeff said he'd be back any day. And any day maybe my sis is gonna quit. Then I won't be working here no more neither."

"Sounds like a plan," Rita said. She thanked him, even

though Ollie's aunt dying could have been code for all manner of hijinks.

"Have a good one," he said, returning his attention to his phone. He was watching a video on YouTube. A woman teaching how to crochet.

"You learning crochet?" she asked.

His cheeks flushed. "Trying to. Want to make a blanket for my Grams."

"That's sweet. Good luck."

She walked over to the truck and got in, plugging the address Jeff had given her into the GPS. It was within walking distance. She drove anyway.

She arrived at a rundown house with a weed-covered lawn. Dallas was already waiting for her on the porch, cigarette dangling from her mouth, phone in her hand. Clearly Jeff had called.

Rita got out and walked up. And saw why Dallas wasn't at work. Big black eye.

Chapter Forty-Six

Before Rita even made it to the porch, Dallas said, "I don't know 'em."

"Jeez, Dallas. I haven't even asked you yet," Rita said.

Dallas sighed, took a drag of her cigarette, then dropped the butt on the wood porch, squishing it with her bare toe. "Come on in."

Rita followed her inside. The place was immaculate. Secondhand furniture. But it had charm and character. More style than Rita's place.

"Cute," Rita said.

Dallas looked at her. "You think?"

Rita nodded. "Wanna try your hand at my place?"

"You serious?"

Rita thought about it. Then nodded. "Yeah."

"What's your number?"

Rita pulled her notebook, wrote it down, and passed it over.

"I'm not saying I will. Just that I'll think about it," Dallas said.

"Sounds good to me." Then she pulled out her phone,

flicked to the photos of the Apex Three. "Can you at least look at the photos for me, Dallas?"

Dallas gestured to the couch. Rita sat and it was far more comfortable than she would have expected. "Carly."

Rita blinked. "Carly?"

"Dallas is my stage name."

Right.

She sat in the chair next to Rita. "Whatever happened to Serenity? Did you catch her killer?"

She meant Lisa.

"Yeah, I did."

"He get what was coming to him?"

Rita nodded. "He died a horrible death."

Carly stared at her. "You kill him?"

"His company did. Poison."

"Shit."

"Yeah, shit."

That seemed to cinch her decision. "Alright, who d'you wanna ask me about?"

"It's an old case. Three men that went missing in Still County four years back."

Rita showed her the photos.

Carly scrolled through them faster than Jeff or Al. Then flipped back between Patrick and Scott.

"I remember these two. Thought all us dancers were prostitutes, so Jeff kicked them out."

"So, no sex work out of the Rawhide?"

Carly looked at her, eyes narrowed.

Rita raised her hands. "Not my jurisdiction. I'm just trying to figure out what happened to these guys."

She nodded. "I'm not saying the women don't, but only if Jeff gets a cut of the action."

"Cut of the action. Does that include money or sex?"

Carly flattened her lips. "Bit of both. But not back

then. Business was better. Jeff hadn't run it into the ground yet."

"So, where would guys go if they were looking for some companionship?"

"Companionship?"

Rita grinned. "Being respectful."

"For a respectful cop, you sure are out of the loop."

"I don't leave Still County unless I need to."

"The Stroll."

"Where's that?"

Carly made a writing motion. Rita got out her notebook and pen and passed them over. Carly wrote down an address. Handed both back.

"I don't know that you'll find anyone who was working there four years ago. Heidi was the longest. But I think she's moved on to Casper. Although Samantha's still around. Hold on, lemme call her to make sure she's down to talk."

Carly got up and made the call from the kitchen.

Then she came back. "Alright, let's go."

Rita and Carly walked outside to the truck.

"Hell no," Carly said. She pointed to the green Volkswagen bug in the driveway. Rita walked around to the passenger side and got in.

Carly drove out to the Bison River State Park parking lot. It was about twenty minutes from Carly and Jeff's.

When they arrived, she and Carly got out and waited.

Carly pointed to her eye. "Thanks for not asking about this."

"Can't say I wasn't tempted."

"I gave as good as I got."

"I dunno. I didn't see Jeff limping."

Carly laughed.

"You can use my number for non-interior designing purposes if you ever need to," Rita said.

Carly grimaced. "I got it handled."

Rita nodded.

A few minutes later, a maroon Jeep Cherokee pulled into the lot and parked beside the bug.

Samantha got out. She was full-figured, mid-thirties, looking more like a soccer mom than a sex worker.

She hugged Carly and shook Rita's hand. "Morning, Sheriff. Carly said you needed help regarding some missing men?"

Rita nodded.

"Must say I'm missing some men myself." Samantha laughed at her own joke.

Rita grinned and showed her the photos. "These are the guys."

"I recognize these two." Patrick and Scott. "But there was a third man with them."

Probably Ken. But he'd said he dropped them off. She pulled up the Apex website for Still. Found a staff photo. Homed in on Ken.

Showed that to Samantha. She studied it for a long time. "Could have been him."

"You mind telling me what happened with them that night?"

"Nothing."

"Nothing?"

"I turned down their business. Wasn't into what they were looking for."

"Which was?"

"They wanted me to be unconscious while they fucked me. And the third guy was going to film us."

Rita stared at her. "What?"

"Not the weirdest request I've had. But I don't get unconscious with my clients. That's some fucking bad news."

"So what happened after you said no?"

"They left. Third guy took them away. Although Scottie-boy didn't look happy about it. They're part of why I moved my business indoors. More safety. For me and my girls." So much for Ken saying he dropped them off.

"Anything else you remember?"

Samantha shook her head. "They're dead?"

"They are."

"Good."

Rita raised a brow.

"Anyone that makes a request like that? Means they've done it before. I feel better knowing they ain't around."

"Thanks for talking with me."

"Carly's my girl. Only reason I said yes."

"I appreciate that."

Samantha gave Carly another hug and they started whispering. So Rita got into the car and waited.

A few minutes later, Samantha drove off, then Carly joined Rita, taking her back to the house.

"Thanks," Rita said when Carly pulled into the driveway.

"Don't tell Jeff I spoke with you."

"He won't hear it from me," Rita said. But there was a woman watching them through her kitchen window. "Not sure about your neighbors."

"Louise will keep it buttoned," Carly said. "She hates Jeff."

"Remember, if you wanna chat"—Rita pointed to her own eye—"you know how to contact me."

Carly didn't take the bait. "Take care, Sheriff."

Rita got out and went back to the truck. Seconds later, she was pulling out of the drive and headed for her meeting with Marnie.

Chapter Forty-Seven

RITA PULLED UP TO THE AUTO PARTS STORE WHERE MARNIE had asked her to meet. She parked in one of the customer stalls and texted that she was there.

She waited for a response, watching an old couple slowly walk toward the store. The man was the more frail of the two. The woman, presumably his wife, patiently held his hand and guided him towards a ramp.

Something about seeing old married couples pulled at Rita's heartstrings. She'd never seen her parents like that. Not that she ever saw them express love to one another when they were younger.

All she remembered was the arguing. She presumed they must have cared for each other at one point.

Now, who the hell knew where Carol was. And her own relationship with Otto was shit. She'd moved back to Still County to look after him, which proved to be a lot harder than she thought. Seeing him opened old wounds. And the matter of him having a secret daughter didn't help things between them.

And then there was Helen.

She pulled up her messages. Scrolled through to his name. Then she typed out: *Sorry.*

She hit send.

She didn't want to.

But it wasn't as though they had a lot of time left together. He was dying. The doctors knew it. Otto knew it. And so did Rita.

Coming.

For a moment she thought Otto had texted her back. Then she realized it was Marnie. The couple had disappeared into the shop and Marnie stepped out, carrying a tool kit.

Rita put her phone in her pocket and got out.

Marnie walked to a van, opened the back, and slid her tool kit inside. Rita walked over to meet her there.

"Nice to see you, Sheriff. Mary Lou said you wanted to talk about a Porsche?"

"Yeah."

"You know they're keyless, right?"

"I have discovered that." She pulled up her photo of the Apex Three and held it out.

"Ah. Those assholes."

"You remember them."

"I'll say."

"What happened?"

"Apex called me and told me to take a new key out from the dealership because they didn't have staff available to deliver one until the next day. So I was made to do it."

"Why you?"

"I was working for Apex. Just happened to be in Casper."

"You worked for Apex?"

"Sure did. I installed their doors and gates during the construction phase. But I realized pretty soon I was supposed to be at their beck and call. He"—she tapped Scott's photo—"hit on me. I rejected him. Next day, he called, demanding to speak to my manager. Wanting to complain. Little shit didn't know I owned the business. So I tore him a new asshole over the phone. Then hung up and cancelled the contract."

"Anything else you remember?"

She pointed at Ethan. "That guy."

"Ethan?"

"He was out of it."

"Drunk?"

"I don't think so. He looked like he'd been dosed with GHB. I had a girlfriend who got drugged in a bar once, and that's exactly what Ethan looked like."

Rita flipped to another photo. The one of the necklace with the "M" charm. "You ever seen this before?"

Marnie shook her head. "Nope."

"So it's not yours?"

Marnie grinned at her. "Never seen it before."

"Thanks."

"You got it."

Rita walked back to her truck. She checked her phone again. Still no response from Otto. Maybe he'd blocked her.

That took care of everything she needed in Beaumont. So she drove back to Still. She was about halfway there when Tilda called.

Rita hit the speaker. "Just on my way back to Still. What's up?"

"The phone you turned over to me."

"You get it working?"

"I did. And Shane was able to break the passcode. We

found a couple of videos that you need to see. Sent them to your office Dropbox."

"Thanks. I'll take a look at them when I get back."

"Don't thank me. You'll wish you never had to watch them."

Chapter Forty-Eight

RITA GOT BACK TO THE SCSO WELL AFTER LUNCH.

She was famished.

Walter and Jason were both at their desks. Edith Mae was at hers as well, typing away on her laptop, head bobbing along to the music in her headphones.

"Tilda get a hold of you?" Mary Lou asked.

"She did." Rita said. "Jason, can you access the Dropbox?"

He nodded, following her to her office.

Walter trailed after them. "I spoke to the rental place."

"What'd they have to say?"

"They don't have the Porsche. Sold it two years ago. And they confirmed Marnie simply picked up a spare pair of keys and drove them out to Still."

"Okay, thanks." There was a protein bar on her desk, a leftover from their hike. She ripped off the wrapping and ate it in two bites.

Walter stared at her.

"What? I'm famished."

Rita closed her door, then walked around to her chair.

Walter pulled up the one that usually sat in front of her desk.

Jason looked over at her. "Ready?"

She nodded.

He clicked on the first of the two thumbnails.

The video began to play.

It was a hotel room with the same wood walls and general decor as the Still Haven Inn. The light source, probably a bathroom light, was too far away, making the video grainy.

There was a man on the bed, having sex with a woman. Even though Rita couldn't see her face, it was obvious that the woman was not conscious.

She remembered what Samantha had said about them wanting her to be unconscious. If the girl on the bed was faking, she deserved an Oscar.

"Jesus," Walter said. "What the hell is this?"

Jason stared. "Is she dead?"

"I don't think so," Rita said.

The man grunted, then got off. She could now see his face. It was Scott. He gestured to the cameraman. "Your turn, pal."

The camera switched hands. Patrick walked into view. He was already naked. He went to the bed and climbed on top of the woman.

Rita felt like she might vomit. She shouldn't have had that protein bar. She wanted to turn off the video. This woman didn't deserve any part of this. Including them watching.

Scott laughed. Then he stepped closer, zooming in on the woman's face.

Rita felt like she'd been kicked in the gut.

Margot. From the bank.

Scott reached down, pulled open Margot's eye,

revealing that she was, in fact, not conscious. Then he let it go.

"Fuckers," Walter said.

More laughter from both men. Rita turned the sound off.

Jason's eyes welled up. "I … I'm sorry. I can't…" He left the room, closing the door behind him.

Rita hit pause. Looked at Walter. "You good to continue?"

He nodded. "Go on."

The video ended soon after. But not before they'd rolled Margot over onto her stomach. Then they switched places again. But the video cut out. Whether deliberately or accidentally, she had no idea.

Rita hit play on the second video. And immediately recognized the location as Low Peak Mine. This time both Patrick and Scott were in frame. They stood over a woman laid out on the blanket. She was naked and unconscious. Her face was hidden in shadow. But it didn't look like Margot.

This woman seemed to have longer limbs.

Rita stopped the video, turned to Walter. "Who the fuck is holding the camera?"

"It has to be Ethan."

"No one said a woman went with them, right?"

"Nope. Not unless they were there another day."

Rita hit play.

A male voice cut in. "I don't want to do this — "

Scott's voice cut him off, angry. "Don't be such a pussy, Ethan."

So it was him holding the camera.

"It isn't right."

"You didn't object last time. In fact, you were a more than willing participant, ain't that right?" Patrick laughed.

"You got me drunk. I don't even remember doing anything."

"Yeah, keep telling yourself that, pal," Scott said.

Patrick glared at the camera. "Bad enough you ruined the last video."

"Didn't ruin it. Deleted it."

The woman stirred, voice slurred, moaning as she started to come to.

"Jesus Christ, she's waking up."

Scott spoke with the calm demeanor of either a sociopath or a sadist. "Relax. Just give her another drink."

Patrick grabbed a bottle of what looked like water, kneeled beside her, and held it to her lips. But he was blocking her face.

One of her hands tried to hit him.

"Just drink it," Patrick said. "You'll feel better."

She must've done what she was told, because moments later, she slid back to the blanket. Patrick turned to the camera with a relieved look and a smile. "She's out. Let's do this."

Ethan stepped forward. "Nope. I'm taking her home."

"Shut the fuck up and keep filming or I'll send Melinda a copy of your video."

"No," Ethan said. The video now showed rock.

A second later, Rita heard what sounded like a fight.

The phone hit the ground.

Ethan's voice. "Get away from her!"

The sound of glass breaking.

Someone picked up the phone, stopped recording.

A chill iced down Rita's spine.

"Jesus Christ." Walter stared at the monitor, jaw clenching and unclenching. "Do you think—"

He didn't finish the thought. He didn't need to.

Chapter Forty-Nine

RITA WATCHED THE VIDEOS EIGHT MORE TIMES, THE LAST few times without the sound so that she could concentrate on the images.

Jason joined them shortly after. "Sorry."

"Don't be," Rita said. "Nobody needs to see this shit. Especially after Lisa."

He gave her a wobbly smile, but she could tell he was upset he wasn't able to continue.

Rita turned to Walter. "Any women go missing around this time period?"

Walter shook his head. "Not that I know of."

"Double check. Also the neighboring counties."

"Will do."

"What can I do?" Jason asked.

"Get a hold of Tilda. See if they can get a clearer picture of the second woman."

He nodded.

"And then get a hold of Milly. I want to know about the blanket. But especially why she didn't tell us a woman had gone with them that day. Find out if it was her." Rita stood. "I'm going to visit Margot."

Neither of them said anything.

Margot.

Rita walked out of the station and down the street to Elk Mountain Equity.

There, she noticed there was only one teller working — Annemarie. And there was a longer line than normal. Rita glanced at Margot's office. The door was open, but the lights were off, nobody inside.

Rita skipped the line and made her way to the counter. Much to the annoyance of the next customer.

"Margot in?"

Annemarie shook her head. "No. It's not like her to miss a day. I'm worried her mother might have taken ill again. But she usually calls."

"You have an address for Margot?"

Annemarie retrieved a piece of paper, then wrote it out. Added a few more lines, then tapped the paper. "If she's not there, that's her mother's address and phone number. Arlene."

"Thanks, Annemarie."

Rita returned to the office and retrieved the truck. Within ten minutes, she had arrived at a cozy ranch style house. It had a red brick facade and a well-manicured lawn. Even a white picket fence. Stone paving steps led to a front door that was trimmed in black wood and had three inset windows.

A white Toyota sat in the driveway.

Rita pulled in behind the Toyota and parked. Then she got out and walked up the driveway to the front door.

She knocked.

No answer.

Rita peered through the door's windows, but saw no activity in the house.

She knocked again. Waited.

No response.

Rita looked around the porch. It had cute ceramic cat planters that she bet Mary Lou would love. She bent down and checked under them. Sure enough, she found a house key. She grabbed it and unlocked the door.

Opening it. "Margot? It's Sheriff Jonas."

Still no response.

She stepped inside, closing the door behind her. She checked the living room and kitchen before entering the hallway that led to the bedrooms.

She passed Margot's bedroom and a home office which had been turned into crafts room. The bathroom was also empty.

"Margot?"

No response.

Rita entered the bedroom. There was another door. Probably the en suite. She walked over to it and knocked.

No answer.

"Margot?"

She opened the door and her stomach plunged into a free-fall.

Margot lay in the bathtub, the water a rusty red. An empty bottle of wine sat on the ground next to it, an empty bottle of pills on the edge of the tub.

"Jesus."

Rita lunged, hauling Margot out of the bath. But she was cold. And dead weight. Rita pulled her out nonetheless. Long slices marred both her forearms. Rita knew there was a knife at the bottom of the tub, hidden by that red water.

Rita lay Margot on the floor, feeling for a pulse. But it was obvious she had been dead awhile.

Rita set a hand on Margot's forehead.

A note propped up on the bathroom counter read: "Mom, I'm sorry. I tried."

Rita wanted to punch something. If Scott and Patrick hadn't been dead already, she probably would have tracked them down and killed them.

She felt like everyone had failed Margot.

Her dad.

Walter.

Pants.

Even Rita herself.

If only they had gone out to the mine sooner. They would have found the phone. Maybe Margot might still be alive.

Fuck.

She wanted to scream.

Instead, she called Mary Lou.

"I'm at Margot's." Her voice was hoarse. "Get Dylan Bruce for me? I have a body."

Mary Lou was silent. "Not Margot."

"Yeah."

Mary Lou gave a soft sob. "She wouldn't hurt a fly."

"Send Walter or Jason over as well."

"I will."

Rita hung up. Then she got onto her knees and pulled the plug on the tub, draining the water. And there it was. A sharp paring knife located in the deep end.

She grabbed a towel and lay it over Margot's head and chest. Then she walked outside. Gulping down the fresh air.

She went to the truck and sat in the driver's seat.

Within a few minutes, both Walter and Jason pulled up

in front of the house. Jason walked over to her. Rita rolled down the window.

"She's dead?" Jason asked.

"Yeah."

"Fuck," Walter said. "She was so damn nice."

"Do me a favor, Walter? Get the suicide note for me?"

He nodded, then disappeared into the house.

"Why did she do it?" Jason asked.

"Because we walked into her trauma, stirring up shit all over the place," Rita said. "Even if she didn't know the recording existed and we might find it, it must have been horrifying to have everyone talking about the men. Wondering who killed them. And here she was, a victim of them. Christ. Margot."

She sighed.

"I got ahold of Milly."

"Yeah? What'd she say?"

"She had no idea a woman went with them. The chef only packed three lunches. And she never noticed a blanket was missing."

"So it wasn't her at the mine?"

"She says not. She was at the inn all day. And I think it's the truth. I read through all of the statements Otto took, and staff noticed her around."

Rita nodded. "Okay. So obviously the men didn't tell her a fourth was going."

"No," Jason said. "And we know why."

Rita nodded.

Walter stepped out of the house and walked over with the note, handing it to her.

"Thanks."

He nodded.

"I'm going to notify Margot's mom. Walter, stay here until Dylan arrives to retrieve the body. Jason, can you notify Elk Mountain? Annemarie is worried. She'll need some support."

He hesitated.

"No details," Rita said. "You can simply tell her we found Margot and she's deceased."

He nodded.

"Meet you at the office after."

She reversed down the driveway, hands tight on the steering wheel. She didn't drive fast. She wanted to keep Margot alive for her mother, just a few minutes longer.

Chapter Fifty

RITA PULLED UP TO THE HOUSE IN BEAUMONT. IT WAS A single-family ranch house from the 1950s and looked significantly worse than Margot's. It was covered in faded white aluminum siding, and the lawn was overgrown in weeds. There was no car, but rather some rusted out washers and dryers sitting beneath a rickety carport that looked like it might collapse with the next winter snow.

Rita parked on a giant patch of cracked pavement that served as the driveway.

She got out and walked up a rotting wooden ramp and stopped at the front door. It was open, a screen door doing the work of keeping bugs out. An older woman in a wheelchair sat at a small kitchen table, sipping a glass of lemonade.

Rita knocked, lightly.

The woman turned, looked at Rita.

Then she rolled to the door and unlocked it. Pushing the screen open.

"Arlene?" Rita asked.

The woman nodded. "It's Margot, isn't it? She killed herself?"

Rita froze. Then nodded.

"Best you come in," Arlene said.

Rita stepped inside. Arlene rolled back to the kitchen table. Rita followed her. "Can I get you anything?"

"Some tea?"

Rita nodded. Walked to the counter and got the kettle. Pouring in water. And plugging it in.

Then she went and sat on one of the yellow chairs. Pulling out Margot's note. "She left you this."

Arlene took it, reading it. Then handed it back. Tears shining in her eyes

Rita said the same thing she said every time she had to deliver this news. "I'm so sorry."

Like sorry did a single damned thing. It did nothing for the pain. Or the heartbreak. Or the sheer unfairness of a life cut short.

"She never got over it," Arlene said.

"The rape."

Arlene swallowed a lump in her throat, nodded.

"She didn't report it."

"No. She was afraid to."

"Why?"

"Back then, she hung out at the bar, was a bit more of a party girl. She was afraid people would say she was asking for it."

Probably because they would.

"She was never the same after that." Arlene rolled into the other room. Rita watched the water boil in the kettle. It clicked off, so she poured out the water into a tea pot. Opened up a canister labelled *tea*. She selected a bag and dumped it in.

Then carried it to the table. Searched the cupboards and found two mugs.

Arlene returned with a photo. "That's her, before. Around five years ago."

The photo was of a markedly different woman. Vivacious, healthier, fuller face. Sparkling eyes. Nice full smile. She looked happy in the photo, sitting at a table about to blow out birthday cake candles.

Once again, Rita wanted to punch the men took that light from her eyes.

"Growing up, she was such an outgoing people person. She'd talk to anyone. Loved meeting people, hearing about their lives. Her dream was to travel the world and meet interesting people, get to know other cultures. After the rape, she changed. Became withdrawn, afraid of people. She didn't want to travel. Managed to get a decent job, got the promotion. I felt like she was finally putting it all behind her."

"Did she tell you who raped her?"

"Someone at Apex. She'd said something about the company back then that made me put two and two together, but I can't remember what it was."

Rita pulled up a photo of the necklace with the "M" charm.

"Was this Margot's?"

She studied it. "Was it silver?"

"No."

"Then it wouldn't have been. She's allergic to nickel. Was allergic."

Rita looked down at the suicide note that was on the kitchen table. "Why did she say she was sorry, she tried?"

Arlene's mouth turned down. "She tried to kill herself when it happened. Twice. I asked her to try harder to find her way back. And I thought she had, for a while. But with the Apex Three all over the news, I guess it brought back old memories." Arlene stopped, a light going off in her eyes. "Was one of those men her attacker?"

"Yes."

"Well, I hope he rots."

"Me too."

She gave Rita a grateful smile.

"Do you think Margot could've killed them?"

"What?" Arlene looked shocked by the question.

Rita shrugged. "Revenge for the rape."

Arlene gave a rueful laugh. "I wish she had. No, Margot wasn't violent."

Rita poured out two cups of tea. They sat drinking in silence for a long time.

Finally Rita broke the impasse. "Is there someone who could come stay with you?"

She nodded. "I'll call my son. He's in Cheyenne."

They finished their tea. Then Arlene escorted Rita to the door. On the way out, Rita stopped. "How long have you been in the wheelchair, Mrs. Hawley?"

"Nearly twenty years. Drunk driver."

Rita didn't tell her she'd asked in order to rule her out as a suspect in the murders.

"I'll probably pack up and move to Cheyenne now," Arlene said. "Be closer to my grandkids. I only stayed local because of Margot."

"If you need anything, give us a call."

She handed Arlene a card. Then made her way down to her truck. She had a text from Mary Lou. *Information on Scott's family just came in.*

Rita dialed her. "Hey."

"Vancouver police were able to track down a number for Scott's sister. You want me to call?"

"No," Rita said. "I'll do it. I'm headed back now."

"Have you eaten?"

"No."

"I'll pick something up for you from Bighorn Bean."

"Thanks."

Rita started up the truck, reversed. And then began the lonely drive back to Still County.

Chapter Fifty-One

MARY LOU HAD PICKED UP A SELECTION OF MUFFINS FROM the Bighorn Bean. Walter and Jason were just getting back. They had cleaned up the bathroom at Margot's so that Arlene wouldn't have to see her daughter's blood.

Rita entered the office and grabbed a blueberry muffin, devouring it in just a few bites. While she ate, she updated Jason and Walter on what Arlene had told her.

Walter looked sad. "She didn't report it."

Edith Mae glared at him. "Are you surprised?"

"Otto would have investigated. Hell, I would have."

"Doesn't make it any easier for the victim."

"But we knew Margot," he said. "She handled payroll."

"Maybe that made it harder for her," Edith Mae said.

Rita squeezed her shoulder and selected another muffin. This one lemon poppyseed. Then she went into her office, closing the door behind her. She stared down at the pink message paper.

The name was Grace Macdonald, and it was accompanied by a telephone number.

Rita picked up the phone and dialed.

A woman answered. "Hello?"

"Grace Macdonald? Scott Macdonald's sister?"

Three was silence.

For a moment she wondered if she had hung up.

"Grace?"

"I'm here."

"This is Sheriff Jonas of Still County Sheriff's Office, Still County, Wyoming. I take it the Vancouver Police have been in touch?"

"They have. They said my brother's remains may have been located."

"It's been confirmed."

Silence again.

But then she heard Grace say to someone in a muffled voice, "They found Scott. He's dead."

Rita waited.

Then Grace was back. "Did they clear the cave?"

"His body was found in town. Buried in an empty lot. He was shot." She was brutal, but this was an odd conversation. She was hoping to provoke some more emotion from Grace.

"Shot?"

"Yes."

Rita heard a man whisper, "He was killed?"

"Did your brother have any enemies?"

"No. I can't imagine why anybody would want to kill him."

"What about his wife? We're still trying to track her down."

"Wife?" She almost laughed. "Scott wasn't married."

"Scott was married?" the man asked.

Grace shushed him. About goddamn time. "He was wearing a wedding ring at the time of death."

"Well, if he was married, he sure as hell didn't tell me."

"When was the last time you spoke to your brother?" Rita asked.

"God, I don't know. A few months before he disappeared, I guess. We hadn't been in touch for a while. He was busy bouncing around the world for work, and I was traveling in Europe. Our paths went in different directions."

"What kind of person was your brother?"

"What do you mean?"

"Just trying to understand why someone might kill him."

Rita could imagine Grace's shrug. "He drank. And slept around ... a lot. But——" She broke off, not offering anything more.

"Did Scott tell you he was coming to Still?"

"No, I think we'd stopped talking then."

"Stopped talking?"

"Fell out of touch."

Rita felt like there was something more, but she was hesitant to push and make Grace clam up altogether. "Anything else you can think of?"

"No. I really wasn't involved in my brother's life, Sheriff."

"Do you know who his next of kin was?"

"Probably me."

"Casper PD will want to make arrangements for the body."

"You can give them my number. Is that everything?"

"It is."

Grace disconnected.

Well, there was obviously no love lost between the two of them. But why? Rita set her phone down. Wanting to call back. Or visit in person. But she didn't think she'd get approval to travel to Vancouver for an interview.

God, did anyone have a happy family anymore? Maybe Mary Lou and Brian. Although, they had been through their fair share of shit. She didn't know much about Mary Lou's husband. Just that he had died when Brian was a kid. Pancreatic cancer, she thought.

Rita brought up Otto's number. He still hadn't responded to her text. Maybe she should call him or stop by the house?

But an argument with Otto would just be a cherry on top of a shit sundae.

Her phone rang, startling her.

She looked at the screen, then answered. "Hey Tilda."

"Jason said you watched your videos."

"Unfortunately."

"Yeah. We weren't able to get any additional identifiers on the second woman."

"Okay."

"But we did match dust traces on the men's remains to the Low Peak mine. And the bullet in the tree was from a .38. But we didn't find anything else. Four years is a long time for an outdoor crime scene to remain pristine. Too bad."

Rita agreed. Too bad the bodies hadn't been discovered. The second mine hadn't been searched. Margot hadn't felt safe to come forward.

"You find your first victim?"

Rita rubbed her forehead. "She killed herself."

"Jesus. Poor thing."

"Yeah."

"Call me if you need anything more."

"I will."

Rita hung up.

A knock on her door. Mary Lou. She leaned against the doorframe, a piece of paper in her hand.

"What's up?"

"I've been looking up information on Angela Ruiz. Want to know Angela's middle name?"

"Hit me."

Mary Lou walked over and set the paper on Rita's desk.

"Mary. Spelled the same as me."

"Mary as in the 'M' necklace?"

"Yep."

Rita tried to fit Angela into the puzzle. She had met with the men at the inn. Had worked closely with them in scouting sites. Had something more happened? Had Scott tried raping her? "It's worth a shot."

Mary Lou made a face.

"Poor choice of words," Rita said. "Can you call Peggy and schedule a meeting?"

"Already done. She had a window open up this afternoon."

Jason popped up behind her. "Ken just called about an Apex van burning on Poison Spider Road. He wants to meet us there."

"Why? That's Beaumont."

Jason shrugged. "I dunno. But he said 'please.'"

Chapter Fifty-Two

THE VAN WAS A MESS OF BURNED CHEMICALS AND CHARRED steel. Ken stood on the side of the road, talking on the phone.

A Beaumont police officer was trying to get his attention, but he was ignoring him.

Rita got out. It stunk.

Ken eyed them, said something into the phone. Then he hung up and turned on his heel, walking over to them.

"What happened?" Rita asked.

"It's not one of ours."

"What do you mean, it's not one of yours?" She looked past him to the burnt truck. Even though the paint was blistered along most of the vehicle, she could still make out the Apex logo on the side.

"I don't know whose truck this is, but it doesn't belong to Apex."

The Beaumont police officer spotted them and strode over. His nameplate read Constable. He barely looked twenty, and he had a cross expression on his face. "This is Beaumont's case."

Rita raised her hands. "I'm just a tourist."

He blinked. Then smoothed down his hair. Her answer seemed to placate him somewhat. "Sorry. I figured with Apex being involved, you might want to take it."

Rita shook her head. "Nope. I try to keep as far away from them as possible. No offense, Ken."

The Beaumont fire chief approached, held out his hand to Rita. "Roy Banks."

She gestured to Constable. "It's his. For some reason, I'm here as a guest of Apex."

"Well, whoever snags it, you might wanna take a look in the back."

Rita and Constable both looked at one another. Then they followed Roy over to the van.

As they neared, the noxious stench got worse. And it smelled familiar. Meth.

Roy gestured to the open back of the van. It was filled with lab equipment of a different kind, as well as destroyed product.

Constable looked at her.

"Meth," Rita said, thanking her stars that Jason had more sense than this Beaumont version of him. Then she turned to Ken. "Any idea why someone would be using an Apex van as a meth lab?"

"It's not an Apex van. I keep telling you that. Look." He pointed to back bumper. "Apex trucks have numbers here." Then he led them around front to the windshield. "And we've got coded stickers here. And the logo, while a good facsimile, is too big."

Now that she was closer, she could see what Ken meant about the logo. It was like a bad copy of a copy of a copy, blown out, somewhat pixelated. And it was giant, taking up nearly the whole side of the van.

She thought back to the ones in the Apex parking lot.

They were usually smaller, and not quite so glaringly obvious.

She turned back to Ken. "So why am I here?"

"Someone is smearing the company name."

"How?"

"Hiding their drug business behind Apex."

"And what am I supposed to do about it?"

He stared at her.

"This is Beaumont's jurisdiction."

"And you know full well it's related to what's been going on in Still."

Rita gestured for him to follow her and walked over to a spot where they wouldn't be overhead. Ken scuffed along behind her.

"Any news on the men who broke into my station?"

"You refusing to help unless I give you information?"

"Not refusing anything. I'm asking a question."

He scuffed his foot against the ground. "If it was Apex—"

"We know it was."

"— he didn't leave a trace of it behind."

"Philip?"

Ken nodded. "He acted alone. Without board approval. So there is no trace."

Rita frowned. Fuck. "And where is Philip?"

He shrugged. "Yachting in the Mediterranean, I think."

"Mediterranean?"

He nodded.

That was different than what Angela had told her. She wondered which one was true. Or if both were wrong. And if Philip was pushing up daisies alongside Boyd somewhere. Much as she detested Ken, she wasn't about to get him killed by pushing him on the matter.

"What do you want me to do about this?" She jerked her head towards the van. "Talk to Angela?"

He looked relieved. "That'd be great."

"I can do that. I'm seeing her this afternoon."

"Maybe you can tell her I'm doing a good job."

"I wouldn't go that far."

He glared at her.

"Jesus, Ken. I'm kidding." Then she eyed him. She'd just had a thought. "What kind of weapon does Apex police use?"

"Glock 19."

She pursed her lips. "Not a .38 or .22?"

He shook his head. "No, but there's .22s available to company employees if they want them."

Rita blinked. "What?"

"Yeah."

"Why?"

He shrugged. "Long distance travel, remote roads, dangerous wildlife."

"Any unaccounted for from four years ago?"

"I don't know."

"Find out?"

He opened his mouth as though to argue.

"In the interest of greater cooperation," Rita said.

"I'll have to run it by Angela."

"Fine with me."

He nodded, then headed back to his vehicle. She caught Jason's eye and waved. Together, they walked back to the truck.

While Jason drove, she relayed what Ken had told her about the weapons.

"Interesting."

"I'll say." Then she grew quiet. Thinking about her conversation with Arnold.

"What's up?" Jason asked.

"Arnold said that he didn't steal the truck."

"Yeah?"

"Well, what do we know about the vandals?"

"There's two of them."

"Yeah."

"So maybe Arnold wasn't the one that stole it. Didn't mean he wasn't along for the ride." She rang Mary Lou.

She answered at once. "Sheriff."

"You find Eleanor's number?"

"Hello to you too."

"Sorry."

Mary Lou snorted, then rattled off a bunch of numbers.

"Hold on." Rita dug out her notebook and pen. "Again, please."

Mary Lou repeated it.

"Thank you." Rita disconnected and then dialed.

"Myers residence."

Rita had a feeling it was the maid. "Eleanor Myers, please. It's Sheriff Jonas from Still. I stopped by the other evening for a chat."

"Mrs. Myers is at a meeting. I'll have her return—"

"Actually," Rita broke in, "you might be able to help me. Is Arnold there?"

"Young Mr. Myers hasn't been with us for some time now."

"So he didn't come to the house yesterday?"

"He did not."

"Thank you." Rita rang off. "That little shit."

Jason glanced at her. "You expected different?"

"I did. Stop at the Myers house on the way back to the office. Arnold was staying there. I want to see if he's returned." Hopefully Heather replaced the key. Unless she bought the house.

He glanced over at her. "You look worried."

"I am." She gestured back towards Beaumont. "Say the boys stole the van, thinking it was an Apex vehicle. Only it's not. You think whoever is running that vehicle through Still County is gonna be happy they lost their meth?"

"Shit."

"Yeah, shit. If this was Arnold and his accomplice, they don't have just Apex looking for them now."

Jason pressed his foot down, increasing their speed.

When they arrived at the house, a sold marker sat on the For Sale sign in the yard. She wondered if the home now belonged to Heather.

They got out and went to the front door.

Rita knocked.

No answer.

Rita accessed the lockbox, fetching the key. She opened the front door. "Arnold?"

No answer.

"Check the kitchen?"

Jason nodded.

Rita made her way up the stairs. There was no sign that Arnold had returned after vacating.

She walked back downstairs and met Jason at the front door. He shook his head.

They exited, and Rita returned the key to the lockbox. She figured he had his own key. But if not, she wanted him to be able to get inside.

"Let's check with Lydia," she said.

Jason didn't move. "Maybe I shouldn't come with you."

"Why not?"

He shrugged. "She didn't say the kindest things when Mom told her about me."

Rita narrowed her eyes. "Come on."

She strode to Lydia's and banged on the door.

Lydia answered with a scowl, her eyes skating over Jason to land to Rita. "What do you want, Sheriff?"

"You wake up this irritable or reserve the attitude especially for us?" Rita couldn't help it. She knew she was taking her anger for Esther out on Lydia. "My deputy has some questions for you."

Lydia's face tightened further.

Jason looked panicked. Rita turned to him. "Go ahead."

He cleared his throat. "We're looking for Arnold."

Lydia looked at Rita. "Why don't you leave that boy alone? He's not hurting anyone."

"Do you know where he is, or would you like me to arrest you for impeding an investigation?"

Lydia's jaw fell open. "You wouldn't dare."

"I wouldn't," Rita said. "But my deputy follows all the rules. So I can't speak for him."

"I have no idea where Arnold is," Lydia said. "I haven't seen him since you chased him away the other day."

So he had gone somewhere. "There was no chasing involved," Rita said.

Lydia pinched her lips together. Making it obvious that even if she knew anything, she wasn't about to share.

"Any more questions, deputy?" Rita asked.

Jason thought for a moment. Then shook his head. Lydia banged back into the house, door slamming behind her.

He winced.

"Good job," Rita said.

They made their way back to the police truck. As they

did, a silver pickup approached on the street, slowed, then barreled past them. She caught a glimpse of Arnold.

"Goddamnit."

She held out her hand.

Jason tossed her the keys.

They jumped in and she started it up. Sirens. Lights. But by the time she reached the end of the road, the truck was gone. And she was not about to give chase.

"You get a plate?" she asked Jason.

"Smeared with mud."

Of course it was. She hit the indicator and turned right. No matter how much she didn't want to, it was time to talk to Helen.

Chapter Fifty-Three

RITA DROVE TO THE RANCHER'S PANTRY AND PARKED NEAR the entrance. Together, they went inside. Rita scanned the store and spotted Helen working one of the cash registers.

She approached just as a customer arrived.

A man with a cart full of beer and snacks pulled into Helen's lane. Rita stepped in front of him. "She's closed."

He let out a sigh, then rolled around to another lane.

Helen stared at her. "Come to gloat?"

"Don't know what you're talking about," Rita said.

"Otto kicked me out."

Jason glanced at Rita.

"And you think that's my fault?"

"You know it is. You told him lies."

"See, I don't think I did," Rita said.

"Well, what do you want? Destroying my life wasn't enough? You're here to wreck my job?"

"It's about Arnold."

"Arnold? Arnold's in Casper with George's parents."

"He's not. He left there weeks ago."

"Bullshit."

"It's not bullshit. He's been crashing at your house."

She stared at Rita in disbelief. It was apparent that Helen didn't know. She truly looked surprised.

"Call Lydia if you don't believe me."

"Lydia knew?"

Rita nodded.

"Bitch." She said it under her breath, but Rita caught it nonetheless.

"You two not friends anymore?"

Helen sniffed. "She thought it was too soon for me to move in with Otto."

"She might have had a point. Are you back at the house now?" It hadn't seemed like anyone was living there.

"Still Haven. The house sold yesterday. And I'm not going back."

"Not even for Arnold's sake?"

Helen didn't answer.

"About Arnold," Jason said.

"How am I supposed to know where he is?" Helen asked. She looked annoyed. Or maybe worried. "I thought he was in Casper."

"When did you last talk to him?"

She had to think. "Last week, I think."

"Jesus, Helen."

"You have no idea how hard it's been for me since Lisa died."

"And what about Arnold?"

She pinched her lips again.

"Any friends from school that he might be staying with?"

She shook her head.

"No best friend?"

"He lives in Beaumont."

"Who?"

"Adrian Hutch."

Rita blinked. "Walter's son?"

Helen nodded.

"Jesus Christ. Does Adrian own a silver pickup?"

"I don't know."

"Arnold have a cell phone?"

"Of course."

Rita held out her hand. "I need his number." For a moment, Helen looked like she wouldn't provide it. But then she sighed, ripped a corner off a Rancher's Pantry flyer, and scribbled down the number.

"Thanks," Rita said. "And I'm sorry about Otto."

She wasn't sure about that last part, but it seemed like something a mature person would say.

Helen's eyes flashed, and she turned back to her till.

Rita called Arnold's number as she and Jason left the store. It went straight to voicemail. "Hey, Arnold. It's Sheriff Jonas. I need you to call me back, pronto."

She left her number at the end of the message, then hung up.

Her next call was to Walter. "Adrian drive a vehicle?"

"Yeah."

"What is it?"

"A silver F-150. Why?"

"I think he's involved with the vandalism with Arnold Myers."

Silence. "What?"

"And they just targeted a meth lab they thought was an Apex truck. So I imagine Apex isn't the only one looking for them right now."

"Fuck."

Walter hung up. She imagined he was calling his son.

Rita checked the time. It was almost time to meet with Angela.

"Get me back to the SCSO?"

Jason nodded. Seconds later, they were headed to the office.

Chapter Fifty-Four

Rita arrived at the station to find Angela had already arrived and was pacing the lobby. She looked irritated to have been kept waiting.

"Sorry. It's been a shit day," Rita said.

"Is this about the meth truck? A call would have sufficed."

"No."

Peggy's absence was strikingly evident. Rita gestured. "Where's your shadow?"

"Working."

"Isn't the work wherever you are?"

Angela merely smiled.

Rita led her into the office, stopping by Mary Lou's desk. "Walter?"

"Off to look for Adrian. He couldn't reach him by phone."

Rita nodded. Then she took Angela past where Edith Mae was typing away at her laptop, bopping her head to music and blowing bubbles. Angela looked at her, eyebrow raised.

"Hiring young?"

"Intern," Rita said, closing the door behind them. She walked around the desk to her chair and sat.

She gestured to the chair opposite.

Angela sighed and sat. "So what's this about?"

"The Apex Three."

"Still no answers?"

"Getting closer. Were you in town when they disappeared?"

"I told you that I was. Well, not that Saturday. Peggy and I were in New York. We returned when I heard they were missing. Helped organize the search with your father."

"You'll send me confirmation of that?"

"I will."

Rita nodded. "Right. Did Ken ask you about—"

"— the guns?"

Rita nodded.

"Yes. And I double checked. All accounted for."

"And the records from that time? Of who checked them out?"

"We no longer have those. They are four years old. Nor do we still have the same guns. They were upgraded a year or two ago."

"You ever sign one of those guns out?"

Angela laughed. "You think I killed them?"

Rita didn't laugh.

Angela sighed again. "Once or twice, I'm sure."

"Ever have cause to fire one?"

"No. I don't like guns." She adjusted her seat. "What's this really about, Sheriff? I sense a hostility about you."

"You ever hear of a woman named Margot Hawley?"

Angela thought. "The bank."

Rita nodded.

"What about her?"

"Scott and Patrick raped her four years ago. She killed herself yesterday."

Angela's face paled. "What?"

"There was at least one other victim. Possibly more."

Angela sat in silence. Rita couldn't tell if she was feigning shock or was just a practiced liar.

"Any Human Resources issues, complaints, actions? Any record of anything untoward?"

Angela picked at a piece of fluff on her skirt. If Rita hadn't known better, she would have thought Angela was nervous. "Scott."

"What about him?"

"He'd been accused of sexual harassment."

Rita tamped down her anger. "Only one complaint?"

Again Angela took her time. "Several."

"So, why the fuck was he still employed at Apex?"

Angela's eyes flashed. "Why the hell do you think? He said, she said. And when does anyone ever believe the she? You think I liked it?"

"You couldn't fire him?"

"Wasn't my department. You think this woman killed them?"

Rita ignored the question. "Did you have any first-hand experience of Scott's harassment?"

"You mean did he target me?"

Rita nodded.

"No. But then again, I was above him in the pecking order. Predators seek out the weak and vulnerable."

"And that wasn't you?"

"No. When I started with Apex, I dealt with my fair share of the sharks. Trying to evade the aggressors, while not being labeled difficult. I'm sure you know what it's like."

Rita nodded. She did. NYPD was a large force. And had more than its share of rotten apples.

"Besides—"

Rita raised her brows.

"—he was friends with Philip."

"Ah. So you were aware of Scott's track record?"

"I was. I thought I could keep an eye on him."

"And this is why I hate your goddamn company. You put a fucking predator in our backyard and don't tell us."

"I agree. It's horrific."

"I don't want you agreeing with me."

"Why not?"

"Because I want to rage at someone. And I can't do that if you're being reasonable. Fuck."

Angela smiled, but there was a sadness to it. "Can I make a donation to the victim's family?"

She thought about Lisa's Place. "Is that what Apex does when they fuck up? Donate money?"

"You'd be surprised how well it works." They were silent for a moment. "I wish I could fire him for you, Rita. Or make it so that he never came here. But I wasn't in charge of staffing."

"And you wanted Philip's job, so weren't about to make waves."

Angela didn't answer.

"How did he fare in Brazil? Did he target anyone there?"

"Why do you think we pulled them out and brought the team to Still?"

"Jesus." Rita got out her phone and drew up the photo of the "M" charm and necklace. "Do you recognize this?"

At least Angela studied it. She zoomed in, then shook her head. "No."

Rita took her phone back.

"Anything else, Rita?"

"Ken wants me to tell you he's doing a good job."

Angela laughed. "That might be going a bit far, don't you think?"

"Exactly what I said. But you should know, he is a good lap dog." To hell with it. She might as well recommend him for the job. After all, the devil you knew.

"I'll keep that in mind."

Angela got up. Rita walked her out to the black Audi. Ken was seated in the driver's seat. He popped out and opened the back passenger door.

Rita walked back inside and to Mary Lou's desk. It was now just the three of them in the office. "Jason?"

"Went to help Walter look for Adrian."

Rita nodded.

"You off, Edith Mae?"

She nodded, snapped her gum. "Crashing at Gail's tonight. She's on her way to pick me up."

"And who is Gail?"

"A friend."

"Why aren't you going home?"

"I'm not living with a bigot."

Rita couldn't argue with that. "You know Walter's son?"

"Adrian?"

Rita nodded.

"Vaguely. He was two grades ahead of me at school. And then he moved to Beaumont to be with his mom."

"And Arnold?"

"Same. Before he dropped out."

Rita blinked. "Arnold dropped out?"

She nodded. "After Lisa died."

Jesus. Helen hadn't told her that.

"What were they like?"

"Nerdy boys. Always into gaming. I dunno. I never talked to them much. When Adrian left, Arnold just kind of kept to himself."

"Well, if you see either of them around town, let me know?"

Edith Mae nodded.

"'Night, Mary Lou. Don't stay late."

"Just until the child leaves."

Edith Mae glared at her. "I'm sixteen."

Rita laughed and walked out back to her Honda. She got inside and dialed Ken.

He answered on the first ring. "Thanks for talking to Angela."

"You're welcome. But I'm calling in the favor."

"What do you want?"

"Meet me at The Shaft in ten minutes." And then she hung up before he could respond.

Chapter Fifty-Five

RITA ARRIVED FIRST AND ORDERED A BURGER AND FRIES TO go. Then she took her usual seat and watched the door.

Ken arrived a few minutes later.

He scanned the tables, spotting her and walking over. He raised a hand, signaling their server. "The usual."

She nodded and headed for the bar.

Then Ken joined Rita at her table and sat. By the time he settled, the server was back with a beer.

"You order?" he asked.

"To go," she said. She might have to work with the guy, but she wasn't going to break bread with him.

"I'll take the steak and mashed potato special for here," he said. When their server departed, he took a breath. "So, I take it this isn't a social call?"

"Nope."

"Okay."

"Why'd you really leave Patrick and Scott that night in Beaumont?"

"I told you."

"No bullshit, Ken. Come on. A woman is dead because of them."

"What?"

Rita nodded. "They raped her. She killed herself."

"Jesus."

"So…"

"They asked me to film them having sex with a woman, but I didn't want to do it."

"Why?"

He hesitated. "They wanted to drug her."

"Wanted her unconscious."

He nodded.

"You report that to Apex?"

"Hell no."

"Why not?"

"I told you I was a trainee. These guys were — established."

"Friends of Philip."

"Yeah. I was still on probation. Probably why they chose me." She didn't imagine he was wrong about that.

The server interrupted them. Handed Ken his plate. Set Rita's brown paper bag on the table.

Rita handed her a twenty. "Keep the change." God, if she kept this up, she was going to be broke. "You hear any rumors about a woman going with them the day they went out to High Peak?"

He shook his head. Then sliced a chunk from his steak. Chewed slowly.

"Did you see Scott target any women at Apex?"

He swallowed his steak, then pushed his plate back. She didn't blame him. The conversation wasn't exactly palatable.

"No. You think a woman killed them?"

Rita didn't answer. She fingered her brown paper bag. "Thanks, Ken."

He seemed startled. "That's it?"

"It wasn't a date."

He flushed. "Didn't think it was."

"Enjoy your meal." He looked down at his food, but still looked uninterested.

Rita went out to the Honda and ate her dinner in the parking lot. She'd have to detract maturity points for this.

But she didn't want to go home until she spoke to Adrian or Arnold. And she didn't want to eat with Ken.

She finished her fries, wiping her hands on the paper napkin Ruby Joe provided. Then she called Jason.

"Hey."

"Any news on the boys?"

"Nope."

Rita pulled out her notebook and pen. "Got Adrian's plate number?"

Jason rattled it off.

Rita wrote it down.

"Where are you?"

"Down near Beaumont," he said.

"And Walter?"

"Out towards Casper."

"I'll head north. Call me with any updates. Otherwise, we'll touch base in an hour."

"10-4." He sounded serious. They were all feeling it. Two kids in over their head.

She turned left out of the parking lot and made her way down to Main. Then she headed left, following the road out towards the mountains.

She passed a few F-150s, but none of them silver. She drove for about an hour, then pulled off the highway at a rest stop. She pulled out her phone to call Jason.

Just as an Apex van drove by on the highway. She glanced at the rear. It was missing the numbers that were supposed to be on the bumper.

Rita hit the gas.

Turned out onto the highway.

She pulled her cell phone. Rang Jason. "Apex van. Headed south on 196."

"Plate?"

She hit the gas. Read the digits.

Two seconds later, Jason was back. "Stolen."

The van had spotted her. It pulled away. She kept pace.

"They're running."

"I'm on my way," Jason said.

"10-4."

She tossed the phone onto the passenger seat. Keeping the line open to Jason. The van turned off the highway, careening onto a crossroad.

She called out each road as they passed.

Farmland turned to woodlands on either side of her. Rita had a feeling the paved roads weren't going to last long. Seconds later, the van tires kicked up clouds of dirt, flinging pebbles towards the windshield.

She was a few car lengths behind, unable to see anything other than the van's ass.

She rolled down her window, then stuck her arm out and gestured for them to pull over.

The van didn't slow. If anything, it sped up.

She matched its speed, the steering wheel rattling, the entire SUV jostling as it bumped up and down.

The van hit the brakes.

She took a hard left.

But she veered too far. Pumping the brakes, trying to keep the Honda on the road. But it was too late. All she could do was hold on for the ride and hope the car didn't go airborne.

It stayed grounded, but careened straight off the dirt road into brush and weeds.

She was still accelerating, headed straight toward a line of trees.

Rita braced for impact.

And the vehicle slid to a stop. Her body bucked hard against the seatbelt. For a moment, she sat in silence.

Christ, she'd survived.

Might have a few more bruises though.

She glanced in the rear-view mirror. The van reversed. She tried to catch a glimpse of a driver or passenger. But they were too far away now.

She threw the Honda in reverse.

The rear wheels spun, trying to find purchase on loose gravel.

"Come on!"

The SUV hitched and bucked, almost breaking free of the ditch.

She pumped the gas, trying to will the car forward on nothing but a wing and a prayer.

Goddamnit. What would Otto do?

Apparently, that was the magic thought. The truck shot forward, gravel spitting.

She was back on the road again.

"Where are you?" Jason asked.

She updated him on her location.

"I'll be there in ten minutes."

"I might have lost them," she said.

She shot down the road. The cloud of dirt was gone. The road went on for another hundred yards before ending at a junction.

She chose a route. It ended in a fork.

The road in either direction was just winding enough that she couldn't see too far along.

Right or left. Again.

If she chose wrong, she'd lose the van. She studied the air. And then she saw it. A slight haze to the right. Like a vehicle kicking up dust.

"Got you, asshole."

She took the right road. Following the twisting path, keeping her eyes open for the Apex van. Keeping Jason updated.

She drove fast, trying to catch up. But it seemed to take forever. And she was starting to wonder if she had chosen wrong.

What if she was actually putting more distance between herself and the van?

But it was no time for doubt.

She was committed.

Rita kept to the road. It seemed to grow narrower and more deserted, but then the woods started thinning, revealing more farmlands and homesteads.

This seemed to be some kind of private road.

She had no idea what it was named.

Then it dead-ended in a dirt driveway. Shit. That was it. She'd hit the end.

And lost the van. It must have turned off at one of the properties. She balled her hand into a fist and struck the steering wheel.

Goddamnit.

"I'm almost there," Jason's voice crackled over the speaker. "Walter too."

"Keep your eyes open for it."

And then she noticed the driveway. Soft impressions in the dirt. She glanced up at the property. Two houses. No lights on, no vehicles or signs of activity. No animals.

Abandoned?

Maybe. Maybe not.

She glanced over at a dilapidated mailbox.

"I'm at 808 on whatever road this is."

"Barn? Two houses?" Jason asked.

"Yeah, that's it."

"The old Blake place," he said.

"Anyone live here?"

"Not anymore."

"Well, there's tire tracks leading up."

"Be there in five," Jason said.

"10-4."

She turned onto the property. And pulled up the long curving drive that led up to the houses.

Chapter Fifty-Six

Rita made her way up the driveway. The tracks branched right along a path leading to a barn. She followed them, pulling in front of the structure.

The roof had partially fallen down.

But there, inside the barn, was the Apex van. The taillights were off, and both the driver and passenger doors were wide open.

Rita grabbed her phone. "I have them."

"Three minutes out," Jason said.

"10-4."

She got out of the SUV, pulling her weapon, training it on the van. "Sheriff's office. Come out with your hands raised."

No response.

"Still County Sheriff's Office. Come out with your hands raised."

Nothing.

She made her way up to the driver's seat. Empty. As was the passenger seat. Keys weren't in the ignition.

She didn't bother to check the back of the van. It

wasn't one of Apex's. Now that she was up close and could see the logo, she knew for certain it was a fake.

"Still County Sheriff's Office. Come out."

Nothing.

She heard a sound off to her left. It came from a row of stables. She checked each of them. All empty. And then she saw a shadow move. She turned.

A huge stack of hay bales toppled towards her.

Rita bolted.

Too late.

One struck her in the back, knocking her to the ground. But she retained control of her weapon.

Two figures darted past her and ran to the van. Climbing inside.

She kicked the hay away, rolling to her knees. Aiming her weapon at the driver. They wore balaclavas. Neither were armed.

She scrambled to her feet. "Get out of the van."

He turned the ignition.

"Out."

The doors closed.

The driver gave her the finger, then threw the vehicle into reverse. Goddamnit. She wasn't going to shoot at unarmed men.

They reversed right into the Honda.

There was a loud crash.

Rita sprinted towards them.

The driver spun around, rocketing down the driveway. Rita ran to the SUV. One of the tires was now flat.

"Goddamnit."

Rita opened the door and grabbed her phone. "They're fleeing."

"Walter's spotted them," Jason said.

Well, thank God.

"You okay?"

"I'm gonna need a tow."

"I'll be right there."

She spotted the police cruiser at the bottom of the drive. Jason pulled up and parked. He got out of the vehicle. "Walter lost them. Couldn't get turned around in time."

Rita blew out a breath. "Let 'em go. We'll catch 'em another way."

She examined the dent in the side of the Honda. The door had sprung open. She tried to close it. Nope. She dialed Randy at Bighorn Towing. Gave him directions on where to find it.

Then she and Jason walked back to the barn. She took a look around to see if her suspects had left anything behind. But she found nothing.

Walter pulled up shortly after. He surveyed the damage to the Honda.

"You think that was intentional?"

She shook her head. "No, I think they were just in a goddamn hurry."

"Was it Arnold and Adrian?"

"No." Even with the masks. Both of these men had larger, more defined musculature. Besides, she didn't think either kid would have the skills to drive like that.

"Well, thank Christ for small mercies."

"You haven't been able to get a hold of them yet?" Rita asked.

"No. But when I do, I'll give him the hiding of his life."

"Maybe keep that to yourself," Rita said.

Walter rubbed his jaw. "Little punk. He's going right back to his mother's."

Why did that not surprise her?

"Let's check the house," Rita said. She didn't think the

van belonged to this residence. It was pretty obvious they either chose the location because they knew it was abandoned or because they were simply desperate and out of options and lucked into it.

Rita walked over to the first house. A sign on the door claimed it was now owned by Elk Mountain Equity. It was locked up tight.

They checked the second house. It was insecure and looked as though squatters had been staying there at some point. Discarded beer cans and some drug paraphernalia, but nothing that looked recent.

"You should get home, Walter," Rita said. "In case Adrian returns."

"What about you?"

"I've got Randy coming for the Honda."

"I'll wait with her," Jason said.

"Alright." Walter looked reluctant to leave. Maybe he didn't want to deal with his son. He ran a hand through his hair. "If it was Adrian doing the vandalism…"

"I'm pretty sure he was just supporting Arnold," Rita said. "And that kid is running on a potent mix of anger and grief at the moment. Don't be too hard on him. Just keep him out of sight until we figure out the meth angle."

Walter ducked his head, gave them a wave, and got back into his truck.

Within seconds he was gone, only a trail of dust to indicate he'd been there.

Rita turned to Jason. "If you want to leave—"

"I'll wait."

She nodded, grateful.

She pulled out her phone and rang Ken. It rang four times, and she expected it to go to voicemail. But then he answered. He was obviously still at The Shaft. It was noisy.

"There's another van," she said.

"What?"

"Another van."

"Shit." The noise lessened. He must have gone outside. "Where?"

"Don't know at the moment," she said. "It got away. But Apex should know there's another copycat. You might want to put a notification in the paper telling residents what to look for."

"What would that do?"

"Expose them. Not give them a place to hide. You'll have a bunch of folks looking out for those vans. Calling it in."

"That's not a bad idea."

"Occasionally I have been known for them," Rita said, then disconnected. Then she went and joined Jason in his Kia.

"Who do you think is running those vans?" he asked.

"No fucking clue," she said. "But I want to know. Let's check with Beaumont in the morning. See if they got any forensics on the one they found burned. Or got any idea on who is running meth in these parts."

Jason nodded.

Not long after that, Randy pulled up the drive. He didn't say much. Just hooked up the Honda and advised them he'd be taking it into Casper for repair.

When he'd left, Jason drove her back to Still.

He dropped her at the apartment.

She went right in and had a shower. Changed into jean shorts and a t-shirt.

She supposed she should be tired.

It had been a hell of a day.

But she felt wired.

The adrenaline of the car chase, pulling her weapon — it was all still coursing through her.

And she was hungry. Despite the burger and fries she'd had earlier.

She walked to the fridge, opened it.

She didn't want anything inside.

So she slid into her runners. Locked up and went downstairs, then started walking.

She tried to tell herself there was no purpose to her steps. But she was lying.

Before she knew it, she was walking up his street.

She didn't know what she would do if she found Heather there.

Cry?

Because her heart would probably break a little.

She stopped outside his house.

Only his truck was in the driveway.

This was stupid.

She should go home.

But she didn't.

She walked up to his front door. Rita was about to knock when he opened it. He was shirtless. Wearing jeans. Drinking a cold beer.

He looked her over. "You're sweaty."

She scowled at him. "'Cause I'm hot."

He grinned. "I've been telling you that for years."

"Don't be an idiot. Let me in."

He took a swallow of beer. It looked so cold. She wanted to snatch it from him and down the whole thing.

"I dunno. Someone told me you were seen at The Shaft knocking back drinks with an Apex goon. I might be jealous."

"Who told you that? Heather?"

He didn't answer. Okay, that was petty.

Rita sighed. "I was there. He was drinking. I was working."

"That supposed to make me feel better?"

"It's the truth. You don't believe me?"

"I do. Only because I know how much you hate Apex."

"So can I come in?" She wiped the sweat from her brow.

"Depends on what you want."

"That beer would be a good start."

He held it up. "This one?"

She reached for it, but he twisted. Setting the cold bottle against her neck. Her toes curled. Then he rolled it against her skin.

Fuck it.

He knew her too well.

She lunged at him. He caught her, slamming the door behind her. She heard the bottle fall to the floor.

He tugged her towards his bedroom.

But she didn't want to be there. It was too intimate. Too familiar.

She tried to push him into the living room. They'd used the couch before. It had just worked just fine.

Cash pulled his mouth from hers. Looked into her eyes. "Bed."

She hesitated.

To hell with it.

She nodded. He hoisted her up, carrying her. As though afraid she might change her mind.

He dropped her on the bed.

Seconds later her clothes were off, flung across the room.

And he was on top of her.

And inside of her.

And her world felt momentarily perfect.

Chapter Fifty-Seven

RITA WOKE ALONE IN CASH'S BED.

She rolled over, groaning. She was sore. They'd gone at it all night. And it had been a hell of a workout.

Nothing like the first time they'd had sex in here. That had been awkward and embarrassing. Neither of them really knowing what they were doing. And then the time his mother caught them.

After that, they'd gone elsewhere. The reservoir, the room he'd rented when he'd moved away from home. They'd never been together at Otto's.

She wasn't sure why.

Cash wasn't scared of Otto.

But maybe she had been.

She glanced at the clock. It was 6.30 a.m.

Rita got up and entered the en suite. She went to the toilet, then took a shower. When she got out, her shorts, underwear, and t-shirt were laundered and folded neatly at the edge of his bed.

She got dressed, then walked out to the kitchen.

He glanced over at her and smiled. Her stomach flip-flopped. She wondered if this is what it would be like living with him. He'd wear her out every night, and feed her every morning.

He plated some bacon and eggs and held it out to her.

"You did my laundry and made me breakfast."

"Oh, I did more than that," he said.

She flushed. "Better watch out. I might put a ring on that finger."

He laughed. "You missed your chance." There was a moment of awkward silence. "Sorry, bad joke."

"It's okay," she said, taking the plate. She walked to the table and sat. He already had orange juice waiting for her.

He fixed his own plate, then walked over and sat opposite.

Then they looked at each other.

"Last night was—" He broke off.

Rita shrugged. "I was running on adrenaline."

He grinned. "I am not complaining. Only wondering how I can keep you in that state."

She scowled at him.

He raised his hands. "Just kidding."

Rita dug into the food. The scrambled eggs were just the right amount of fluffy, not overcooked like she'd always managed to do. The bacon was crispy perfection.

"This is really good."

"Grandma taught me well."

"Can you take me home this morning?"

"Too sore to walk?"

She flicked scrambled eggs at him.

He laughed.

She grinned.

They finished up breakfast, and by 7:15, he was pulling around into the back parking lot behind Bighorn Bean.

"Thanks." She reached for the door handle.

"Rita."

She glanced at him.

"What are we doing?"

"What do you mean?"

"Don't play dumb."

She sighed. "I don't know. What do you think we're doing?"

"Fucking."

"Okay. If you want to put it that way."

"I want more than that."

She felt a jolt of fear. Her heart lurched into her throat. *Not ready. Not ready.*

He reached out and took her hand. "You don't have to be ready."

God. Did he have to read her mind?

"But I am. So whenever you are, let me know. But just promise me one thing."

"What's that?"

"If it's not what you want, you don't fucking run. I'm not sure I could take that again."

"I promise."

He looked surprised. "What? No argument?"

"I'm trying to change, Cash." She held tight to his fingers. "Or at least I hope I am."

He smiled. "That's all I ask."

She studied him. "And you're sure you don't want Heather?" She didn't say the rest. But she wouldn't be able to handle it. She didn't want to come second to him. She wanted to be first. Even if she wasn't ready to say it.

"I'm certain. After all, you were the reason we divorced."

She blinked. "Me?"

"Don't you remember I said, 'other things'?"

Rita nodded. "I was the 'other thing'?"

"She felt like I never fell out of love with you."

"Is that true?"

"Not telling."

"Asshole."

He grinned. She slid out of the truck. He got out as well, walking around to her. He cupped her head, leaning in. Kissing her. Until her world had shrunk to just his touch. And all she knew was the taste of him.

Then he released her, spun her around, and tapped her bottom. "Have a good day."

God, she felt like she was still vibrating. She turned around and met his eyes. "I don't have to be in the office until 9."

Rita had no idea how she unlocked the door, got up the stairs, unlocked the other door, and made it to her bedroom fully clothed. Although, making it to the bedroom wasn't entirely true.

They wound up naked on the floor.

And this time, neither of them cared.

Chapter Fifty-Eight

When Cash left, Rita limped to the bathroom.

She had another shower, letting the hot water soothe her sore muscles. Then she toweled off, dried her hair, dressed, and went downstairs to the Bighorn Bean.

Skyler had an iced coffee waiting for her. "Figured you'd need to cool down."

Rita raised her brows.

"Saw Cash leave," Skyler said.

Rita tried very hard not to flush. "You're getting awfully observant."

"Want to know if I heard anything as well?" Skyler asked, grinning.

"Hell no," Rita said. She grabbed her ice coffee, tossed her money in the tip jar, and hurried out.

She took the crosswalk and made her way to the office.

Mary Lou looked her over when she entered. "Hope I don't have to make another trip to Merritt's for you."

This time Rita did flush. "No. We were careful."

"Good."

"Who told this time?"

"Claudia Perkins spotted his truck out back of your place."

"And who the hell is Claudia Perkins?" Rita asked.

"Real estate."

"Why is she calling you?"

Mary Lou shrugged. "Thought I might be interested."

"Jesus Christ, this town."

Jason was petting Ted and looking from one of them to the other.

"It's nothing," Rita said.

She went into her office, grateful for the cool air.

The phone rang. A second later, Mary Lou was at her door.

"Scott's sister is on the line."

"Grace?"

She nodded. "And she sounds drunk."

"Put her through."

Mary Lou nodded, returning to her desk. A moment later Rita's phone rang. She answered. "Sheriff Jonas."

Silence.

"Hello? Grace?"

"It's me." She slurred the words.

"Are you alright?"

"I lied."

"About?"

"Scott. He was not a good person." She paused after each word as though for emphasis, or because she was having trouble finding the right ones.

Rita waited.

She sniffed. "Scott was the golden child growing up. He could do no wrong in our parent's eyes. Valedictorian, honor roll, class president. Excelled in football and soccer, was offered scholarships to all the big schools. Everybody fucking loved him."

She paused to sniff back more tears. Rita heard the rattle of ice cubes. She was taking another drink.

"You still there?" Grace asked?

"I am," Rita said.

"He wasn't a good brother, Sheriff. He started molesting me when I was five. Said he'd kill me if I ever told. And then when I said I didn't care if he did, he said he'd kill our parents."

"Jesus. Did they ever know?"

"Of course. I said something when I was twelve, I think. But neither of them believed me. Not their precious boy, a sexual predator. I must have misunderstood. Or been confused. Or made it up."

"I'm sorry."

"I didn't want anything to do with him. Last time I saw him was seven years ago when he was home for a conference. I don't know why I even met up with him; guilt, maybe? Parental pressure?"

"How did it go when you saw him?"

"He behaved like he had never done a fucking thing to me. He was with this other guy. Worshipped his every word. I can't remember his name."

"Patrick?"

"Yeah, Patrick. Fucker. He——" She broke off, crying.

"Grace?"

"I'm fine. Dennis is here."

"That your husband?"

"Boyfriend. He knows everything."

"You were starting to tell me something about Patrick."

Grace cleared her throat. "I went to the washroom. But then changed my mind and headed back to the table. I saw Patrick drop something in my drink."

Rita bit back her curse. "Did Scott see?"

Grace laughed. It was a sound Rita never wanted to

hear again. "Scott fucking mixed the pill in with a spoon. He was the one that handed it to me when I got back to the table."

"Jesus Christ."

"Yeah. That's the kind of brother I had, Sheriff. One willing to drug me for his friend to fuck." And Scott too, most likely. Not that Rita was going to say that out loud.

"So when you find out who killed my brother, Sheriff? I'd like to know their name, because I wanna shake their goddamn hand. And whatever I can do to keep him out of jail, fair warning, I'll do it." Grace sniffed again. "And he wasn't married. He wore a wedding ring so women thought he was."

"Why?"

"So women would be more comfortable around him. A wolf in sheep's clothing sort of thing."

"Thank you, Grace. And I hate to ask you this question."

"Did I kill my brother?"

"Yes."

"No. I wouldn't even be able to point to Wyoming on a map."

"What were you doing when he disappeared?"

She thought for a moment. "Four years ago? June?"

"July."

"I had just gotten back from Spain. It's where I met Dennis, actually."

"You keep your plane tickets?"

"I keep everything, Sheriff. I'll email them through."

"Thanks."

She was quiet a moment. "I wish I did kill him. Years earlier. Saved myself and other women a whole lot of pain."

"Listen, if you don't wanna collect his body…"

"Yeah?"

"I can have the county bury him in an unmarked grave."

Grace was silent a moment. "Can you send me the DNA confirmation that it's him? Because I need to know for sure he's dead."

"I can do that."

"Then dump him wherever you like."

Rita smiled. "Thank you, Grace. This must have been a hard phone call to make."

She sniffed. "I blocked most of my childhood out. And to be honest, Sheriff, I don't want you to catch his killer. I'm glad he's fucking dead."

She hung up.

Rita sat, holding the receiver.

Jason appeared in the door. "How did it go?"

Rita shared the details of the call.

"You think she did it?"

"No. I believe that she was in Spain. It makes zero sense for her to have killed him. She hasn't seen him in three years, decides to catch a plane to Wyoming, drive to Still, murder her brother and two others, then retrace her steps all without leaving a trace? No. But it does make me wonder."

She looked up the phone number for the Vancouver Police Department. After explaining why she was calling, she was put through to a Detective Emma Nelson.

She only got voicemail. So she left a message explaining why she called. Then she hung up. Her stomach grumbled.

"Breakfast?" Jason asked.

Rita really didn't want to face Skyler again so soon. "Get me a muffin?"

"Will do."

He headed out of the office. Rita picked up her phone and dialed Otto. There was no response. This time she left a message. "Dad, it's me. Call me back, please. I spoke with Helen."

She wasn't sure if she should have added that part. But it was too late now. Her phone rang.

A Canadian number.

"Sheriff Jonas."

"Hi, this is Detective Nelson. I got your message. You're telling me Scott Macdonald is dead?"

"He is. Murdered four years ago. We just found his body. I take it you had history with him?"

"Unfortunately," Nelson said. "Interviewed the greasy prick seven years ago. Smug as hell. Not even threatening him with DNA caused him to pause. He was simply used to getting his own way."

"But charges didn't stick?"

"No, my victim declined to prosecute. I think she was scared of him."

"Can you tell me anything about her?"

"I called her before I called you," Nelson said. "She wants to talk. I've got her number."

Rita wrote it down. "Thank you. I appreciate the call."

"Going to be completely honest with you, Sheriff. At the time, I felt like it was only a matter of time before Scott killed one of his victims. If he's dead? It's a very good thing."

She hung up.

Rita called the number Nelson had given her.

The phone was answered immediately. "Jennifer."

"Hi Jennifer, this is Sheriff Jonas."

"Has Scott assaulted someone else?"

"He has."

"Fuck. I was scared that would happen."

"Can you tell me what happened to you?"

"Yeah." There was a moment of silence and then she began. "I was at an architecture conference, having drinks at the bar, when he introduced himself. Seemed a nice enough guy. I saw the ring on his finger, didn't think he was looking for anything more than conversation. Boy, was I wrong about that."

"So you didn't know him prior?"

"No. I knew he was in the business, had seen him at the conference earlier that day, but I didn't *know* know him. Everyone seemed to think he was hot shit. I was kind of surprised he sat with me. Then flattered, I suppose. He said he'd read my thesis. And he had. Knew all about it."

"You let your guard down," Rita said.

"I did. He must've spiked my drink. Next thing I knew, I was in a hotel room. Scott was raping me. I tried to get him off, but he put a hand over my mouth. I couldn't breathe. Thought I was going to die. I woke up in my own room the next morning."

"I hate to ask this, but do you think he had someone film it?"

"How did you know that? You find the recording?"

"No. We found a couple others."

"Asshole."

"You reported it."

"Right away."

"Did they do a rape kit?"

"Yes, but no DNA was found. He must have used a condom. And I didn't know what room he'd raped me in. Wasn't his own. Because they tested those sheets as well."

"They didn't check other rooms?"

"There were over a thousand of us. Hotel had stripped most of the beds by the time I woke up and made the report. They did find GHB in my bloodstream."

"Was he arrested?"

"I don't know if he was arrested. But he was questioned. I picked him out of a lineup."

"But you chose not to go forward?"

"Someone sent me a copy of the video from that night. I don't know who. Probably a fake email address. But I looked like a willing participant. He said he'd send it to my husband. My mother. I guess he accessed my phone while I was unconscious. My mom was undergoing chemotherapy at the time. And I didn't want her to see it."

"So you chose not to proceed?"

"Yeah. Detective Nelson was amazing. She didn't try to push me. We don't have a statute of limitations on sexual assault here, so she said when I changed my mind, she'd go forward. But it was entirely in my hands."

"I'm so sorry."

She laughed grimly. "You know, I should have gone through with it. Because my life went to hell anyway. I started having panic attacks whenever I left the house. I couldn't touch my husband without being repulsed. Couldn't do my job. Couldn't even go to the office. I was so scared I'd see Scott. Then my mother died, my husband left. Like, I did nothing wrong, and yet I paid in fucking blood."

She was silent a long time, her breathing heavy.

"There's not a night I don't question that decision to not press charges. I feel like it's my fault those other women were hurt."

"Only one person at fault. Scott."

"It doesn't feel that way."

"How are you doing now?"

"Working for a smaller architectural company now. It's a good place. My boss knows about what happened to me. She's very protective."

"I'm glad."

"I still have nightmares though. That one night he'll show up at my apartment. And I won't be able to fight him off again."

"Then I have good news for you. Scott's dead."

There was complete silence. "What?"

"He was murdered four years ago."

"How? Where?"

"Shot in the head. Buried in an unmarked grave in Nowhere, Wyoming."

"Nowhere?"

"Well, it's actually called Still County, and I love the damn place, but it may as well be Nowhere."

"And Scott's dead?"

"Along with two others. One a man named Patrick, who seems to have participated in his penchant for harm, and another."

"Did he suffer?"

"I don't know."

"I hope he did. I hope he was fucking scared. I hope he shit his pants." Then she gave a little laugh. "You probably think I did it."

"No, but I wouldn't be doing my job if I didn't ask."

"What was the date again?"

Rita told her.

"Hold on."

There was silence for a few moments. "I was hospitalized at the time. My second suicide attempt. I can send you my discharge paperwork."

"That won't be necessary. I believe you."

"You're not lying? He's really dead?"

"He is. And I'm not sure if this will make you feel better. But he's moving from one unmarked grave to another."

"It doesn't. But I appreciate the attempt, Sheriff."

"Take it easy, Jennifer."

"Thank you."

Rita hung up. She pulled up the email Peggy had sent her of Scott's schedule over his time at Apex. He had spent most of his time at Apex in South America. Where he was no doubt able to assault women at leisure.

It enraged her.

Chapter Fifty-Nine

RITA WALKED OUT INTO THE BULLPEN. SHE UNCLIPPED THE photos of the vandalism and dropped them on Walter's desk.

Then she glanced over at Mary Lou. "He not back yet?"

"Still out searching. I think he went to Beaumont to talk to Winona."

"Winona?"

"His ex."

Rita nodded. Then she wrote names on the whiteboard. *Arlene, Margot, Milly, Angela, Peggy, Marnie, Jennifer, and Melinda.*

She printed out the photograph of the "M" charm and necklace. The Porsche fob. The phone. The skeletons. Adding everything to the board with magnets.

Then she wrote. *Ethan, Scott, Patrick.* Adding a timeline of events and the locations they were aware of. She wrote "TWO GUNS. WHY?"

Jason handed her a photo of the Porsche. She pinned that up as well. Edith Mae pulled off her headphones, watching.

"Okay," Rita said. "This is what we know. Scott and Patrick are predators. They went out to High Peak with a woman. They wanted to rape her and have Ethan film it."

Edith Mae curled her lip with disgust.

"But why did Ethan go with them?" Jason asked. "He hated them."

"Scott used the film he made of Jennifer to blackmail her into silence. What if he did the same thing to Ethan?"

"What do you mean?"

"Remember when Ruby Joe kicked them out? Marnie said Ethan didn't look drunk. He looked drugged. Eventually he wound up in a cell, sleeping it off. But before that, they could have met up with Peggy. Drugged her. Then made the two of them think they'd sleep together. Took some photos. Convinced them both they were drunk."

"Yeah."

Rita kept staring at that damned "M" charm. "Who the fuck does this necklace belong to? It's not Margot's, Milly's, Melinda's, or even Angela's."

Edith Mae snapped her gum. "What about Peggy?"

Jason glanced at her. "Peggy starts with a 'P.'"

"It's an old-fashioned nickname for Margaret."

Rita stared at her. She felt as if the wind had been knocked out of her. Everything Peggy had ever signed had been with "Peggy," not "Margaret."

Rita walked to her office and retrieved the newspaper clipping from the Casper Chronicle. She squinted, focusing on Peggy's neckline. But the photo was too blurry.

She headed back out to the others. Handed the clipping to Jason. "Can you see if she's wearing a necklace?"

He shook his head. "We might be able to get a better copy from the paper."

"Who took the photo?"

He turned it around and pointed to the name: *Blaze Wright.*

She pulled out her phone.

Jason googled the number for the paper. She dialed it, navigating an extensive phone tree. Eventually the phone rang for his extension.

She was certain she'd get voicemail.

But to her surprise, he picked up the phone.

"Blaze speaking. If you've got breaking news, I want to hear it."

"Sheriff Jonas, SCSO. We met the other day."

"I remember."

"I need a favor."

"Oh?" He sounded rather pleased. "Go on."

"You took a photo four years ago."

"The one in Still of the Apex crew."

"Yes. You have the original?"

"Of course."

"I need a copy."

"That'll take some time. You'll need to speak to the photo licensing department."

"I'm not looking to license the photo. I just want to see the original."

"Why?"

Rita sighed. "Is there someone else I can talk to?"

"No, wait."

"Yes?"

"I give you a copy of the photo without a warrant, will you give me an exclusive interview?"

"This isn't a negotiation," Rita said.

"Think of it as the start of a beautiful new friendship."

"I dunno if I want a new friend."

"Come on, Sheriff."

"I'll do my best." There was no harm in tossing him a

bone. It wasn't as if there were a lot of other papers competing for news in these parts. It might help to have him in her pocket.

"That's all I can ask for."

Maybe he wasn't as much as a nuisance as she originally judged him to be.

"Email?"

She gave the general email, then hung up. Pacing. Ted hopped onto the desk closest to her and purred. She glanced at him, then rubbed his head. "Oh, now you've forgiven me?"

Ted yowled.

Rita turned to Mary Lou. "Any word from Walter yet?"

"No." She shook her head. "Still out looking for Adrian."

"He worried?"

Mary Lou answered. "Pissed, I'd say."

Jason's computer dinged. "Got it."

He opened the email from Blaze. It was a much higher resolution. He zoomed in on Peggy's neck. She appeared to be wearing some kind of necklace.

But it was still too small to be identified. "Jason?"

He peered close. But ultimately shook his head.

"Shit."

"But there's one thing we know," he said.

"And what's that?" Rita asked.

"That she hasn't been wearing a necklace since we saw her."

Rita straightened. "You're right."

"So it could be hers."

She turned to Mary Lou. "I want everything we can get on Peggy. Background, how long she was with Apex, where she was when the men went missing. Everything."

Mary Lou nodded.

Rita turned her attention back to the whiteboard. "Angela told me that she wasn't targeted by Scott because she's above his pay grade. So maybe—"

"He found easier prey."

Rita nodded. "Maybe he went after Peggy to get at Angela. Because she rejected him." Rita curled her lip. Everything about Scott was vile. "Or he simply targeted her because her boss was out of town and she was vulnerable."

Rita looked at the dates she'd written on the board. "We confirmed Angela was out of town when the men went missing?"

Jason nodded. "She came back on the Sunday. Flight records support that."

"And Peggy was with her?"

Jason looked over his notes. "That's what she said. But she never sent through any corroborating information."

"Call Ken. See if he can confirm it one way or the other."

Jason nodded and picked up his phone. Dialing. Rita continued to pace.

Jason hung up. "He wasn't in. Left a voicemail."

Rita walked back to the board, feeling the pieces fall into place. "So let's posit. Angela goes back to New York but, unlike they told us, Peggy stays here."

"Why would Angela lie?"

"It's Apex. They protect their own." She walked to Walter's chair and sat. "Scott and Patrick invite her to go out to the mine with them. And she says yes, because she didn't know they'd already raped her. She thought she'd slept with Ethan. There must have been another video. Ethan found it and deleted it. So when he heard they invited her, he knew exactly what they were planning. So he went with them to make sure nothing happened. And she felt safe around Ethan. He was someone she trusted."

"Why didn't he just tell Peggy what they'd done?"

"That's a helluva thing to drop on her. Especially when they were about to leave town. Maybe he wanted to save her some grief."

"What was Scott doing with these recordings anyway?" Jason asked.

Edith Mae wrinkled her nose. "Posting them online?"

"I hope to hell he wasn't," Rita said.

"The dark web posts everything," she said.

"I don't even want to know how you know that," Rita said. Ted jumped up beside her. She scratched his ears. "How do we figure out if Scott had files in the cloud?"

Edith Mae shook her head. "If he's been dead four years, the files will probably be gone."

"Are there other types of storage? More robust?"

She nodded. "There are some that are lifetime storage."

"Call Tilda," Rita said. "See if they can find anything like a cloud account on Scott's phone. And if so, is there a password?"

Jason was already dialing.

Chapter Sixty

THE LONG-TERM STORAGE SYSTEM WAS CALLED StoneDrive. Tilda had given them a username, but not a password. Edith Mae had her headphones on, laptop open, and was doing her best to figure it out.

The phone rang.

Mary Lou answered. Then snapped her fingers. "I've got Ken for you."

Rita picked up Jason's line. A moment later, Mary Lou patched him through.

"Sheriff."

"Peggy," Rita said.

"What about her?"

"You know where she was when the Apex Three went missing?"

"That was four years ago."

"Was she with Angela in New York?"

There was a long pause. Was he thinking? "No."

"How can you be sure?"

"Trainee, remember? I was the one that drove Angela to the airport."

"And Peggy didn't go with her?"

"No. You think she killed them? Peggy?"

Rita ignored his question. "Thanks, Ken."

She hung up.

"She wasn't in New York?" Jason asked.

Rita shook her head.

"So she could have been the woman in the second video."

"Yep."

"Okay," Jason said. "But if she felt safe going with them, why take the gun?"

"She didn't," Rita said. "That was Ethan. He took precautions. Red coat, food, filed a plan with Milly. Guaranteed he signed out the weapon for the day in case they ran into any wildlife. And they did. Only it wasn't the four-legged kind."

"They gave Peggy water, drugging her, only she didn't drink enough and woke up," Jason said. "Heard them talking about raping her."

Rita nodded.

"So she killed them?" Jason asked.

Rita got up, pacing some more. "Yeah. Patrick tried to give her more. But what if she didn't drink it? Ethan and the men get into a fight. He prevails. Gets Peggy sober-ish. But she remembers what Scott and Patrick tried to do. They get back to the car, but she still feels threatened. So she gets the gun from Scott's glove compartment and tries killing them, but she's still drugged and misses."

Jason walked up to the board, looking closer at the timeline. "So were they dead at High Peak or in town?"

"Any blood found in the car?"

Jason shook his head.

"Maybe she just scared them. They all pile in the car

and drive back to town. The whole way back, they're trying to convince Peggy not to tell."

"What does it matter if she tells? By all accounts, they've got Victor protecting them."

Rita walked some more. Then stopped. "The phone."

Jason looked at her.

"Scott thought she had his phone. That's evidence. Proof of what he did. Victor might protect him. But I know goddamn well that if Otto had seen that video, he would have arrested that motherfucker."

"So they get back to town and stop at Moses' place. Why?"

Rita shook her head. "Maybe she had the gun on them the whole time. And maybe, just maybe, Ethan had the other gun. They knew there was a hole. That nothing was going to happen with the land for some time. If the men were discovered, they would be long gone."

Jason grabbed a bottle of water from his desk and took a drink. "Okay. Let's say Ethan helped her. How did he wind up dead? Peggy just turn on him?"

Rita paced more. Back and forth, counting her steps. And then she stopped. "Remember when Scott and Ethan were arguing? Scott said Ethan had participated 'last time'? Now Peggy's thinking this man she trusted also raped her. And Ethan's now unsure what happened. I'm pretty sure Scott and Patrick were manipulating the fuck out of both of them. But Peggy's still suffering the effect of the drugs and feels further betrayed. So she lets him help her kill Scott and Patrick, and then she kills him. Jesus Christ, she straight up told me her father was a farmer. She probably knows how to operate heavy machinery."

Mary Lou waved at them. "Walter just texted. He's on his way back from Beaumont."

"Adrian?"

"No sign of him."

Rita glanced at Edith Mae. "How's the hack going?"

"Going."

"Keep at it."

Edith Mae popped a bubble and nodded.

"I'm going out to Apex," Rita said. "I think it's time we bring Peggy in for a chat."

"Want me to come?" Jason asked.

Rita shook her head. "No. I think it's best I go alone. See if you can track down Helen for me. See if she's heard from either Arnold or Adrian."

He nodded.

Rita rubbed her forehead. "Grace told me she hoped I never found who killed her brother."

"And?"

"I kind of agree with her."

Chapter Sixty-One

RITA GATHERED A COUPLE OF THE PHOTOS FROM THE whiteboard and made her way out to the police truck.

She got inside and sat for a moment, thinking about Peggy.

Always in the background.

Assisting. Helping those around her.

Kind of like Lisa to some extent.

Why was it that the ones who were helpful and kind became victims? Christ, Scott had destroyed so many lives. Margot. Arlene. Grace. Jennifer. Melinda and her kids. Peggy. Ethan. Even Patrick had somehow got swept up in Scott's horror.

And he just walked through the world, tainting everyone he touched. At first protected by his parents. And then by his company.

Angela had known this.

But so had Victor.

And Rita ultimately placed the blame at his feet.

She turned the ignition on. And drove out. She didn't race. In fact, she drove slowly. It didn't seem fair. Not to

Rita even. That this man had been allowed to freely terrorize woman. And now a woman was going to pay.

Maybe it was self-defense? The evidence didn't show that. But Rita would support it.

Poor Ethan.

He got caught in something he didn't understand. He thought he was helping a friend, and it cost him his life.

Rita hit the indicator and turned into the lot.

A guard met her.

"I'm here to see Angela," Rita said.

"You have an appointment?"

"I do not," she said. It was the first time ever she was grateful for Apex's security. She was content to wait while he called up to Angela and advised her Rita was here.

He was back a few minutes later, lifting the security bar.

She drove on through and parked in her usual spot. She half expected Ken to be waiting for her in the lobby. But he wasn't.

Nor was Peggy.

She walked over to the reception desk. The woman behind the counter was someone Rita hadn't met before. She gestured to the elevators.

"Go on up. Top floor."

Rita nodded. Headed for the elevator. She pressed the button, wondering what that day must have been like for Peggy.

Off on an adventure, a hike, with work friends.

Next thing, she's groggy. Waking up naked in a dark mine. Listening to three men talk about raping her. And not only about it happening in the future. But that it had already happened. And been filmed. And she had no idea. No memory of it. And they're laughing.

Christ, she must have been scared out of her mind.

Rita remembered what it was like when Clyde and Ken came for her down at the reservoir.

There was a second there when she thought Clyde meant to rape her. And she didn't know that she was capable of fighting him off. That feeling was going to stick with her awhile longer.

God, this company was evil.

They hired the worst.

They destroyed the best.

As long as she was sheriff in Still, she'd do her best to protect her people against them. She understood more than ever why Otto quit. He'd seen into the heart of Apex and understood it was going to be a battle.

And he already had one he to fight. The cancer. There simply wasn't energy for two wars.

Finally, the glass elevator stopped and the doors opened. Rita stepped out, turned left, and headed to the boardroom, also known as Angela's office.

The door was wide open.

Angela was sitting in her chair, looking out at the mountains. A bottle of white wine sat on the table behind her. She turned towards Rita. "Come on in."

Rita entered.

Angela poured out two glasses of wine. "Mouton Rothschild 2000."

"That expensive or something?"

"It's expensive."

Rita walked over. "This isn't a social call."

Angela shrugged. "Help me out. I hate drinking alone."

"I'm beginning to realize that," Rita said. She almost declined. But this was a shit day. So she sat and picked up her glass. Angela took hers. They clinked.

"Salud," Angela said.

"Salud," Rita said.

They both took a drink.

Then Angela nodded at the envelope Rita held. "What's that?"

Rita handed it to her.

Angela took a sip of wine, then set her glass on the table. She pulled the first photo out of the envelope. It was the one with the necklace and the "M" charm.

"Could have told me Peggy's real name was Margaret," Rita said.

"It's not."

"Bullshit."

Angela shook her head. "It's really not. However, Margaret was her grandmother's name. So, she was named after her. This pendant was hers. Peggy inherited it when she died."

Rita sat next to her. "I knew you recognized it."

"And yet you didn't press."

"Spirit of cooperation."

"Ah."

"Besides, I would have been guessing. And I hate guessing."

Angela fingered the photo. "I asked her how it wound up buried with the bodies."

"What did she say?"

Angela set the photo down and collected her wine glass. Drinking some more.

Rita twirled her glass between her fingers. Finally, she took a sip. It tasted expensive. She set the glass on the table.

Angela glanced over. Her eyes were bright. Like she was fighting back tears. "I'm responsible, you know. I knew what he was like. And I left her here with him. She was finishing up some reports. Was supposed to fly back to the office on Monday."

Rita settled back in her chair. "Kinda getting tired of women telling me they felt responsible for the terrible shit Scott did."

"I suppose it is backwards."

"Ass backwards," Rita said. "He's the one that was the problem."

"Yes, but I suppose as women, we do our best to protect one another. And ourselves. It's just sometimes goddamn exhausting."

"Did Peggy mention Ethan?"

Angela took another sip of wine. "She said he was there. Ethan didn't strike me as that kind of a man. But then maybe they're all shit. And what do I know?"

"I don't think he raped her."

Angela straightened. "What?"

Rita shook her head. "I think Scott and Patrick drugged the two of them. They raped Peggy. But the next morning, they told Ethan and Peggy they got drunk and slept together. And they bought it."

"Jesus Christ," Angela said.

"But Ethan figured it out. Maybe found the video Scott made. And he knew it was all lies. He deleted it. And no doubt tried to talk Peggy out of going with them to the mines. But what was he supposed to tell her? That they'd raped her and were planning to do it again? So he chose to go along. To keep her safe. And he did. But—"

"She got mixed up. Thought he was a part of it."

"Is that what she said?"

Angela smiled. "I'm theorizing."

"Well, it's my theory as well."

"Great minds."

They sat for a moment in silence. Rita stared out at the

mountains. They were beautiful. Made her feel safe. But that was a lie. Peggy had been in those mountains. They hadn't kept her safe.

"I need to speak to Peggy."

"I know. Give me a few more minutes to process this."

"Want to tell me what she told you?"

Angelia drummed her fingers on the table. "She went for a hike with friends. They gave her water, she felt dizzy. Woke up in the mine."

Rita took a drink of water. Couldn't imagine that feeling of helplessness.

"Overheard that they had raped her and were planning to do it again. When Ethan tried to intervene, he got into a fight with Scott. Which is when she grabbed his jacket and made a break for it. Running down the mountain to the car. She knew Scott's .38 was in the glove compartment. She got it out."

"How? His keys were left at the mine."

"There was a spare set in Ethan's jacket. He brought them along because Scott was always losing his. She shot Scott when he followed her."

"There was no blood in the car."

"Peggy said it was the strangest thing. She missed him with the first shot. But got him with the second. He went down. And she thought he was faking. There was hardly any blood. But he was dead. They put him in the back seat. Ethan had the .22 and made Patrick drive them back to Still. They were planning on burying Scott on Moses' land."

"And Patrick?"

"She said he didn't know."

"Bullshit."

Angela shrugged.

"But when they got to town, she killed him as well."

Angela nodded. "Ethan had the .22. Handed it to her because he went to start the digger. But as soon as he turned around, she shot him."

Rita's cell phone buzzed. Helen. She rejected the call. "What about the mirror pieces found in their throats? What was that from?"

"It was Peggy's. It got broken in the mine. Ethan cleaned up the pieces."

"Did she feel they died too fast? Needed to suffer?"

Angela smiled.

"Did she break into my apartment as well?"

Angela nodded. "She was scared."

Rita raised her brows. "She was scared?"

"That's what she said."

Rita glanced at the time. "Where is Peggy, Angela? She's always at your side."

"Gone."

She straightened. "What?"

"I recalled her."

"You mean transferred her."

"Ken's taking her to the airport."

Ken. That fucker. "He told you I called to check her schedule."

"He did. As you said, he might not be the smartest stick in the shed, but he's goddamn loyal. Peggy is on her way to Apex, Brazil. I'll be joining her there shortly. The operation in Still doesn't need me hovering over them anymore. And Peggy doesn't deserve to be in jail."

"That's not your decision to make."

"No, it's yours. But I know you, Rita."

"What does that mean?"

"That you should come work for me."

Rita blinked. "I beg your pardon?"

"You really don't want to be a cop."

366

"You know nothing about me."

"You're sitting here drinking wine with me instead of searching our building for your suspect."

"I believed in your cooperation speech."

"No, you didn't. But you tolerated it. Come work for Apex. Take Boyd's job."

Rita simply stared at her. "Take Boyd's job?"

"Yes."

"I can't do that."

"Why not?"

Rita opened her mouth. Closed it again.

"I'll pay you double your current salary. Triple. It's a lot to think about, I know. Why don't I give you two weeks? You can let me know. You have my email and cell."

Join the enemy? She couldn't, could she? What would Mary Lou and Jason say? She'd be betraying them.

"Bring any staff you feel you'd need."

"Is this some kind of ploy to destroy the SCSO?"

Angela laughed. "Heavens, no. But I made my reputation by choosing the right people for the job. And you're the right person for Apex Security, Rita."

"I hate Apex."

"Exactly."

Rita blinked. "Pardon me?"

"But you also chafe at rules. You hate regulations."

"You mean the law? I happen to believe in that."

Angela smiled. "Do you really want to arrest Peggy?"

"Ms. Ruiz—"

"You can run Apex Security however you want. Clean it up. Pare it down. I trust you."

"The answer is no."

"Two weeks."

"I won't change my mind."

"A lot can happen in that time."

Angela got to her feet. Rita stood as well.

Angela gestured to the wine bottle. "Stay, enjoy. I need to head to the airport."

Rita felt like she should be doing more. "I could arrest you for helping Peggy escape."

"Escape? I merely transferred an employee. It's been on the schedule for weeks."

Rita almost snorted. No doubt someone was doctoring the paperwork as they spoke.

Angela stopped in the doorway. "I almost forgot. You may be pleased to know that Lisa's Place is being fast-tracked. It may have started as a corporate version of a mea culpa, and it can't possibly honor her memory enough, but..." She shrugged. "I am truly sorry about your sister."

Rita didn't say anything.

"I hope to hear from you in two weeks, Rita." And then she disappeared out the door.

Rita had the distinct impression that she was being bribed. Work for Apex? No, work for Angela. There was a subtle difference there. But Rita understood it.

Angela protected those she cared about despite the law.

That was a powerful draw.

But she couldn't.

Could she?

Apex had the latest equipment. Beholden to corporate interests. Not community.

God, if Still hated her before, they would despise her now.

But what did she owe any of them?

Mary Lou.

Jason.

She felt like she would break their hearts.

So why was she still standing here, considering it?

Because it was probably the last time she'd ever be in this room and have this view. She stood, watching the light play on the mountains for a few more minutes.

Then she turned and walked out of the boardroom.

But when she hit the door, she stopped and retraced her steps. Grabbing the wine bottle. Last time she'd ever drink Mouton Rothschild 2000 as well. No sense in letting it go to waste.

Chapter Sixty-Two

Rita left Apex feeling emotionally exhausted.

She texted Mary Lou: *On my way back. Stopping at Wandering Elms.*

Then she drove. She didn't remember the drive. One moment she was at Apex, the next she was at the bed and breakfast.

She parked outside, drumming her fingertips on the steering wheel. How much did she want to tell Melinda?

There wasn't going to be a trial. Not unless Peggy returned to the U.S. And she was fairly certain Angela would never let that happen.

So there wasn't going to be any disclosure. But Melinda deserved to know what happened to her husband. She got out of the vehicle, grabbed the bottle of wine, then walked around to the back of the house and knocked.

Melinda answered. She no longer carried the carton of tissues. Her eyes looked clearer. Her nose and cheeks were no longer red.

"You look rested," Rita said.

Melinda nodded. Opening the door wider. A man sat

on the couch. His appearance startled Rita. Brown hair. Thick rimmed glasses. In the light, he looked a little like Ethan. Rita could see why Melinda had chosen him. Or maybe she was just tired.

"Please, come in," Melinda said.

Rita entered, closing the door behind her. She held out the wine bottle. "Mouton Rothschild 2000."

Simon got to his feet and took the bottle. "That's expensive shit."

"It's been opened," Rita said. "But I only had a sip."

"You sure you don't want it?" Melinda asked.

Rita shook her head. No, it felt like a gift from the devil. "I have news about Ethan."

Simon set the bottle of wine on the coffee table, and then he and Melinda sat. Rita walked over and joined them.

What the fuck was she supposed to say?

"You can tell me, Sheriff," Melinda said. "Did Ethan kill those men?"

"He did not," Rita said.

Relief blossomed across Melinda's face.

"It's a little complicated what happened. But basically, the two men buried with him raped another Apex employee. Ethan tried to help her. And the situations went sideways."

Melinda clasped her hands to her cheeks. "He was killed by accident?"

Rita couldn't have put it better herself. "Yes, he was."

Melinda turned to Simon. "I knew he would never have hurt anyone." Simon squeezed her hand. "And did you figure out what happened when he called me crying that night, saying he'd done something terrible?"

Rita nodded. "The men he was with? They drugged a

woman and raped her. He wasn't able to stop it from happening because they drugged him as well."

"Jesus Christ," Simon said. "These men are dead now?"

"They are."

"So who killed Melinda's husband?" Simon asked.

"Unfortunately, it was the woman they raped. They were trying to do it again. Ethan stopped them. But she was confused by the drugs they'd given her. She shot him."

"That poor woman," Melinda said. "What's going to happen to her?"

Rita hesitated. "How much do you know about the way Apex works?"

Melinda straightened. "They didn't hurt her, did they?"

"No. Her boss flew her to Brazil. She's going to be safe there. But Ethan won't get justice."

Melinda sat in silence. Both Simon and Rita waited for her to speak.

"He died doing something good," Melinda finally said. "Even if she didn't understand. That has to mean something, right, Sheriff?"

"Yes. I think it does."

Melinda nodded. "After all, Ethan would be alive if it weren't for those men. It's them I blame."

"Me as well," Rita said. She got to her feet. "Have a safe trip home."

"Thank you." Melinda's voice was getting wobbly again. Rita imagined there would be more tears once she left.

"Enjoy the wine."

"We will," Simon said.

Rita let herself out. And walked down to the truck. She got in and sat again, thinking. Then she pulled out her phone and scrolled to Angela's contact details. *I want Peggy to know the truth about Ethan. That he was trying to help her, not hurt her. Ethan's wife and kids deserve that.*

She hit send.

Waited.

And waited.

I'll tell her.

Rita didn't want to say thank you. But in the spirit of cooperation, she typed it out and hit send.

Three dots appeared. Angela was writing out a response. But it wasn't a text that came through. It was screenshot from an online article. *Ex-Apex CEO Drowns in Bahamas Island Tragedy.*

Rita scanned the text. Victor Price had been lost off the side of his yacht two days ago. His body had just been recovered.

Jesus.

And then a final text came through: *talk to you in two weeks.*

Rita set the phone down. Her hands were shaking.

Had Angela had Victor killed?

Vengeance for Peggy?

Is that what kind of power she was offering Rita?

She picked up her phone. Read the article again. But she didn't know how to respond. She closed messages.

Noted she had a voicemail.

Right.

Helen had called.

But she was the last person that Rita wanted to talk to.

She started the car and drove back to the office. Walter peeled out of the parking lot just as she arrived.

She waved, but he didn't see her.

Rita parked and went into the office. "Walter's in a rush."

Mary Lou glanced at her. "Adrian and Arnold were spotted out near Apex."

Rita blinked. "I didn't see them when I left."

Mary Lou shrugged.

Jason glanced over at her. "No Peggy?"

Rita shook her head. "She's on her way to Brazil."

Mary Lou's jaw fell open. "You're kidding."

"When do I kid about Apex?"

"Never."

"I'm glad she's gone," Edith Mae said. Tears glittered in her eyes. "She deserves an award for killing those assholes."

"What's going on, Edith Mae?"

She swung her laptop around. "There's thirty-nine files."

Rita blinked. "What?"

Edith Mae nodded. And suddenly looked very child-like. "But I don't want to watch them."

"Nor will you. Download them for me. We'll have to start identifying victims. Getting them some kind of closure."

Edith Mae sniffed. "I can do that."

"Meanwhile," Rita said, "let's go have a chat with Adrian and Arnold. Out near Apex?"

Jason nodded.

She tossed him the keys.

They went out back and got in the truck. Rita leaned her head back against the seat rest. She felt like she was going to sleep for a week after this. Maybe she could get Tilda to help her with the videos. It wasn't something she wanted to do alone.

Jason glanced at her. "You okay, Rita?"

"Angela offered me a job."

Jason paled, his foot braking. "Are you gonna take it?"

"No, of course not."

"You should consider it."

"You want the job of Sheriff that bad?"

"No, but it's your career. You shouldn't discount them just 'cause it's Apex. You seem to like Angela."

She did.

"Maybe you could do some good."

"You think so?"

He shrugged.

"Now I know you want my job."

He smiled. "Are we going to try and get Peggy extradited?"

"I'll talk to Hunter. He'll know what's involved. And ultimately, it's his decision. He'll be the one prosecuting her."

An Apex van raced towards them, passing in a blur. Rita turned. The back of the vehicle was all bashed in.

"It's the one from the other night."

Jason braked. "You want me to chase it?"

Rita shook her head. "Nope."

She wasn't about to engage in a high-speed pursuit through town. Besides, she wanted to talk to Adrian and Arnold. That was more important than chasing a van across the County.

They neared the road to the reservoir. Spotted Walter's truck. Jason flicked the indicator and slowed. Turning left onto the gravel road.

He pulled off to the side and parked behind the vehicle. Then his phone rang.

"Hey Walter."

Rita could hear Walter's voice. He sounded hysterical. But she couldn't make out what he was saying.

"Calm down, Walter. We're here. Walter? Walter?" He glanced over at Rita and shook her head.

"What's happening?" she asked.

He shook his head. "I couldn't make it out. Something about Arnold being hurt."

Rita got out of the truck and ran down the gravel road, Jason behind her. At the bottom, near the water, was a silver pickup truck.

The windshield was spattered in blood.

Walter was on the ground beside the open passenger door. There was a body on the ground. Walter was leaning over it.

"I can't find him! I can't find him!"

Rita ran, dropping to her knees, beside Walter.

It was Arnold on the ground.

Walter was applying pressure to Arnold's chest. "I can't find Adrian."

Rita jumped up, pulled her weapon, turned to Jason. "Ambulance!"

Jason nodded, pulling his radio.

Then Rita ran around to the driver's side. The door was open. More blood spatter here. But the seat was empty.

She examined the ground, but there was no sign of a blood trail or of Adrian.

She pulled her radio. Got Mary Lou. "Get Casper PD. Get Apex. I want roadblocks all over Still County. Out to Beaumont. And even as far away as Casper. We're looking for an Apex Van, dented exterior, stolen plates." Rita gave her the license number of the plates. "And Mary Lou, they might have taken Adrian. And they're armed."

"Adrian?"

"Yeah."

"Jesus Christ. Walter—"

"Is falling apart."

"I'm on it," Mary Lou said.

"Rita!" Walter sounded frantic.

Rita ran back around the truck. Arnold made a funny wheezing sound. She dropped beside him.

Arnold grabbed her wrist. "Ma—"

And then nothing.

"Ambulance, Jason. Now!"

"They're coming."

Walter started CPR with mouth-to-mouth while Rita did chest compressions.

She heard sirens.

They grew nearer.

Jason went sprinting up the gravel road. A second later, the ambulance arrived. The vehicle bounced down the road, and two attendants exploded from the doors.

"At least three GSWs," Rita said. "And he's not breathing."

She and Walter shuffled back to let the EMTs take over.

Walter grabbed her arm. "Where is my son, Rita? Where is he?"

She wiped blood from his face. Only got more on him. "I don't know, Walter. But if those motherfuckers took him, we'll get him back."

Walter was shaking. In shock.

The EMTs loaded Arnold into the back of the ambulance. Walter went with them. But when they left, there were no sirens. No need for them.

Because Arnold was dead.

Rita strode up to Jason. "Keep control of the scene. Call Ken. Get Apex's help."

He nodded.

She got in the truck. And drove. Following the ambulance to the hospital.

Her fingers were wet.

Arnold's blood.

She wiped them on her pants.

Christ, she was going to have to tell Helen. And George. Both of their kids dead. Because of Apex.

She felts a hit of rage spike through her.

She clenched her fingers.

Her phone rang.

Helen again.

Jesus Fucking Christ.

Rita pulled over to the side of the road. Grabbed her phone. "Helen?"

But she'd hung up.

Rita hit her messages.

She punched her code and played Helen's voicemail. "I know you don't want to talk to me right now. But Otto has collapsed and is non-responsive. Cash is driving us into Casper. We don't know if he's going to make it. You need to come now."

The End

About the Author

Lauren Street has always loved a mystery. As a kid growing up in Bible Belt country she devoured every whodunit book she could get her sticky little hands on and secretly investigated all of her (seemingly) normal boring neighbors. Sometimes their pets and farm animals too. All grown up now and living in the UK with her thoroughly unsuspicious (and often unsuspecting) husband, she writes domestic psychological thrillers about families torn apart by secrets and lies. And she sometimes still peers over garden walls to check up on the neighbors.

Also By Lauren Street

The Still County Thrillers

Still Here

Still Buried

The Bishop Smoky Mountain Thrillers

Hide Me Away

Fuel To The Flame

Closer By The Hour

A Gamble Either Way

Calling My Children Home

Too Far Gone

Here You Come Again

A Friend Like You

The Company You Keep

One By One

Come Back To Me

Replaced with Nolon King

Replaced

In Her Place

Irreplaceable

The Salazar Redwood Forest Thrillers

The Girl Who Couldn't Stop Dying

The Girl Who Couldn't Get Out

The Girl Who Couldn't Be Found

Standalone Novels

Postpartum